MODERN DAY FABLES

JASON PETERSEN
AARTI PATEL

ISBN: 978-0-9967759-2-2

TABLE OF CONTENTS

"Nature is busy creating absolutely unique individuals, whereas culture has invented a single mold to which all must conform. It is grotesque."
— U.G. Krishnamurti

"Do not let your fire go out, spark by irreplaceable spark in the hopeless swamps of the not-quite, the not-yet, and the not-at-all. Do not let the hero in your soul perish in lonely frustration for the life you deserved and have never been able to reach. The world you desire can be won. It exists . . . it is real . . . it is possible . . . it's yours."
— Ayn Rand

SCREEN

MISHA SAT CROSS-LEGGED on the floor and examined her fingers as she always did when she returned. One of her fingernails was longer than the rest, and this was the first time she had noticed but otherwise all was fine. Misha's fluffy white dog, Poof, sniffed her fingers as he enjoyed partaking in any shared activity. His floppy ears flew up and down as he yipped excitedly in circles around her. The amount of time that had passed was still mysterious to her, so Misha wandered to the small adjoining kitchen, her joints a little stiff and unyielding to her weight as if they had taken time off from supporting her body. It was one o' clock, not a second too early or too late. Sometimes she wished the clock would develop a mind of its own and fool everyone.

Here at home, the skies were clear and blended easily with the sunshine for a perfect San Francisco afternoon. You could stick your hand out and imagine it on a two-dimensional plane with the rest of the world around you, like a postcard. Not real enough. Misha sighed and flipped on the big screen, bypassing her inbox, task lists, and everything else so she could catch some entertaining shows for a change. A re-run of Trivia Time aired on channel 7, three digital contestants mounted on podiums and ready to buzz in the correct answer. India was currently in the lead, but Japan was a close second as the dapper host flashed the next question on the Trivia screen. "Who was the first celebrity actor to fly to the moon during the year 2013?"

Misha stared at the digital contestants as each screen tallied the corresponding country's correct answers. "How boring," thought Misha. She turned off the big screen and sat on the couch for a second. Her nerves were tingling a little too much these days and were keeping her up at night. A buzz ran from her neck to her shoulder blades, and would shoot off to unexpected places from there. Rummaging through her purse, she picked up a small bottle and ran her finger around the cap. This bottle was illegal, but it had helped her get through the past two years of her life. The body buzz was getting worse, and she didn't know what it was ultimately progressing toward. Some people fried slowly, others short-circuited abruptly. She knew her buzz was a warning from her body, but she was scared to attend to it and didn't know what to do anyway. As these thoughts lingered on her nerve endings, they seemed to fry the synapses even more. After all, the buzz had taken the place of cancer as the leading cause of death in the world. Almost everyone had it to some extent. She couldn't handle too much more today, Misha thought, as she heard her phone ring on the big screen.

Misha followed the sound of the incessant phone beeping toward the living room and hovered her finger above the phone application icon on the big screen. "Hello?" Misha's face scrunched up with the question. It had been close to ten years since she enjoyed interacting with other human beings, but she had not uttered this to anyone except Poof. Misha paused in silence as the person on the other end seemed to be communicating something with returned silence. "Hello?" Misha quickly tired of these games. She had noticed a trend starting when she was in college and it had gotten worse ever since: People would call you and have nothing to say when you answered the phone. The telephone seemed obsolete, electronic mail had turned into drifted smoke never to be read or answered, and mailed letters had died off decades ago, at least from what Misha had learned at the city's Technological History Museum.

It had been months since anyone had called her, and certainly cancelling the phone app would save her a little money; in this world, a little was a lot. Misha rolled her eyes and made one more attempt. "Hello? Hello?" Someone cleared her throat delicately on the other end. "Can you hear me?" Misha asked. "Yes . . ." the response trailed from the caller. Misha felt a little relief and continued, "How can I help you?"

"Misha," the caller attempted, "this is Tsai." Misha felt a softening of all her nerve endings, as if a perfect breeze had picked up from underneath some window and had stripped her of all rigid defenses with its ease of lightness. The name 'Tsai' catapulted her years back to a time she could hardly recall, it had been so long. Tsai had been the Taiwanese last name of her close friend, Ann. Misha had rarely called her friend "Ann," preferring instead to call her "Tee-sai," a mispronunciation of Ann's last name. Tsai used to think it was funny. Misha's brain tapped at her urgently to close the memory back up. Family members had reconnected with her in years past, and friends had unexpectedly been in touch, each time bringing back that familiar yet historical feeling of interaction. Yet the communications that had been set in motion each time had somehow been foiled, muddled and confused like a trail or a scent never to be traced again. After all this time, Misha could not grasp who destroyed the evidence or thwarted it after its very inception.

"Misha, it's really me—Tsai. Please don't hang up." Misha had no intention of hanging up. She was just too paralyzed to know what action to take next. The history between her and Tsai was not easy to sum up, and after the movement of the world in its own direction, it was hard to know what turn the friendship had taken. While plenty of people still immersed themselves in social activity through the big screen, Misha's social life was virtually empty.

"Hi Tsai...how've you been?" Misha was nervous and her heart began to beat unwittingly as if clear and imminent danger were present. Tsai was obviously nervous too, and she strung together a bunch of ums and uhs as she began to explain her reason for calling. Misha interrupted her abruptly, "Tsai, it's okay. It's been a long time." Tsai sighed and continued, "Misha, I've thought about you so often and I wanted to call you so many times. You're one of the only people who still has a phone, it would have been so easy. I'm sorry, I chickened out. You've been on my mind. Can we meet?"

Misha's mind blasted to what she imagined for their proposed meeting. Out of anyone she could see right now, she most welcomed a meeting with Tsai. "Sure, how about one o' clock tomorrow at Minnie's, where Chestnut meets the Embarcadero? It's a real coffee shop, not one in the big screen. Do you still live around here?"

"I do—I can meet you then." Their conversation ended and both girls hung up, sitting respectively in expectant silence wondering what tomorrow's meeting was going to lead to. For Misha, there was no need to eke out a phone conversation that was fifteen years too late in its ability to be casual. As a young girl, Misha would have described a lot of her human interactions as both awkward and natural all at once. These days, she didn't know how to describe them and felt inept for it. Her family no longer contacted her, as she seemed to make their lives scarier and more precarious somehow. Not that she meant to.

Poof turned up at Misha's knee as she knelt on the carpet, rubbing against it like a cat. Poof had always been more like a cat than a dog. He also had a keen sense for significant human moments when they broke the monotony of days strung together, much like a cat. Poof looked at Misha inquisitively, asking for some sign of what it was all about. Misha reached into a bag of dog treats instead as the dog would be unable to process any human answer. She had managed to skip her own lunch as usual, and it was already time to head back to work.

THE BIG SCREEN LOOMED in the distance in her living room, never quite fitting into or setting décor for the space. Its dimensions almost reached the proportions of the wall it stood against, yet some homes had even larger ones or those that covered multiple walls. A circular blue "zoom" mat stood arm's distance from the screen and had been calibrated by some high-tech company exactly for Misha's weight and build. It was to send her into the screen, where her job was located. Misha snuggled her dog affectionately before leaving — it was never easy for her to tear herself away from the natural feel of four real walls, a sensitive canine, and smells. Beyond the screen, the world was devoid of scent, leaving the body absent of one of its important sensory skills.

As Misha stepped onto the zoom mat, the mat calibrated to standardized dimensions and accepted her weight and build as unique identification. After the screen performed a quick dental scan, the horizon of the virtual world melted with that of reality in less than a second, without Misha having to press a single button. The clock was set to zoom her into the screen environment at the exact appointed second, and if she was not present—well, she knew from experience what would take place in that event. Her nerve endings vibrated and she developed a poignant eye twitch in her right eye. The eye twitch spread like wildfire through her whole body as the two environments married into one.

Misha examined her fingers, and noticed the same fingernail that needed clipping. She liked to check in with her body after each zooming to make sure she was all there. There were days she forgot to self-calibrate in this way, but on the days she did so, she felt healthier and needed less medication for her buzz. Misha worked for a company called Mind Memo. She could hardly remember what she'd been working on before leaving for lunch break. Seated up on her desk to the right was Carol Myer, her legs crossed and a report hanging off her fingertips like a snotty tissue. It would have been refreshing if one day at two o'clock, Carol wasn't seated in that position. "Hey!" Carol chirped.

Carol was a step above Misha in Mind Memo's elaborate company hierarchy, but that step was impediment enough to Misha performing her job freely. As Misha reached for the report, Carol jerked it a few inches away. "What?" Misha snapped. Carol's eyes pierced into her knowingly and smiled. "Oh—it's just that Lydia wants to see you in her office about this report." Carol batted her eyes playfully and Misha knew that Carol had a hand in whatever issue Lydia wanted to discuss. Misha's stomach tried to turn, but real anxiety was hard to feel in the screen.

Misha snatched the report and walked over to Lydia's office door. The screen on the door scanned her face and offered her a waiting time of two minutes. Waiting in the hallway in front of Lydia's door produced some of the most loathed moments in Misha's week. A short Asian man named Alex scurried past her with some files, giving her a quick salute. Though not in a smiling mood, Misha smiled at him. It felt good sometimes, to stretch the mouth into that facial expression. As Alex passed and she released it, her jaw felt sore.

Lydia's door silently glided open and Misha caught the first hints of Lydia's silver hair, her pitted face, her sleek business suit, her cluttered desk, and finally her blue eyes. Misha entered the office and turned around to shut the door so she could avoid the ugly gaze that had met hers, forgetting that the doors in this building were automatic. She slowly turned back around and sat down in the seat in front of Lydia's desk. At times, Misha pictured there were invisible physical restraints built into this chair, as it somehow sucked the breath out of her and allowed no free movement.

Lydia's face got uglier by the day, and the act of zooming into this world didn't seem to help matters. Her uneven black eyeliner shifted up and down as she blinked and her mouth twitched into absurd expressions when the buzz got a hold of her too suddenly. The promise of the tense discussion ahead was locked in her eyes, and she seemed to have all the accusations and rebuttals planned out in advance. Lydia waited and watched Misha squirm just long enough before she started speaking.

"Misha—do you know what we do here?" The question hung in the air like an insult instead of a question. Misha churned the question over in her mind and realized that she had no idea what they did there—at least not what it amounted to. But she knew the expected reply and gave it without pretense. "We clean computer databases for companies that have been lazy over the years in doing so. We organize the information in new ways for easier storage and retrieval. We set up Mind Memos that will remind employees from those companies how to maintain these databases on their own. Mind Memos are a big screen application, so we have to tailor the app to fit each company." How tedious, thought Misha to herself.

Lydia looked displeased. "Take a look at your report," she commanded. Misha looked at the report in her lap. It had taken her two weeks to finish it. She looked back up at Lydia and waited some more. She often wondered if people knew how much time they could save by just saying what they wanted to say. "Misha—you have worked here for two years. There is still no reflection in your work that you have grasped the significance of the screen in daily life and business. Carol pointed this out to me in your quarterly evaluation. As we taught you extensively during training, the screen is essential to our business model. It's the platform upon which the whole world runs. That should be self-evident, even to you."

Misha said nothing. Lydia was right; she didn't understand what was important about the screen. She knew she was currently inside of it, and it helped her earn a living. "Is there something I can change in the report?" asked Misha earnestly. Lydia shook her head. "Misha—it's disappointing. You're one of our best writers and programmers. There's nothing technically wrong with your report. However, it just doesn't reflect current trends in screen industry. You haven't grown at Mind Memo and you haven't grown with the times. You also haven't kept up with technological advances. I still have to contact you using a telephone app. That's so 2008. Can you tell me what's going on?"

Misha blinked, she felt helpless in this environment, truly without answers. "Lydia, this is my best work. I'll go for more training if you need me to." She really was trying. Lydia shook her head again. "I'm sorry, Misha, we have to let you go. There are more qualified applicants at the moment who are able to keep up with the screen. You don't belong here." And just like that, Misha was handed her last paycheck and the automatic door slid open for her exit. The tiny glimmer of Lydia's humanity slammed shut as she went back to her work and the black eyeliner resumed its skimming of screen reports.

Misha's report slid off her lap and onto the floor as she got up to go. "Misha?" Lydia called to her as she was almost out the door. "Yes?" Misha replied, hopeful. "Please meet with security to disable your screen access codes before you leave." Her thin cracked lips pressed together in a final impatient smile.

CAROL MYER STOOD by the water cooler outside Lydia's office, self-consciously sipping water from a paper cup. "How'd the meeting go?" she asked Misha nonchalantly. Misha walked past her and rounded the maze of cubicles to her own desk, with Carol following a few steps behind. "Maybe we can re-work that report together. I have some ideas. Do you wanna grab some lunch?" Misha emptied out the contents of her desk. Carol was oozing loneliness all over the place. People chose strange times to be friendly or vulnerable, even more so in the screen. "Carol—you know I just lost my job. You helped make it happen." Misha wanted to get out of there as fast as she could. "What? No!" As Carol's face was rounded into an incredulous O shape, Misha walked to the elevators and caught the next one going down to the security department.

The security department was situated in the back of the basement and was so dimly lit that it was hard for Misha to see her hand in front of her face. Mind Memo saved money by cutting corners in bizarre ways. Some floors were so brightly illuminated that it was like staring into the sun, and others were treated like dungeons. "Earl?" Misha called out the head security guard's name so she could follow his voice to the correct office. "Yes?" A voice came bellowing out of room B11. Earl was a tall elderly black man with a shiny head and huge hands. As he shook Misha's hand, his body heat emanated to warm the air all around her. In the screen environment, where so much stood stagnant and cold, anything comforting felt accentuated a hundred fold. Earl smiled, experiencing a similar effect from Misha's presence.

Misha was a rare Mind Memo employee in being privy to Earl's secret wisdom down there in the basement. Earl shared his pearls of real conversation, depth, and history with her alone. When Misha first started working at the company, she had visited the security department intending to leave in ten minutes with a name tag and had ended up staying for a full lunch hour. During her repeated visits, Earl told her of his days growing up in a world without the screen. His stories described people who truly enjoyed each other's company, or truly detested it—but they showed it either way. Earl explained the big screen's timeline, how in its nascent phase it was just a television for entertainment purposes. Its versatility grew with the advent of computers and advanced programming. The internet gave the screen extra meaning in people's lives as a way to access information, spread new or regurgitated information in an instant, and most importantly—connect with one another around the world. People began to carry around tablets of miniature screens that allowed them to use these features wherever they went. For many, if a friend wasn't around, well…technically a tablet offered enough entertainment and activities to fill an entire weekend.

Technology began to blend, morph, and borrow, such that devices like phones and cameras were no longer useful as just single purchases and were being bundled into more advanced gadgets by manufacturers. Once the technology age's momentum started, its growth skyrocketed faster than anyone thought it would. What was new on the market would become outdated two months later, or even less. Technology began to "sense" things increasingly, with built-in programming to enable screens to detect the push of a finger or the wave of a hand. Scientists and engineers together dreamt of the day they could breathe enough life into technology to create a *truly* virtual reality.

Then one day the Sacred Touch Company, who had designed the first electronic news publication in holographic touch-screen tablet form, came up with the solution and did a public demonstration to prove it. The event was covered extensively by the media and so the scheduled nightly programming was interrupted on that fateful Monday to showcase a brave individual serving as the guinea pig for the highly prized new technology. A famous celebrity yogini, Hali Seltzer, had volunteered to be the first person to travel inside the screen and show the world what an enriching environment was contained within, and how safe it was to travel there and back.

Hali was dressed in flowing yoga pants with a jingly gold coin belt around her middle. Her hair flowed in long ringlets around her face and down her back. She supported spirituality in every way whether it was to a higher being, heart-centered, or even technological. Barefoot and smiling, she stepped onto the blue zoom mat as the lead inventor, Matt Stills, explained how the big screen worked.

Scientists had finally found a common thread between electric energy flowing through computer circuitry and the living electricity flowing through the human nervous system, Stills began. They had isolated a specific way in which both computers and humans could think, and therefore sense, alike. Sacred Touch had researched this emerging technology for close to a decade with much funding help from the government and undisclosed grants. Using their discovery, they had created a virtual environment inside the screen, much like in a very realistic three-dimensional video game. The environment ceased to be simply virtual, however, when the screen's circuitry tapped into the human nervous system and introduced a subject's sensory perception straight into the environment. It was essentially a *bundling* of two very advanced gadgets, Stills chuckled wittily, flashing a charming smile.

The audience roared in unanimous applause and in the broadcast, countless were seen giving Matt Stills a standing ovation for his speech. To understand what he was saying was to be intelligent and tech savvy, a mark of a truly enlightened individual. Hali nodded and clapped along, content that she was contributing to history and to the evolution of human beings into a more unified species. Stills then turned on the big screen to the hush of the crowd. He asked Hali whether she was ready to go, and in response Hali closed her eyes and pressed together the palms of her hands in prayer form. She lowered her head and softly uttered, "Namaste," which translated from the Hindi language to mean, "The divine in me bows to the divine in you." Matt Stills solemnly returned the gesture, failing to see that Hali had been conveying the sentiment toward the screen.

Stills pushed the power button to activate the system and numbers flashed on the screen, representing Hali's height, weight, and dimensions. A thin blue neon line appeared, moving from left to right and scanning Hali's teeth without her having to open her mouth. An environment suddenly flashed on the screen, a coffee hall with high ceilings, chandelier lighting, and knotted wood tables. A bar curved around one wall, and a diverse night crowd gathered in small groups to chat or show off pictures and videos on their phones. Hands started to shoot up in the amphitheater, all clambering to ask Stills questions about what they were seeing. He waved them away for the moment and pressed a remote control button, unveiling large screens all around the hall.

"What we see now is Hali moving through the coffee hall environment, actually experiencing it as if it's real." Stills's voice echoed through the audience as their eyes turned toward the large screens. The scene on the screens looked like a movie, with the camera perspective shifting and turning as Hali wound her way through the crowd. Everyone could look through Hali's eyes as she hailed a bar-barista and was handed a foaming drink topped with whipped cream and a drizzle of chocolate sauce. Hali's voice boomed through the speakers as she gushed, "Thank you so much!" The audience observed Hali's live body on the stage with mounting confusion, wondering how she was still standing upright.

The crowd was becoming antsy and a voice shot out from the front to ask, "Is Hali really drinking that?" Stills smiled. "She thinks she is," he replied. Other questions followed, "Why is her body still upright?" Stills explained how her conscious human mind was mostly in the screen, while her physical body remained semi-paralyzed out in the real world. "How are people using phones and video features in the virtual environment?" Stills had anticipated this question and beamed about the research currently being done to make technology available to users inside the virtual environment. "How will virtual technology correlate with technology in the real world?" Stills explained how all virtual data would be stored in a master database connected to the real world. One day people would be able to hold full-time jobs in virtual environments. "Are the other people in the coffee house real?" Stills shook his head and described the simulated beings that would populate the screen until enough live members like Hali moved in and took over.

In Earl's memory, one audience member's question stood out more than any other. A tall bronzed young man with clear eyes and spiky black hair shouted out his question during one of the silent pauses and it cut through the amphitheater like a knife through air. Unlike the other questions that had reverberated in the big hall, his question was punctuated with a period and hung in the air like a taunt. "Who is she while she's in the screen?" For the first time, Stills's eyes roamed the crowd to see who was asking the question. An attendant pointed out to him who the culprit was. Stills looked down from the stage with his hands on his hips and answered matter-of-factly, "Why, she is herself, of course."

EARL SIGHED AND SLOWLY shook his head, "I got the order from Lydia a few minutes ago. I'm sorry, Shorty." Earl had always called her Shorty as she stood only slightly above five feet tall. "It's okay, Earl, I sensed it coming for a while now," Misha assured him. They looked at each other in helpless understanding of the world in which their virtual selves now stood. "What now?" Earl asked her. Misha shrugged her shoulders, she really didn't know. It had gotten increasingly difficult to find a viable job in this world without becoming a slave to the screen. She had never taken a liking to this environment and had tried to work positions out in the real world as long as she could, but they kept dwindling in number. Maybe she should apply for a waitress position at Minnie's, thought Misha. What did this world produce anymore? What did it do for a living? Misha had learned a long time ago that endless questioning led nowhere.

"Earl—thanks for being my friend," Misha concluded. Earl nodded, adding, "Likewise. I'll miss your visits." Out in the real world, there was little chance of them bumping into one another. Earl took Misha's nametag and stuck it in the obliterator. It was as if she had never existed at this company, according to the system. Anything tied to her identity would be destroyed or if it proved useful, would be archived in the master database. "Misha, call me if you ever need anything. I have a phone too." Earl handed her a business card and winked, and she turned to leave the basement forever with five minutes left to zoom out to her house. Back when she was in her more sentimental years, she would say goodbye to spaces she would never see again. The offices of Mind Memo left her no such desire and she stepped onto the blue mat by the elevators without ceremony.

Poof licked Misha's fingers on her return. "Thanks, you," Misha patted him. Searching for jobs would now replace waiting outside Lydia's office as her most loathed activity. For now, she decided to check her phone messages instead. Ever since Tsai had called, the old bug had returned to check the phone for any signs of life. Earl had told her once that when cell phones fully took hold of society ages ago, they were people's best friends next to dogs. A citizen would be joined-at-the-hip with a portable phone and check it constantly, trying to materialize phone calls and messages. They would even get in car wrecks trying to interact with their phones. Misha felt some desperation today to receive more phone calls, knowing at the same time that society hardly used phones anymore.

She hovered her finger over the phone app, waiting for the familiar empty tinkle that indicated zero phone calls and messages. Instead, a solid ding sounded from the screen and showed Misha that she had fifteen missed calls. Misha stared at the news incredulously. Who was trying to reach her today, and for what purpose? She scrolled slowly through the call log and couldn't believe her eyes. They were all from the same phone number, marked "Undisclosed." Her nerves began naggingly buzzing at her, and she felt instantly worried. She pulled a pill out of her purse and gulped it down, sitting still on her couch.

Okay, she thought, maybe this is nothing. It could have been a wrong number, it happens. But unfortunately, nothing unexpected ever happened anymore. Within the big screen, it was highly possible to control it all—at least for most people. Misha suddenly remembered how neurotic she had been two years ago before she had started taking the pills. Her mind crossed over terrains of worst case scenarios regarding the phone calls, and then considered scenarios that were even worse than those. Her stomach did a full turn and her hands itched to reach out and fix the problem, whatever it was. She got back up and walked over to the big screen, which today resembled a curse. She wanted to smash it in with a bat and watch it cry out or exhibit some emotion. Real people were in that screen, why didn't it feel anything?

MISHA TOSSED AND TURNED in her sleep, waking up throughout the night to find her T-shirt drenched in sweat. Her dreams had been too vivid and real.

She had seen a laboratory. Stadium seating surrounded the steel floor and was filled with spectators holding remote controls. A chair stood in the middle of the room, an exact replica of the one in front of Lydia's desk. Misha scanned the lab and found there were no exit doors. A man with silver hair grabbed her wrist and flung her into the chair. The chair had straps and a screen stood a foot away from it. Classical music filled the room and she could not hear anything else. She cried out with all her strength and felt a painful ·buzz rise in her throat, threatening to suffocate her. The silver-haired man's countenance morphed from one face into another rapidly, without any expression to hold on to. Misha tried frantically to communicate with him but could never tell who he really was. His face crept closer and closer to hers, mouthing words like ammunition that were all deaf to her ears as the classical music became louder. Suddenly, only one large eyeball was visible to her and in it, she saw the cruelest form of laughter and ridicule she had ever seen.

Misha's heart lurched her upright in bed with its

pounding and she searched the room for the silver-haired man and the steel floor. With great hesitance, she began to realize she was in her own bedroom with Poof curled around her feet. Poof snored softly as if nothing alarming had happened and slowly Misha began to believe it too. Her guard was not yet fully lowered, however. She had never advertised the fact, but some of her past dreams had held uncanny resemblance to real life. Her college roommate, who had gotten to know her well, used to call her "Dream Child." It was funny at the time, as it seemed Misha's dreams played out short prophetic episodes. These occurrences had become stronger and more frequent over time and Misha found it less funny now.

Misha traveled uncertainly to the bathroom and threw some cold water on her feverish cheeks. She stared up into the mirror as if for help, and caught an eye twitch grab both of her eyelids. She gripped the edge of the sink. What was happening?

IT WAS RAINING the next morning as Misha got ready to meet Tsai. Misha was starting not to care about this meeting, an apathy that had been borne of disappointing encounters with friends in the past. Tsai was probably hitting a slump in her own life and craved seeing a friend worse off and more depressed than her. The other possibility was that Tsai needed something. In this world of big screens and gadget bundling, there were few people left to turn to for a simple favor. Everyone was absorbed by screen pixels and dispersed into the stratosphere. If Tsai had assumed Misha was one person she could still ask for a favor, she would be right. Misha sometimes wished it weren't that way.

With a couple hours left to kill, Misha downed a pill and sat in her familiar position on the couch. The buzz encircling her eyebrows simmered down to a tolerable level that still promised its future return in a few hours. As Misha's mind cleared, the question posed by the young man on the night of the big screen unveiling popped into her thoughts. *Who are people when they're in the screen?* Misha had asked herself the same overarching question from a young age, but there was no one to talk to about it. Once, she had tried with her mother and the result had been awkward. For a split second, Misha had thought she saw a glimmer of shared sentiment in her mom's face. But the words that left her mouth amounted to, "You'll see when you grow up." But Misha didn't come to see. She didn't see in kindergarten, seated around other children who were inductees like herself into a new world nebulously called the Screen. She didn't see as she entered her thirties and continued to work thankless and pointless jobs in the screen environment, not knowing a single soul around her. She had nearly become convinced that she simply lacked the wisdom to see, but was not fully sold on that either. In her mind, but also seemingly out in the world, it was forbidden to talk about it. Maybe she was crazy.

Or was she? There actually was someone out there to talk to. She had known it all along, but had been scared to act on the implicit invitation. Maybe now she could. Misha walked over to the fridge and rearranged magnets, photos, and receipts until she found what she was looking for. Standing in front of the big screen, she typed the necessary digits into the phone app. The line rang five times and just as Misha was about to give up and end the call, she heard a click and a familiar voice greeting her. "Earl, it's me—Misha." Earl replied immediately without the typical delay of most responses, "Wait."

"I can call back if you're busy," Misha offered and Earl interrupted her quickly. "Hold on." She had never heard this level of assertiveness or urgency in his voice and wondered immediately what was wrong. Had she been ill-advised to call Earl? "Turn over and read the back of the card," Earl spoke softly after a moment. What was Earl talking about? Misha looked at her hand and the business card she was holding there. On the front of the card, it displayed Earl's contact information at Mind Memo and the small light bulb logo that represented the company. Upon turning it over to the back, she found one line of large words hastily scrawled in pencil and scrunched into the small white rectangular space. It read, "Who is she while she's in the screen?" Misha looked up from the card and saw small flecks of color enter her vision.

She wondered again like the night before, what was happening? Earl had known she was going to call. He had written her question on the card. She didn't know what to say next. Before she could figure it out Earl continued, "We have to meet. Morton's tomorrow at three. I'll see you then." He abruptly hung up. Misha could not take enough pills lately to stave off the buzz and it had now begun to return in small pangs everywhere. She yanked herself from reaching for the pill bottle and closed her eyes for a moment. It was time to stop. If the buzz was going to come, it was going to come. Her meeting with Tsai was fast approaching and time was ticking out on the screen's reminder system. How did the screen know she had a meeting with Tsai when she had never entered it in? With all questions suspended in the living room, Misha walked outside into the brisk air that propelled her toward an uncertain future.

THE CITY STREETS contained technological stragglers who still worked jobs in the few remaining office buildings and shops. People were returning to work heavy-lidded after short and unfulfilling lunch breaks. Some services still had to be conducted outside the big screen, for now. Health care was one that had not made a full transition to the virtual world, as people could not find a substitute there for surgery, dialysis, or anything else that required a hookup in the hospital. Acupuncture had made an easy transition into the virtual world and was currently thriving there. For the rise of the buzz in the population, the Centers for Disease Control had announced that increased time spent in the big screen would eventually normalize the symptoms and that everyone's adjustment period was different.

Out of nowhere, a homeless man across the street yelled out to Misha, "Naughty girl! Naughty girl!" Misha avoided eye contact and started walking faster, yet the bum began to walk in her direction and kept calling her "naughty" in an uninterrupted string of words until it sounded like "teenaught" instead. He stopped in the middle of the street, shaking his head and giving her the 'shame-shame' hand gesture, running one index finger along the other like scraping ice off a windshield. "Naughty, naughty girl. Wandering the old streets of San Francisco. Naughty like Saran Wrap. Remember Saran Wrap? It never does what you want it to. Sarannnnn…"

Misha remembered Saran Wrap, and it was true it never did what you wanted it to. Only soccer moms and chefs knew how to expertly use it. For a moment, Misha's buzz somehow felt calmed by the homeless man's insights. She turned back once to look at him and he stood there in the middle of the street expressionless and seeming to discover he did not know where he was. The way he looked described how Misha felt today and she remembered that she still had to meet up with Tsai.

As Misha reached the intersection of the Embarcadero and Chestnut Street, she could see that only a handful of people were seated inside Minnie's. One of them would turn out to be Tsai. Tsai had been a one-of-a-kind friend in her life, one that had redefined in Misha's mind what a friend could be. Fifteen years ago, they had worked together in a tense and pompous office setting doing research for the most prestigious and trusted medical community in the nation, Ballard's Holistic Medical Group. It had been the nation's premier medical establishment that combined conventional and alternative health care into one approach, without the two groups wringing each other's necks.

Somehow even with a bunch of diverse and eclectic doctors working together, the white coat stench of orthodox medical training still hung in the air and made patients' blood pressures consistently rise in the office. The positions that Misha and Tsai were hired for had been their first jobs out of college and they'd been very enthusiastic and bright-eyed about the place—for about three months. After that, the two friends became frustrated by the lack of challenge at work, the low pay, the workplace drama, and the pushiness of medical professionals. The worse things got at work, the closer the two friends became and the more they tried to find humor in what happened around them. With creatively doctored paperwork, they convinced the research department to pay for their "work-related" education at the Ballard University, including courses on how to make ice cream, draw self-portraits, and do the quick step. They drew caricatures of the doctors they worked for and hung them up behind the office door. They set up elaborate baskets to shoot crumpled paper balls into.

Misha and Tsai only saw each other at work, but they knew everything about each other's lives. When Misha learned she had to get a root canal treatment, Tsai was the first person she told and Tsai offered to accompany her to the painful appointment for moral support. The two came to take it for granted, but they actually looked forward to going to work at their stuffy jobs in a weird way. Misha stood in front of Minnie's and wondered what had happened. Fifteen long years had gone by, and she didn't know why she and Tsai hadn't talked since the days of Ballard. But the question almost seemed moot considering no one talked anymore.

Misha walked through the café entrance and saw a petite figure sitting at the coffee bar. Tsai looked smaller than she remembered, hunched over in an awkward position. Misha suddenly felt vulnerable and ill, but continued to walk toward the bar and stopped right behind her friend. "Tsai?" As Tsai turned around, welled up tears left her eyes and traveled down her cheeks. Her eyes were red and her whole face looked swollen as if she was allergic and a bee had stung her. Misha sat down on the barstool next to her, alarmed. "Tsai, what is it?" Tsai limply fell forward and her head landed on Misha's shoulder. The re-introductions had been bypassed for now and Misha patiently waited for Tsai's sobbing to end. "Tsai, what is it? You can trust me, I won't tell anyone. What's wrong?"

Tsai wiped away her tears and began her story as if the two of them were still sitting in their Ballard office uninterrupted from fifteen years ago. "Misha, I have the buzz. I know everyone has the buzz, but mine is getting worse. I'm getting twitches everywhere. My eyes, my knees, my lips…even parts of my body I never knew I had. It's so painful. It's really bad, Misha, I'm so scared. And I've begun to hear things. I think they're trying to enter my brain and read what's there. I feel like I'm going crazy."

Misha sat across from Tsai, wide-eyed. These were the symptoms that she herself had been experiencing too. She wasn't alone or crazy. "Tsai—who's 'they?'" Tsai gulped back her sobs and answered frantically, "I don't know! I'm freaked out, Misha. I feel like they're telling me things and brainwashing me. I'm going to see a doctor, but you have to go with me. Please! I'm too scared to go alone. I can't handle this on my own." Tsai's eyes welled up again and tears plopped like rain into the coffee mug she held in her tiny hands.

"Okay, Tsai," Misha reassured her, "don't worry. I'll come with you. You don't have to go through this on your own." Misha gave Tsai a hug and past Tsai's trembling shoulders, she could see a café patron open up a portable screen on a coffee table with violently twitching hands.

THREE O'CLOCK THE NEXT afternoon, Misha sat across from Earl at Morton's Steakhouse. She felt discombobulated after seeing Tsai the day before and was shocked at how tiring social interaction had become for her. She recalled it being energizing when she was younger. It was okay, she told herself. Reconnecting with Tsai had given her a chance to help an old friend out, one who had helped her years ago.

A waitress dropped off a couple platters of comfort food on the table and left. Misha picked up a napkin and laid it across her lap, then spooned some food onto her plate. Earl did the same and they sat there in silence. The setting of the steakhouse seemed to drop away while a single question rose into the forefront. Misha said it out loud first, "Who is she while she's in the screen, Earl?"

Earl scooted his chair closer to the table and his usually bellowing voice dropped down to barely above a whisper. "Misha, I want you to be careful, okay?" Misha's eyebrows rose in disbelief. "Earl—what are you talking about?" Earl lifted his finger up to his lips to gesture Misha have a more hushed tone. "Don't worry, I'll tell you everything, but you have to keep this between us and watch your back right now. I'm on your side, so promise me." Misha's mind felt dazed and uncertain about everything and everyone. "Yes, I promise," she assured Earl.

Earl nodded and began, "Before the big screen was invented, people were already entering the screen, so to speak. Different websites existed that were collectively part of what was called 'social networking' and people posted their pictures on them, invited friends to join, and chronicled their life experiences. "Real Face" was one of them. People all around the world connected to other people through these sites, both people they knew and those they didn't. Sure, these pages helped old friends reconnect and made it easier for family members to keep in touch across long distances. They even helped some people find dates.

"There were other effects too, though. An identity page allowed an individual to tell others who he or she was, or wasn't. In real life, you can try and guess who someone is when you meet them based on your own perception, but identity pages took the guesswork out of the process. The websites encouraged people to visually balance out the traits they didn't want others to see about them by only highlighting the ones they did. An identity page declared, even demanded, how others should perceive it. If you didn't want to be seen as a smart nerdy type anymore, you could change all that overnight with your identity page. Or if you wanted to spell out for others how the nerdiness should be seen, you could easily do that too. You could sculpt your identity and your blossoming celebrity all at once. If someone didn't buy into what was on the screen, well then—too bad for them. Guilt usually set in for those who didn't believe, because everyone else supposedly did.

"As the big screen entered the world and people grew accustomed to it, identities went beyond Real Face and became larger than life. Hali Seltzer added a yoga studio to the virtual environment, and claimed it was the best yoga she had ever done in her life. She grew even more famous than she was before, and not just for yoga but for anything she wished in the moment to be famous for. It would all magically work out for her overnight: Notoriety for being a bestselling author, acclaim at directing and producing feature films, media attention on her new yoga-inspired cooking show, admiration for her unmatched philanthropy. The dabbling in new areas of work and creation was endless. It was a renaissance—the virtual renaissance. But if you had seen Hali's feature film, it would have made you question whether that was a good thing.

"Other people followed Hali's lead and dove into the screen, hiring programmers to create new virtual environments specifically for them that people could join. People wanted to be famous, and it was never easier than in the virtual world. It was like a drug that never wore off. Except that all drugs wear off eventually. Hali was the first to show signs, but it was not widely publicized what had happened to her—only that she had developed an unnamed neurodegenerative disorder. In other words, she had the buzz. As the buzz increasingly grabbed a hold of Hali's body, her hold on fame both in and out of the virtual world became more tenuous. She and her doctors never attributed the symptoms to living life inside the screen, so she spent more and more time in there. Where once she felt larger than life, she was then at the age of 50 frail and unable to do yoga anymore. She died at age 55.

"Who was she while she was in the screen? I can only speculate, Shorty. I ain't no scientist or researcher. But I'd say that in the screen, personality wears off as it gets sold out in meager portions to others. At first it seems riveting, but eventually everyone learns to act the same, talk the same. Monotony. They speak a new unified language, one I can't understand. They do it, ironically, for protection. So they don't stand out and get in trouble. You can't tell the difference between anyone anymore. People appear to be all put together, but they're more self-conscious than ever. They get lost in there and can't come back here." Earl pointed to the ground. "I think the buzz is the result of a split. One part of the person is in the screen, but the other part is still out here. And I think the part that's left out here gets mad when it's neglected."

Misha's eyelid twitched in response. She stuck a fork into her mashed potatoes and it froze there pointed toward the ceiling. Earl pointed to her and asked, "Who do you think she is while she's in the screen?" Misha felt like she had prepared this answer in her mind over many years, but the actual words were escaping her now. She started talking clumsily anyway, "I just don't trust what I see in the screen. I don't believe people's actions or what they're telling me. Something feels hidden from view, and I can't put my finger on what that is. It doesn't feel real, even though they say that it is. But I've been told by people that I simply don't get it."

"Who told you that?" Earl asked her. Misha rummaged back through her memories. "Well, my mom for starters. Lydia too…" Earl interrupted her thought with, "Lydia? What did she tell you?"

Misha tried to remember how Lydia had put it. "Well, she told me I didn't get what they did there at Mind Memo. I hadn't grasped the importance of the big screen in daily life. She isn't the only one who thinks that about me, though. Others do too, Earl, only they don't say it out loud. I can still tell they're thinking it. What is it that I don't get?"

"Listen, Misha," Earl explained, "when I first met you, I knew I could talk to you. I mean really talk to you, like a real human being. That's rare in the virtual environment. Your personality stood out to me because it wasn't peggable. You can't melt and become one with the depravity and mush that place has turned into. That's a good thing. But today, the thing that can't be pegged makes people scared. I want you to trust no one right now. You need to be your own best friend and look out for yourself and no one else. I think something weird is happening. A few days ago, Lydia asked me for your files, both active and archived. I thought it was just a routine check she was planning to run on all employees, but now I know something's up with your being fired from the company."

"Wasn't Lydia just disappointed with my performance at Mind Memo? That must be why she asked for my files," Misha reminded Earl. Earl shook his head. "No, this is about something else. Trust me. I looked in the master database yesterday and found that your files had been transferred to an undisclosed location.

Nothing should be undisclosed to someone who has access to the database in the first place. Those files went somewhere outside of Mind Memo. And I don't know where."

Undisclosed. Misha had seen that word on her call log two days ago. "Earl, I've gotten phone calls from an undisclosed number. What should I do?"

Earl thought to himself for a moment and then said, "I'm going to look into this more. I've had to be discreet with my searches so far because they can trace what I do at Mind Memo. That's why you and I had to talk out here. But I'll find a way, don't worry. In the meantime, don't talk to anyone else for the next couple days. Stay off the phone unless you see me calling. Okay?"

Misha nodded. "There is a close friend I have to take to the doctor's office—she has the buzz. But I've known her a long time. I won't talk to anyone else." Misha and Earl finally felt relaxed enough to enjoy a delicious dinner at the once famous Morton's and then got ready to leave. Outside the entrance, Misha turned to Earl with one more question, "Earl, what's in those blue pills you gave me a couple years ago for the buzz? They've really helped me feel more myself." Earl smiled at her and winked. "Nothing, Shorty."

MISHA'S WALK HOME SEEMED to take forever. It was definitely longer than her walk to Morton's, she could have sworn, if her watch hadn't told her different. Either the big screen was changing the continuum of time on earth, or her conversation with Earl had slowed down her senses so she could mull over her current predicament. She saw some city birds hanging out under the trees that lined Market Street and wondered if they worried about what each other thought as much as humans did. She was almost positive they did not.

In fact, Misha wondered if she were to administer a survey to everyone on earth asking them what was most important in life, and they had to answer honestly, if the top answer would end up being "what others think about me." Why was it so important to human beings what others thought of them? Misha had felt a slave to this feeling often in her life, starting with what her very own mom thought of her. Did this steal energy from her? Misha sighed. She supposed it was natural to care what others thought, but people were taking it too far when the presentation became more important than the individual.

She arrived at home close to six in the evening, and was greeted by Poof's small yelps accosting her for not refilling his food bowl on time. Misha mentally slapped herself on the wrist, because of course Poof was the king of the household. She refilled Poof's bowl and sauntered lazily to the couch, quite possibly her favorite spot in the world. She flipped on the big screen looking for shows she hated or didn't understand. These shows, while not enjoyable to watch on a primal level, offered her a bird's-eye-view into the world that existed around her.

There was the Love Channel, on which aired an educational program diagramming how love operated on a molecular and physiological level. Love was, the show proclaimed, the most pure source of fuel for the human race. The show went on to describe how love reached a new spiritual dimension in the big screen, according to a team of researchers. Virtual love could cure illnesses like the buzz, promote feelings of well-being and happiness, and lead to equality for all. Misha wanted to vomit out what she was witnessing.

The next channel, called 'Perfect Diet,' dedicated itself to helping humans transition to a spiritually conscious and optimal diet. Refined sugar was currently on a bill pending in Congress to be banned from the human diet completely. Researchers had shown that sugar lowered the I.Q. of newborn babies, destroyed the digestive tract over time, and led to overly aggressive behavior. Nuts also headed the lengthy food hit-list. The Perfect Diet network was one of the highest rated channels on the screen. Misha listened while Kathie Lee Donner, a leading expert in nutrition, explained the benefits of a recently popularized diet. "The Ballard Research Facility has found a direct correlation between the Veggie Popsicle diet and increased intelligence in certain populations…" Kathie held up a ball of frozen broccoli with a popsicle stick poking out the end of it. "These are super easy to make at home…" she chirped as she periodically nibbled on the frozen broccoli ball.

Misha stopped listening to what the expert was saying as Kathie's face began to violently twitch from one facial feature to the next. An eye twitch moved to her nose and then to her earlobes. Kathie's mouth twitched a couple seconds later and quickly spread into a full smile in a hopeless attempt to cover the phenomenon. In response to Kathie's act of suppression, all her features began to twitch in an orchestra of spasmodic buzzing.

Misha switched off the big screen and re-composed her own body. It took her a few minutes to shake off the feeling of veggie popsicles and messages about eternal love. Enough was enough. Maybe it wasn't enough for the rest of the world, but it was for Misha.

Screen

A FEW DAYS LATER, Tsai asked Misha to meet her at the doctor's office. Her specialist was called a "neuroendocrinologist," a fancy name for a doctor who knew the connections between the nervous system and the hormonal system. The doctor's office was located on the curvy and steep Lombard Street, so Misha decided against driving and instead walked there with Poof who hadn't been out in a while. The air had a saturated quality that Misha often felt during a full moon, which was slowly revealing its outline in the twilight. Dusk hours, when the sky turned blue and was still lit by a fleeing sun, were Misha's favorite during the day. Poof seemed to like them a lot too.

Misha tracked street addresses until she arrived at the right one: 411 Lombard. Lombard Street had changed a lot over the years, but staring at the building ahead of her, she was surprised she had never heard of this location before. From the outside, the building hardly looked like a medical establishment and instead resembled a church crossed with a library. The heavy rust-colored bricks suggested there was a lot of universally accepted and important information housed inside. But the stained glass windows held stirring images of spiritual figures and emblems, those long forgotten along with some recent ones. Misha circled the building trying to find some sign that she was at the right place. Other than the number on the curb '411,' there was no professional signage or clinic name displayed.

Misha pulled out her portable screen to call Tsai while Poof urinated on the building's front step. Tsai answered after five rings and said, "Hello?" Misha felt annoyed, but tried to brush the feeling away for the sake of her sick friend. She needed to be there for Tsai today, but of course Tsai should have known who was calling.

The alert "Call From Misha" must have even flashed on Tsai's screen display. There were more than enough clues. Misha chastised herself for thinking these thoughts and quickly got to her point in as gentle a tone as she could muster. "Tsai, I don't know if I'm at the right building. I'm at 411 Lombard, but I don't see a sign and it doesn't look medical to me. Can you tell me which way to go?"

Tsai's voice softened as she answered, "Sorry Misha, I knew it was you. I'm just really scared. You're at the right place, just use the front entrance. I'm in the waiting room filling out paperwork. And Misha—thanks. You're a really good friend." Misha apologized to Poof as she put him into a loose backpack before going in. She didn't want the receptionist to order that Poof be tied up outside. She opened the heavy opaque glass door leading into the building and stepped inside.

The waiting room had four stark white walls and a few decorative paintings. A half dead plant stood on a circular end table near a yellow couch. Five folding chairs accompanied the other furniture and a bunch of health magazines were neatly stacked, untouched, on the coffee table. The carpeting looked like it couldn't have been purchased any thinner and was a grayish brown tone. A water cooler stood next to the receptionist's window with paper cups teetering on top. The receptionist looked up at her when Misha entered and frowned slightly. The only thing missing from the fairly predictable setting was Tsai. Where was she?

Misha walked up to the receptionist and felt a slight chill travel down her spine and limbs. "Hi, I'm actually here for my friend. Her name is Ann Tsai. She said she was filling out paperwork here in the waiting room. Has she gone into her appointment already?" The receptionist's name, Betty, was etched in black on a nametag pinned to her lapel. It looked like a nametag that waiters and waitresses wore at Misha's neighborhood restaurant. Betty was appropriately brunette and bored, not unlike other receptionists Misha had run into at doctors' offices. She snapped her gum and replied, "Your friend Tsai has gone back to provide a urine sample for the lab. Please wait out here for now." She then returned to her screen and whatever she was doing there. Betty should have looked pretty based on her features, but her face was surprisingly loathsome to Misha, and she didn't know why. Again, she felt guilty for snapping to quick judgments about people like she had with Tsai earlier.

As instructed, Misha sat down on the yellow couch and grabbed a magazine called Picture Perfect Abs. She couldn't believe a magazine was dedicated to the topic of abdominal sculpting alone and that it was sitting here in a neuroendocrinologist's office. Poof whined softly in the backpack next to her on the couch. Misha unzipped the bag a little so Poof could stick his face out and whispered for him to stay inside. Betty's eyes shot up and stared at Misha.

Fifteen eventless minutes passed by and Misha wondered how long it took to provide a urine sample these days. When she was younger, you just peed into a cup. Maybe technology had invented fancy gadgets to reduce urine spillage. Misha marveled at the randomness of the thoughts running through her head and knew she wanted to get this experience over and done with as soon as possible. She wanted to be there for Tsai, but she had never liked doctors' offices and this one was no exception. Her eyes glazed over the article in front of her titled "Celebrity Abs in Seconds." Three pictures of chiseled abdominal muscles were displayed next to the article. How much time could people possibly dedicate to their abs?

Finally after fifteen more minutes, what must have been a medical assistant staggered toward Misha like a man who had been inebriated the night before. His nametag displayed the name "Chuck." "You can go back now," he slurred and turned quickly, leaving Misha to catch up with him. Misha walked the twisting hallway from the waiting room to the clinic's innards, following behind the silent medical assistant.

Misha didn't know how long they had walked, but Chuck eventually opened a door and motioned for Misha to wait inside. Leaving her no time to reply, he left and shut the door. Inside the exam room were the typical medical supplies. A high-tech exam table stood in the center covered with crinkly white paper. A sink in the corner was surrounded by clear glass storage canisters containing items such as cotton swabs and tongue depressors. A chair stood lonely close to the door and the floor was superbly clean, without even a stray piece of lint. What was missing from the room, yet again, was Tsai. Misha was starting to get annoyed.

She sat on the exam table hugging her backpack and noticed something that was not standard in most medical exam rooms—video cameras. Two video cameras were mounted in the corners of the room, one by the sink and one close to a generic floral painting. Who was watching her? Misha got out her portable screen again to call Tsai, even though a sign on the wall cautioned "No portable screen calls" within a red circle with a diagonal slash through the words. The phone line began to ring and there was a sudden knock on the door.

Misha's heart skipped a beat as a man entered, wearing a white coat and approaching her with outstretched hand. His hand was warm as Misha shook it and she felt slightly more at ease. His sandy brown dark hair was combed in a stiff gel-sculpted wave to one side, and his pinched nose was framed by a typically handsome face. He looked very familiar to her somehow, as if she had met him before. "Hi Misha, my name is Dr. Little. Sorry about the unusually long wait today. Your friend Tsai felt somewhat ill while we were obtaining her vitals, so she is resting in an exam room and has been administered low-flow oxygen. Rest assured she is in good hands. You can visit her in a few minutes … minutes … minutes … minutes." Misha rubbed her ear. She was suddenly having trouble hearing, echoes resounding through her eardrums. Dr. Little's face spread slowly into a low pitying smile, one that seemed oddly permanent.

Misha felt a sore throb building in her right hand and looked down to discover a small bleeding pin prick on her palm. Nausea cascaded in waves from her eyes to her throat, down to her stomach and then up to her head. Her vision was becoming blurry and confusing, and she became unsure whether Dr. Little was still in the room or not. Misha tried to speak to him and felt panic seize her as she saw his isolated smile flash in front of her eyes. Scraps of color and darkness swam before her like messy paper mache art right before she felt her body involuntarily slump and fall off the table, ending up limply in front of Dr. Little's shiny black shoes.

MISHA AWOKE TO THE SOUND of faint classical music, her body aching from any trace of movement. Dr. Little was stroking her hand and she tried unsuccessfully to pull it back from his reach. Shifting her body weight, she discovered she was securely strapped into a chair and felt her stomach sink into the steel floor. She was in a laboratory. About ten other people were strapped to nearby chairs and were emerging from their own drugged stupors. Scientists and lab technicians busily swarmed the expansive floor like an ant colony, hopping from screen to screen at shiny lab tables. Dr. Little stepped away from Misha and toward a nearby screen, pushing buttons and levers Misha had never seen before. On the wall, Misha saw a silver plaque that read in large digitally rendered letters "SciTech." Leaning against a nearby wall stood Tsai, her eyes averted toward Dr. Little. Poof was nowhere in sight. Misha suddenly spotted her backpack on a lab bench, Poof's trembling nose sticking out.

"Don't worry, Misha. We're all very nice here. We're not going to hurt you. In fact, we're here to help you. How kind it was of you to accompany your friend, Tsai, to her doctor's appointment." Dr. Little's mouth curled into an even deeper smile that conspired with his vacantly glossy eyes as he caught Misha looking toward Tsai. "Go ahead Tsai," Dr. Little continued, "tell Misha how we offered you a little notoriety in exchange for bringing in our little Misha. How you were recruited because of your past friendship. How you assured us that Misha would trust you even after fifteen years. We were easily able to coax out of you the appropriate, and might I add, highly compelling, emotions that were needed for the task. Tears, sentiments, victimhood, familiarity. You even endured the slight discomfort of the injected neurological toxin so that your body could truly mimic severe buzz symptoms. You were great! We couldn't have asked for a better performance. Bravo."

Tsai looked like a little girl who felt both indescribably scared and guilty. "You said you wouldn't hurt her," she whispered. Dr. Little flung his head back and issued a fake laugh. "Don't be so stupid. Tell Misha what you're getting in return, Tsai. How we were planning to air your TV show in exchange. Except we're not. Sorry, your ideas are just dumb. I guess you were fooled too."

Misha blinked back tears as her eyes met Tsai's. It had always hurt to assume people didn't care, but it hurt even more to be tricked into thinking they did. Now was not a good time to cry, she realized. "Why were you looking for me?" she asked Dr. Little. She gestured to the small group around her. "Why were you looking for us?" She suddenly realized who "Dr. Little" really was and why he looked so familiar to her. He was Brent McKenna, the host of the old reality TV singing competition called "Bring It On."

Brent spread his arms wide and projected his voice so that everyone could hear. "Welcome to SciTech, also formerly known as the Sacred Touch Company." He began to applaud. "We are the largest, most advanced biotechnology company in the world. The big screen that you are not a fan of, Misha, was invented by us years ago…pioneered by the computer programmer and entrepreneur, Matt Stills. He was a spiritual and technological visionary and revolutionary. We continue his vision today—toward a more unified and compassionate world." The employees of SciTech nodded and clapped in unison. "I myself have been in the entertainment business for years. You may be familiar with the multitude of shows I hosted and produced. I owe my life to the big screen. Growing up, I was called an "ugly nerd" and ostracized at school. In the big screen, no one could push me around anymore. I was the cool one, the trendsetter, and I called the shots. Using my extensive background and accolades from the big screen, I now stand as the proud figurehead for SciTech." He bowed to more rowdy applause.

"The scientists here at SciTech are the most innovative in the world at running the big screen and keeping it current to the trends. But today we stand together facing a bit of a challenge. As the screen developed and spread across a global audience, copycatting reached unforeseen levels. Television shows that premiered were consistently knockoffs of previous shows. Electronic books became dull and redundant, new authors seldom standing out. Musicians rose to number one overnight and flopped the next week. Only five played out songs ran on the radio, over and over again. This has all affected the economy over time. People are not spending as much money in the virtual environments we created especially for them long ago. We are just not entertaining effectively."

Brent paused to choose his wording carefully. "It seems, people, that real character is lacking today in the big screen. The screen is becoming devoid of a real life force, if you will. True creativity. Daring. Originality. Without these elements, we can't sell anything. We need character back. Don't worry, though, this will all change soon." Brent gestured to the people restrained in front of him. "We'll be extracting character straight from you."

THE GROUP SAT IN SHOCKED silence, trying to interpret what Brent McKenna's sentence meant. "Oh, don't be alarmed," Brent continued, "SciTech has been researching the process for many years. We identified the parts of the brain that most contribute to human character, and we can infuse the energy found there into the screen. The whole thing is much simpler than you would think, using the advanced technology of our day and age." Brent beamed proudly and his face seemed to shine like a brand new yellow light bulb. "The hard part, though, was finding people who had enough character left to extract. We looked long and hard. Most people were too far gone in the screen to be of any use. But not you folks. For some reason, you've been bucking the system, which is pretty annoying. Employers in the virtual world have marked you as essentially unemployable. We've quarantined and examined all your virtual files." Brent shook his head at them. "But at least you have a stockpile of character left for us to 'borrow,' so to speak. We've hand-picked each of you, you should feel honored. When we're through, you'll be better adapted to today's society. Too much character in one individual is never a good thing.

"Don't think of yourselves as special just for having character, though. Everyone in the world has it. Some people have a larger responsibility to the world to share with others and so they run out of it faster. Take me, for example. Character is not unique. Using your brain waves as fodder, SciTech employees will be able to weave your character seamlessly into the screen in real time using mathematical algorithms and equations. It's all a bunch of numbers at the end of the day, that's what is so beautiful about it. The numbers you give us will help SciTech build a more creative platform for sculpting and enhancing the virtual environment. As long as the audience responds once more to what they see in the screen, we have done our job. You can thank us for having had the chance to participate after we're through here. And no—you won't suffer detrimental side effects from the procedure. In fact, you may notice you're new, improved, and better able to adapt to this world."

Brent McKenna pulled on a green lever attached to his screen and Misha felt a small steel dome lower loosely around her head. Around her, she heard everyone screaming as the same happened to them. Electrical wires sprouted from the domes and attached to screens all around the lab. The screens emitted a soft hum of sound while the domes warmed up with electricity. Misha's forehead began to feel warm and unsteady and the screams around her began to die down.

As streams of numbers and letters appeared on the screens, Misha felt her panic rising. What were they going to do? Brent McKenna was seated on what looked like a throne, watching the spectacle as if he were at the movies. Misha's brain felt softer and mushier with each passing minute and she didn't know how much longer she could last. Her body felt like that of a ghost, slowly floating through the air and hovering nearby instead of staying attached to her. She looked at those restrained around her and saw people squirming with what energy they had left. Misha felt like throwing up and saw the Love Channel flash before her eyes. Rock Hard Abs. Veggie Popsicles. Her muscles twitched aggressively in response and a buzz took over her whole body.

Misha tried desperately to remember what she had talked to Earl about the other night at dinner. Her mind slowly pieced together fragmented memories of words and images. The thing that can't be pegged makes people scared. Who was she while she was in the screen? Misha could feel the answer on the tip of her tongue, and then it came hurtling from her throat all at once and she screamed it out with all her might.

"Nobody! Nobody!" The group of faces around her turned and tried to look. "There's nobody in there, in that screen. Own who you are, what you have, and they won't

41

be able to use you for it! Take ownership of what you got. Right now! You already know how!"

Misha's words kept coming and she saw Brent McKenna yelling at his lab techs and rising angrily from his throne. "Shut her up, immediately! She's infecting the screen, she's infecting the virtual environment!" Misha kept shouting at the top of her lungs until she felt her voice would give out, and then she strained to yell out some more. Wisps of smoke started to rise from the screens attached to the group. The wires were beginning to fry and the heat in the helmets covering the group was diminishing in intensity. The lab techs were too slow in responding to Brent's order. They seemed to be mulling over what Misha had said. "Stop her!" Brent shrieked as he started running toward Misha's chair. He was within twenty feet of her when a white blur shot out in front of his foot, tripping him and sending him sprawling to the ground. Poof panted in Misha's direction and decided to finish off the job. He hopped over to Brent's hand and bit down hard. Brent wailed in agony and writhed on the ground. Then Poof went after Brent's nose and was quick enough to get away once the celebrity's face started gushing blood.

Misha looked around her as all the lab screens simultaneously short-circuited and died. The helmet above her head lifted as Poof ran over and jumped in her lap. The small group of individuals around her rose from their constraints and looked at each other in utter amazement of their newfound freedom. The scientists and lab techs were helpless, staring into black screens that no longer communicated with them. Brent cradled his hand on the floor and ordered his team to do something.

A man picked up his blue and red baseball cap from the floor and replaced it on his head. A petite woman shivered and ran her hands over her arms and face, making sure everything was still there. Another lady patted Poof on the head, silently thanking him for his unexpected heroics. A gangly teenager with messy hair and ripped jeans wondered out loud, "What now?" Silence filled the air for a moment as they all shrugged. Misha turned to everyone and said, "I guess we just keep on living. Out here in the world." Misha turned to go retrieve her backpack when she heard commotion over her shoulder.

"Watch out!" The man in the baseball cap blurted out in her direction. Poof yelped in alarm as Misha turned and saw Brent charging at her, his broken and bloody nose leaving a crimson trail behind him on the steel floor. His cool attitude and control had evaporated along with the smoke from the broken screens, and the madman that he really was twisted into all his features. "You aren't worthy, you aren't worthy," he was chanting with wide eyes as he closed the space between himself and Misha.

There may not have been anything inside those blue pills, but Misha knew she had what it took inside of her. And she was ready to end this. Instinctually, she cocked back her fist and released just in time to see it meet square with Brent's face. He staggered back and grabbed his precious nose, which was now fully broken thanks to Misha and Poof's combined efforts. Something intangible had broken inside of Brent too and he crumpled limply to the ground. He had given everything up. A lost soul, his gaze lingered toward a big screen on the wall that could no longer verify his existence for him.

The crowd started to thin as everyone regained their bearings and exited the hall. Misha found an unmarked exit door and left through it with Poof in tow. The two of them welcomed the fresh air of the world around them

43

and stared up at the full moon in the sky. Tree branches were silhouetted against the midnight brightness and birds were unexpectedly chirping as if throwing a party for a new day. The heady scent of spring rode the waves of breeze around them. Misha stopped to sit on a park bench down at the bottom of the hill and, with Poof's help, examined her fingers. They were all there, one of her fingernails longer than the rest.

SADMAN

I F I'D LEARNED ONE THING in all of my limited years, it was this: No one listens to anything. Or I guess I should say no one hears anything. Listening is actually commonplace. You listen to words you've heard before, scan your mind for an appropriate response—perhaps a cheeky quip, a profound insight, a contradicting argument—all said before, all saturated with pre-packaged meaning. Like static or white noise, the words blend together, creating a sound that lulls you to a restless sort of walking sleep. Like an ongoing symphony with a faceless conductor, no beginning and no end, the dynamics purely for the sake of distraction. Meanwhile the pressure just builds.

The castles of the past are falling, and we cheer. The dogmatic doctrines are dissolving and we comfort ourselves by taking tidbits here and there from the wreckage and remolding them, calling ourselves the creators of a new and better world, basking in the false pride of being the catalysts to change.

No one wants to hear this: there is no change. In all probability, it is only getting worse. That is why I decided to leave college.

I took the train out of Boston with just under a thousand dollars to my name and two years of useless coursework under my belt. My parents and I were no longer on speaking terms. You see, they are good people. I am not. Five years of useless haggling and circular arguments had led me to believe that the only thing I was good for was to follow the right path, whatever that was. I witnessed all of my fellow classmates struggle with the same problem, drinking the pressure away on the weekends, pouring their souls into their work in order to end up at the so-called destination of success and acceptance into society. Forcing a smile while carrying a weight too much for any one individual to bear, listening to the same lectures about social responsibility, progress, change. A student on the floor below me went to the hospital for alcohol poisoning. A good friend of mine in pre-med had to have an emergency splenectomy, which is removal of the spleen, whatever that is. I'm guessing it was stress-related. Two years was enough for me.

But where to go when you have no map, no compass?

I ended up in Southern California at a high school friend's apartment. The medical marijuana craze was just getting started, so we grew crops for a local dispensary which paid us nicely for our "donations." Burying myself in all the nuances of growing marijuana provided a nice respite from the pressures of the real world. Seeds, strains, clones, lamps, hydroponics, fertilizers, hybridization—these became my world and I delved deeply. After two years I had over fifty-thousand dollars, mostly cash, which I kept in a safe in my room.

A certain element of danger comes with having that type of cash. No matter how secretive you try to keep your life, people talk, and I guess the wrong people got word of our endeavors. One summer night, three guys with ski masks kicked down the front door and ordered me at gunpoint to open the safe. Note to self: ski masks, good for keeping the face warm on the slopes, equally effective for armed robbery. They took everything I had. I heard through the grapevine one of them was this dude I knew. That was the end of it for me. I took what little I had in my bank account and drove up the coastline.

California is beautiful country. I took the 101, and stopped at many small towns to eat, explore, and swim in the ocean. I saw a gray whale off the coast of Carlsbad one morning after a fitful night of sleeping in my car. A morally questionable but attractive young woman took me in for a few days in Santa Barbara and showed me things I had only seen one night when I was ten-years old and snuck downstairs to watch Cinemax after my parents had gone to sleep. Guess she had a thing for rogue-ishly handsome mysterious drifters. Or weirdos, I don't know. After a month I reached Seattle. And that's where the story really begins.

For those who don't know Seattle, it is a dark and rainy place for nine months out of the year. The climate has given birth to a culture that thrives off of the conflicting traits of suspicion and a goodwill-toward-men rhetoric. I dug the depression of the place. No one smiles at you, or if they do, they look like they are doing it out of pity. It gave me the freedom for the first time to feel sorry for myself, and I dove into that with even more passion and joy than my marijuana growing experience.

I guess you could say that I felt I'd found my calling. What I'd been searching for all this time wasn't happiness, or security, or success, but simply the freedom to feel what I'd been feeling basically all of my life, and that was that life sucks. I grew my hair out, took up guitar. Started singing songs at some local open mics about the meaninglessness of life, the futility of the human pursuit. A lot of people told me they liked my songs. I said thanks,

47

but inside I mocked them for it, told myself that they were only kissing up to me. I drank a lot of coffee. Worked at a movie theater. I watched too many movies. Started wearing tight pants. Bought a scooter.

Life was good…. Until one day when a girl came up to me after I played a few songs and threw a monkey wrench in the works. She had a mischievous glint in her eye and it made me uncomfortable.

"Hey, your songs are pretty good," she said. "Do you have an album?"

"Thanks," I said, immediately finding comfort in being able to dislike her for complimenting me. "Naw, I'm not really interested in making any albums. I just write songs for myself pretty much." I left out the fact that no one had ever asked me to make an album.

"Oh, that's cool. It's important to do things for yourself sometimes."

"Yeah, that's true." Why was I agreeing with her?

She kept looking at me expectantly. I started to fidget with my hair, found an itch on my nose to scratch.

"What?" I asked defensively.

"Huh?" she said, then laughed at me. Definitely not with me.

"What's so funny?"

"You're funny."

"Thanks, I guess," I said.

"You're welcome." She smiled. Her teeth were slightly crooked on the bottom. "I guess."

I was beginning to really dislike this girl. She was short, brown skinned, probably of South American or maybe Middle Eastern origin. Pony tail, little or no makeup, knee-length jean skirt, white T-shirt, small hoop earrings. Cute too, but clearly quite annoying. She was still standing there, just looking at me. She glanced down at my jeans, and suddenly I felt very self-conscious.

"Jonah," I said, holding out my hand to shake hers.

"Lisa," she said back and shook my hand. Daintily, and not a shake really, more like she just gripped my hand and I swear even did a tiny curtsy.

"Well, nice to meet you, Lisa." I looked over to the window as if to examine something more important, then back at her. I think I saw a glimmer of disappointment in her eyes.

"Yeah, nice to meet you too."

I smiled politely and turned to walk away, then heard it, just barely audible.

"Mr. Sadman."

I paused for a second, came this close to asking her what she said, but ended up just walking away. Found myself suddenly wondering if my pants were too tight.

The next three nights I slept poorly. I watched movies but the usual dark-themed plots just didn't get my angst-fueled fire stoked the way they usually did. I kept thinking about what she called me, wondering if I had just imagined it, wondering if there was some sort of meaning to what she said if she had said it. Analyzing it, worrying about it, defending myself against an invisible foe. I wrote a song to put expression to my frustrations, titled it *Annoying Chick*. Finally, I decided I needed to get it out of my system, so I called one of my friends, this dude named Jim.

"Sure, man, let's go. There's this restaurant in the University District called Flowers, you know it?"

"Yeah, I know it." It was one of those all vegetarian café-slash-restaurant-slash-bars.

"Let's meet there at like 9, we can hit up some other spots afterwards."

I met Jim at Flowers. He brought along his gay

friend, Leo. They were neighbors. Jim is a dork who hasn't really realized that he is a dork. He works as a computer programmer, sitting in a cubicle all day typing out code. He's in his late twenties, but could probably pass for forty. Pasty white skin. Likes to talk about politics, especially Libertarianism. I still have yet to figure out what exactly Libertarianism is, but I swear to God Jim looks and acts just like a stuffy Republican. Leo is your quintessential Seattle gay guy, pretty much a diva, works at BCBG, very moody. Asian, I think Vietnamese. Laughs a lot, cries sometimes especially when drunk, basically a basket case, but overall a pretty fun-loving guy.

I always thought it a little odd that such a straight-laced dude like Jim and a flamboyant fellow like Leo were such good friends, but whatever, this is Seattle. People are open-minded.

"What's up, bitches," I said, easing casually into my seat.

"Who you calling a bitch, you skank?" Leo asked, then jumped up out of his chair and kissed me on the cheek. He did that a lot. I learned over time to just go with it.

"Hey, man," Jim said. "You want a drink? Jim Beam on special."

I got one from the waitress in the interest of preserving my manhood, but privately winced at each sip of the harsh liquid. Not much of a hard stuff guy, more comfortable with red wine.

"You hungry?" Jim asked. "I ordered some sweet potato fries, you can have some of mine if you want."

"No, I'm cool. I just had dinner."

"Come on, sweet potato fries! You know I can't eat them all by myself."

"Ok, I'll have a few."

"Hey, Jonah, were you checking out my butt?" Leo asked me. "'Cause I thought I saw you checking out my butt when I got up."

"Yeah, Leo, I was checking out your butt."

"I knew it!"

It went on like this for a bit. I didn't really have much to say. Jim launched into his same old speech about SUV drivers, how they all drove SUV's because IQ is inversely proportional to the size of your car. Leo talked about the latest fashion line at BCBG and how he dumped his boyfriend of two weeks because he found out he was a slut.

Finally, Jim asked me, "So what's up with you?"

My usual response is something along the lines of "Same old shit, you know. Nothing much." Or something like that. But today I decided to change it up a bit.

"Nothing much, same old shit. But..." I paused. "Well, like the other day this girl really pissed me off."

"Why, what'd she do?" Jim asked me, getting this excited look on his face. Jim likes to talk about girls.

"Well, I don't know. She came up to me after I played a few songs at The B and B and was like, I like your songs. I say thanks or whatever and then she starts laughing at me and saying I'm funny. So I say thanks, I guess, and I introduce myself just to kind of end it because she's looking at me all weird. Then as I'm walking away I could've sworn she calls me Mr. Sadman."

"Mr. Sadman?" Leo asked.

"Yeah, that's what it sounded like to me."

"Maybe she said Mr. Sandman," Jim offered.

"Why would she say that, do I look sleepy or something?"

"No, but you do have those dark circles under your eyes all the time," Leo said. "I know this great under-eye cream that could really help you out. I got some you could borrow if you want."

"No thanks, Leo, that's okay. But anyways, you know, it made me kind of mad!"

"Well, did you say anything to her?" Jim asked.

"No."

"Well, maybe she liked you. Girls are weird. Was she cute?"

"Yeah, I guess so. Just annoying."

"Aww, poor Jonah," Leo cooed. "You can come over tonight and cuddle with me if you want."

"Leo, don't make me punch you in the balls." Leo put his hands over his crotch and acted scared.

"I bet she liked you," Jim repeated.

I thought about that for a second. Then I started getting this weird feeling in my stomach, like I was nervous or something. That pissed me off.

"No, I don't think so. Whatever, it's no big deal. Let's get out of here, go somewhere else."

We ended up at a bar up the street called Dante's. It was a Friday night so the place was pretty packed. They were also having an open mic night.

"Hey, Jonah, why don't you play some of your songs?" Leo asked. "Did you bring your guitar?"

"I don't know, I think it might be in my car," I said, knowing full well it was in my trunk as I always kept it there in case I found the opportunity to play a few impromptu songs.

"Go get it!"

I hesitated, pretending to think about it first. "Ok, fine."

I got my guitar and put my name on the list, with three other people ahead of me. The first was this chunky girl who sang about broken heartedness and stuff like that, sounded like she had a bad breakup. With the venom she sang with you could tell she probably still had feelings for the guy. The second was this greasy looking dude with a week-old beard who tried to sound like a cross between Van Morrison and Bob Dylan. The result was you could only understand one out of every five words he sang, but I guess that was supposed to make his songs more profound or something. The third was a white girl with dreads who had somehow managed to combine African tribal music with classical guitar. She liked to beat her guitar like a drum and did a lot of chanting, and it was pretty creative but slightly strange to be honest. I was up next. I felt confident, as usual, that my songs were more deep and meaningful than the others.

I sang one of my go-to songs first, called *Sea of Emptiness*. It was about floating on a sea of… well you know. I could tell by the way the audience's eyes glazed over that I was reaching them, that they were busy plumbing the depths of their souls to find that place where my message was really hitting home. After I finished, I got a sort of lukewarm applause, which was the norm. But I wasn't the type of performer that tried to wow the crowd with all this fancy guitar work or catchy refrains, and really if people got all excited about my songs I would know that they weren't really grasping the meaning behind my lyrics. So I was satisfied.

It was then that I saw her in the crowd. She was in the back, sitting with a couple of girls and some guy, her hair in that same pony tail, same hoop earrings, wearing a red T-shirt this time and some black jeans. She was looking right at me. And god damn it, she was smiling that mischievous smile again! Feeding off of my irritation, I decided right then and there to play my newest song. I strummed a few chords and launched into the first verse of *Annoying Chick.*

Now, to be quite honest, this song wasn't much like my other songs, but I was pretty proud of it. It had some clever lines like, "Nails on chalkboards/ got nothing on you/ think you're so smart/ tell me the truth" and the chorus went "Annoying chick/ You make me sick" and I have to admit it had a bit of a groove to it. It even had a bridge part that stole the popular "Love me, love me, say that you love me" lyrics and turned them into "Bug me, bug me, I say that you bug me."

As I sang, a strange thing began to happen. People started to perk up, some smiling, some even laughing at a few of the lines in the song. Even stranger, I started getting this feeling of excitement as I played, I don't really know how to describe it except to say that I was kind of enjoying myself. I mean it wasn't exactly as profound an experience as with my other songs, but it wasn't so bad either. I didn't look up at Lisa while I played. I guess I wondered if she knew that she was the inspiration.

When I finished, people clapped, enthusiastically this time. I even got some "Woos" and a couple "Yeahs" and that was a first for me. I looked out at the crowd and people were looking at me, laughing, having a good time. The craziest thing of all, I noticed that even I was smiling. So I braved a glance to the back at Lisa. She was on her feet clapping and whistling toward the stage. Weird, this was all just too weird. But it felt good. The top of my scalp was tingling and everything felt kind of like I was under water. I decided then and there why not, I'll just go and say "hi" to her after this. I mean why the hell not?

And then something happened. Jim came up and gave me a slap on the back, saying "Nice work, man." And Leo pranced up, clapping gaily, crying "Yeeeaaa!" and without warning grabbed my face and planted a big fat kiss on me. No—not on the cheek this time. On the lips. Full on. The cheers from the crowd rose up again.

"Leo, you ass!" I hissed at him. He put on a mock look of shock. I guess he was too caught up in the excitement to care much.

I looked up to see Lisa putting on her coat and her friends standing up and getting ready to leave. I quickly put my guitar back in its case and hurried toward the door to try and catch her. I ran into her on the sidewalk just outside the door.

"Hey, Lisa!" I said.

"Oh, hey, Jonah," she replied. "That was a really good song."

I smiled shyly. "Thanks."

"See, I told you you were a funny guy."

"Yeah, I guess. Hey, just so you know—"

"And it's cool too that you have such a supportive boyfriend," she said. She smiled at me. Not the kind of smile I was hoping for.

"Oh, but—"

"Come on Lisa, we gotta go!" one of her girlfriends called to her.

"Sorry, I gotta go, maybe I'll see you around again sometime!"

And she turned to run and catch up with her friends.

"Yeah, okay . . ." I stood there alone, feeling like a total dumbass. A homeless guy sitting against the newspaper bin asked me for some change and I just blankly looked at him.

"Huh? Oh yeah. Sure." I fumbled in my pocket and handed him a dollar bill. At least I think it was a dollar, I don't even know.

"Hey, dude, don't forget your guitar." It was Jim.

"Are you mad at me?" asked Leo coming up behind

him. He must've realized he'd gotten a bit overzealous and had a hang-dog look on his face. For a second I almost started to go off on him, but the image of dorky Jim and sheepish Leo standing there looking at me suddenly seemed very amusing. I could even see myself as if from above, on a random street corner on a random night in the city of Seattle, a young man with many years behind me and even more ahead. Life is weird, that's for sure. I started laughing.

"No, but if you do that again I really will punch you in the balls!"

I GUESS YOU'RE WONDERING if I ever saw Lisa again, and the truth is, I didn't. It bothered me for a while, but I found myself getting caught up in doing my thing and writing some new songs, and after a while I just let it go. I wrote some songs about things I thought were funny, and some about things that were important to me. I wrote a song about stuff that happened to me in Boston and California, about my parents, about working at a movie theater, I even wrote a song about the odd couple, Jim and Leo.

Now, don't get all excited, I wasn't a changed man, I hadn't seen the light or that sort of thing. I still rode a scooter, though I'll admit my pants had gotten a little looser. Overall, I still saw the world the same way I had before.

It's just I wasn't so scared to see it in another way too.

EYE CONTACT

S HOULD YOU BE ALLOWED to play poker with sunglasses on? Roberto didn't think so and he proved to everyone the disadvantages of it with his poker skills that night. Lana Denet wore a fashionable pair of purple shades at the table. But that wasn't her problem. She had become convinced, looking out through the shaded lenses, that women didn't stand a chance in this sport compared to the men. She had prepped to be a badass before the battle. But it was hard to pose without really feeling it, and bits of bravado were shorn off as she hid behind her specs. Maybe her white tank was a little too busty, or she had on too much make up she wondered. Should she have curled her hair tonight? She was the first one out among the top ten.

Gene owned a local dive bar that was failing and hoped to win enough money to save it. A lot was at stake that night, including a scolding from his wife. Gene flexed his biceps out of a tight white wife beater, seeking to intimidate the dark haired broad, one of the only women at the table. His strategy worked, especially as it caught fire like a testosterone wave across the players. Gene was the next to go. The caricature of Gene was too predictable to catch on to, and too easy to defeat.

A few people actually missed Lana and Gene after they left. As the table dwindled and individual players became more recognizable, it proved more costly to make mistakes with your bets. Some could handle it, some couldn't. Poker is a game of spotlights, and how you portray yourself speaks as loudly as your chips. Most people in the room that night had learned new sides of their personalities by playing poker. Ruthless sides came out, those with bravado became quiet at times, and those who would never have self-described as calculating manipulated the table without batting a lash. It was funny what money could do to people. Sometimes it didn't even seem like it was about the money.

Jonah was quick-witted and his opponents were often confused in guessing the cards he was dealt. He never stopped cracking jokes and the humor masked any other tell, if they were even there. As Lana got up from the table, Gene was pretty proud of himself. Jonah catalogued the arrogance wafting off of the man from being the one to do her in. If Gene couldn't avoid his wife's scathing personality, at least he could dish it out to another woman who dared playing poker with a bunch of dudes. Gene kicked back in his chair and received his next hand. A pair of twos. Yikes. Oh well, he was Gene and he could do something with this.

The smell of fear mingled with sweat and testosterone for Gene as he bluffed his way up the betting ladder. The only one left to battle with was Jonah, and Gene wasn't scared of this small fry. "What a little retard..." Gene thought in his head. "This guy couldn't last a day where I was brought up. He'd get his ass beat just goin' to the store." He smiled to himself and was dealt his last card. Drats, no other twos to be had. It didn't matter because Jonah was a pussy. Gene flexed his biceps a few times and gave Jonah that look. "That look" was interchangeable. It could be used for flirtation on women, and when skewed a few degrees to the left served as a threat for men. Gene had used it a bunch before and knew the look's potential from real field work.

Jonah saw the look, and he couldn't help it. Gene actually looked like some cartoon character about to grab his TNT and blast Bugs Bunny out of a hole. It was all too ridiculous. Laughter bubbled up from his belly and he failed to press any brakes as it reached his mouth. The 7-Up swirling in his mouth got a second life as it propelled out through his mouth and nose. A few droplets sprinkled across Gene's face. Gene dropped his cards after just having raised his bet by quite a margin. "What the F—" He started to hammer at Jonah, whose eyes focused on Gene's twos instead of Gene's flared eyeballs.

"Hehe—Sure, I call," were the next words out of Jonah's mouth. His smirk made Gene feel even more murderous. "Why I oughta…" Gene began, and with those words he sparked new peals of laughter from Jonah. Jonah couldn't get enough of the muscle milk from this guy, it was funny as hell. He swiped his arms across the center of the table and pulled Gene's chips toward him along with his own bets. Gene was wiped clean, sprayed with 7-Up, and on his way to his lady whose testosterone had risen higher over the years as his had decreased.

Jonah enjoyed his little triumph, but Gene was mostly right about him. Jonah couldn't really hack it in the real world yet. He was an idealistic, self-centered, and stupid college student who thought he was the smartest person walking on the planet. True, he was enrolled at a highly prestigious school but he still had yet to learn how to use his smarts. Spit-laughing 7-Up on his opponents wouldn't win him all his battles.

Beneath Jonah's perpetual mirth was an insecurity he sometimes forgot about. He was the next to go, of course.

Sometimes when you celebrate too early, you're inadvertently giving away your tells. You're actually giving away more than your tells. Jonah's display of shits and giggles didn't end when it should have and Barry took notice. Barry had no sense of humor and his dryness could be a deadly enemy to the hearty laugh.

Barry's bald head started to gleam in excitement as he and Jonah faced off on this hand. That gleam was one of his only tells. You see, Barry's strength and weakness was that he never took the youth seriously. He truly hated the youngsters for having their whole lives ahead of them. Why did they deserve a second go at it (even though it wasn't their second, and only their first) when he was left in the dust as a bitter middle-aged man? Shooting down young boys at the poker table was one of Barry's favorite sports.

"Right on, Baldy, what you got there?" Jonah smirked for the fiftieth time since his last big pot. He waited for Barry to react, and knew any reaction would be okay and still offer him solid advantage. Annoyance, deflection, a comeback, whatever. Barry barely even glanced at Jonah, and in that off-shore dismissal, Jonah thought of his old pop. "What the? . . ." Jonah thought to himself. He hadn't seen his pop in years, the dude was mostly a blip in Jonah's past now at age 20. What was it about Barry? . . .

It suddenly occurred to Jonah. He felt like he was being ridiculed even though Baldy hadn't uttered a word or hardly looked at him. One memory he did have of pop, the guy knew how to laugh at Jonah in his own head. Somehow that subtle seed planted in pop's head grew into a large oak inside Jonah's. Yeah, the joke was always on him and it started with his dad. He didn't even have siblings he could gang up with, and his mom seemed useless as a defense.

"Yo, Baldy…" Jonah ventured on, "think that head of yours could use a little less waxing if you know what I mean…" Jonah could no longer hear his own words, as he wondered what terrible things Baldy was thinking about him. All of a sudden, Baldy's new watch was shooting glare onto Jonah's eyes. Jonah wanted to shield himself from all of this. Why didn't the guy bat an eyelash, for god's sake would he just say something?

Baldy never did say anything, he just showed his cards as if the outcome were inevitable all along. Next thing Jonah knew, his chips were gone and no one said a word to him as he grabbed his jacket to leave. "Laters, suckers," He threw out haphazardly. Baldy had already sent out over the brain waves that Jonah was radioactive, and no one was going to defy him while trying to win the money that night. Jonah skulked out.

Barry felt good about that last one, but he never let anything show and figured he was set for the night. How did he like to put it? Oh yeah, "The greatest tell is no tell." Enough ha ha's to go around for all. The chips seemed magnetized toward Barry for a while, and the remaining five could tell Barry wasn't really hurting for them anyway. This was all sport to him. Not to Flip.

Flip had no idea what he wanted to do yet in life, but he figured he had time. Mid-twenties, he enjoyed spending time in his small apartment with his "butt boys." He didn't call them that, but others did so in a derogatory manner. So what? At least he had people to play Call of Duty with on a Friday night. There weren't more reliable friends out there. It kind of sucked they wouldn't let him enjoy even a half hour of peace during a date without calling or texting. He didn't have time for a chick anyway. What he did need was that extra change wherever he could find it to pay for that next game.

Barry and Flip had been circling each other for a few rounds, almost like a mental bout "Fight Club" style. Barry hated Flip more than anyone at that table, and it was bothering him so much that his anal sphincter started to spasm involuntarily. What was going on? A stupid guy named Flip, that was all he was. Barry begged his sphincter to relax but the situation only got worse. Baldy felt sure Flip was bluffing this one, but how could you ever tell when Flip was expertly bluffing round after round. The chips were magnetizing closer to Flip these days than Baldy. A poker game could feel like days more than hours, they were all starting to experience the thrilling pain of it.

Baldy knew what it was: Flip was cool! Fuck, this kid needed knocked upside the head, but he was undeniably cool. He somehow commanded more respect at the table than Barry himself. When had the kid last washed his pants, anyway? He had the undeniable look of a video game addict, but Flip smelled fine. Barry was starting to feel like he was the only stinky one there, his pits starting to drip as much as his head now. It felt like the whole table was rooting for Flip, and no one had said a thing. Barry knew, though.

He tried out his look on Flip, and all he felt in return was mockery. Flip seemed to show him respect, but it was so over the top Barry was starting to wonder. "Your go, officer." Flip snapped Barry out of his mind with the comment. Was the boy being serious or facetious? Barry couldn't even tell anymore, the kid was too cool about it.

Turned out Flip wasn't bluffing after all. His hand was phenomenal and Barry had no way of knowing. If Flip had any tells, it was off Barry's radar for sure. The anal spasm subsided as Barry gave up his persona for the night and walked out to his striped red and white Mini Cooper.

Flip turned out to be no match for Nikki, and the defeat happened pretty fast. The butt boys were mostly to blame as Flip had never completed one full date with a girl without their interruptions. Flip was disarmed by Nikki in a way that he hadn't been with Lana. Lana had tried to reach out too overtly to their cocks, thinking she could distract her way toward the pot. Nikki was a lot more subtle than that.

Her curves were clothed, but somehow the style begged each guy to wonder what was under there. Her hair was in a pony tail, not down and in curls like Lana's. She had on a ball cap that just barely shielded the brilliant and cunning color of her eyes. No one noticed her for a while until her spotlight became obvious among only five left. She didn't really do anything cunning to Flip. They were up against each other and Flip was just too nervous to really think. He forgot his hand altogether, had no idea what he was betting, and fumbled around in his mind for a way to ask Nikki out later on. He could use his winnings to take her out somewhere real nice.

Nikki's hand was fair, but it was enough to beat Flip's. Their interaction was brief just like all of Flip's dates, and then he was off to join his butt boys for the night.

Nikki was a strong opponent out of the remaining four. She won a bunch but she was just getting really tired. If she were to be honest, she'd be cool with just splitting the pot four ways right now and calling it a night. What time was it, one or two in the morning? How did people last like this, especially on the fuel of flat beers, bummed cigarettes, and a dinner that happened over six hours ago? Nikki's mind started telling her she had better things to do, like head to bed. She hated that she couldn't be more competitive. She had never played sports as a kid—maybe that was the problem.

David caught on to Nikki's fatigue and pounced. He was the guy with never-ending energy and useless facts. The gene pool this, and the gene pool that. The guy seemed to know statistically who should win this match, and of course the facts supported the victor being David himself. He was in the middle of another factoid when his I.Q. bits completely wore down what was left of Nikki's competitive spirit for the night. "Shit," she thought, "this ain't even fun anymore. I'm outties." Luckily, that hand was bad anyway. She'd have another go at it next time. Even though she was the one leaving, she thought, "Good riddance to David," as she headed toward the exit. She knew that statistically speaking or not, there was no way that guy was going to win tonight. She had her bets on who would, though.

Three left. Someone needed to take down David. It was getting to be way, way too much. When there are only three left, personalities can really grate without the buffer of a fourth person. Nikki's absence was felt as David spewed his sense of conquest all over the table. Jerry couldn't handle it anymore, he needed to take out this dweeb.

Jerry was smooth, and he was good at the art of non-eye contact. He couldn't stand looking at people's eyes for long periods of time. It was like torture. David's eyes looked like they were about to pop out of his head, roll across the table, and continue revealing new epiphanies about the gene pool. Jerry made sure with the art of non-eye contact that David didn't get a good look at his face. David sure did try though. He amped up the muscling of his I.Q., thinking that would force some eye contact out of Jerry. No deal.

Jerry won. His no bullshit attitude put out David's fire and left him soggy and still trying to seek eye contact and validation. The vending fact machine was out for the night. Jerry breathed a sigh of relief. He didn't know if he was happier to pull over his newly won chips or watch the annoyance called David walk out the back door. Which was locked. So David turned and headed out the exit in the front. Which said push, but he pulled. Once he figured it out, he was out into the night.

Jerry turned to the remaining player and thought, who is this? How was it that Roberto had gone mainly unnoticed as the numbers dwindled? Roberto was an eye contact person, that much you could tell. Somehow the eye contact was subtle enough to avoid attention—until you were one-on-one with him. And then it was kind of scary. The guy's eyes were…how to describe it? Seeing and knowing? Knowing and seeing? Jerry's mind played tricks on him looking into Roberto's eyes, telling him Roberto knew everything. It was written right there in those seeing and knowing eyes. Or was it knowing and seeing? Without any verbal factoids, Roberto seemed to be saying that the odds were 100% he was going to win tonight.

The guy was constructed and dressed like an advanced new technological device, like a popular computer or phone. He was setting a trend, and he knew it. His eyes weren't demanding you to look, but they were telling you he wouldn't look away. Not until he had won. He was daring you to look away, and taunting you that it would be your demise because you'd surely miss something. Like his tell, whatever that was. No one had picked it up yet tonight.

"Fuck this," Jerry thought. He reached into his

pocket. The invisible dealer (who was really there but just represented a shuffling and dealing machine) dealt out the hands. Roberto only briefly glanced at his before directing his stare at Jerry. His hands suddenly faltered, nearly imperceptibly but enough that Jerry noticed.

"When had Jerry put on dark sunglasses?" thought Roberto, amazed by his lack of observation. He saw everything. His eyes were wide open. He memorized the players, their props, their strengths, and their tells from the get-go. Why hadn't he seen Jerry's shades before? The guy was just pulling them out now! Didn't he have any sense of ritual?

Roberto was panicking, and he couldn't stop it though it didn't show from the outside. But Jerry had already seen the slight tremble of his hands. Sure, why not switch things up? No one said that your chances go up just because you do the same thing every round. Eyes open, eyes shaded, eyes diverted. Good not to get too predictable and to try something new for a change. Eye contact, shmye shmontact.

Roberto's plan was just too narrow. He had great skills and had gone expertly unnoticed for most the match as he won more and more chips. His eyes were pretty sneaky, awkwardly naked, and kind of scary. Also somewhat desperate and annoying with that whole seeing and knowing, knowing and seeing bull crap. Jerry didn't care much for it and won the first hand right after putting on his shades. No strategy really, he just didn't want to look at those yucky eyes. Who needs that at 3 in the morning?

The disappointment in Roberto's eyes was unmistakable as he lost the rest of his pot and got up to leave. He was trying to stay intact, but having a hard time of it. He also seemed to want some consolation from

Jerry, who wasn't in the mood to give it. Roberto hemmed and hawed near his chair as Jerry finished pulling all the chips toward him. Roberto felt like he wanted to cry, that was a lot of money. Jerry chuckled involuntarily to himself. He looked up and offered as parting words,

"Dude, try some shades next time."

THE IV CLUB

JULIA BARELY HEARD what Kelly was saying. She was too busy internally questioning her choice of putting butterfly barrettes in her hair along with a ponytail this morning. The idea had been to go for the cute and innocent look, but as the day had worn on, her fear that she looked more like a six-year old girl kept growing. She decided to take them out.

With the burden of her big decision finally off her mind, the real world zoomed back into focus, and Julia caught the tail end of what Kelly said while pointing at a flyer taped up on the wall next to the girl's bathroom.

"What? The IV Club?" Julia asked her friend, taking a closer look at the flyer, which showed a simple illustration of a sun rising over a field. "What is that? A bunch of hospital patients getting together to discuss their meds?"

"Innocent Victims Club," replied Kelly, rolling her eyes. "It's new."

"Huh?" Julia was antsy to get to the bathroom and fix her hair.

"Innocent Victims. I actually went last week to their first meeting." Julia arched a skeptical eyebrow toward Kelly.

"The idea is that everyone has a story to tell about

their lives where they have been treated unfairly," she continued. "So you get together and you share your experience. The goal is to realize that you're not alone in what you went through, and to come to understand that you didn't deserve to be treated that way or to experience that. It's a very supportive environment."

Julia laughed unintentionally, then checked herself when she saw how serious Kelly was. "Isn't that kind of personal stuff though?" she asked.

"It is, but in trusting a group of people enough to share some of your deepest pain or fears, you can heal from what you went through. I didn't get to share last week, but the people who did told some amazing stories. I'm going to share my story at the next meeting."

"Wow, I don't think I could do that."

"You should come with me! You might be surprised. It's tomorrow after school in room 304."

Julia knew she didn't want to participate but at the same time, was curious in the same way you would slow down to gawk at a car wreck.

"Yeah, maybe," she said.

AT 3:30 THE NEXT DAY, Julia and Kelly, along with a group of about fifteen other students, sat in a circle of chairs facing each other in room 304 of Glenwood High School.

"Wow," Kelly whispered excitedly to Julia, "Last week there were only seven of us."

Julia didn't reply but instead looked around at the faces of the other students. She knew a few of them casually from classes. Some looked nervous, but others had a look of serenity on their faces, as if even just coming to the meeting had already bestowed upon them some sort of inner peace.

The door to the classroom opened and the willowy Ms. Eddy glided in with a flourish. She was the teacher for AP English, known to be challenging but generally popular by those who had dared to take her class.

"Hello everyone! Sorry I'm late." Ms. Eddy fumbled around for a bit, pushing a strand of short blond hair back behind her ear as she took off her coat and put her bag to the side. She stood up straight and paused to take in the group of students, then breathed in deeply before generating a beaming megawatt smile.

"Welcome to the second meeting of the IV Club!"

Some awkward smiles, a couple of lonely claps, mostly silence.

"I know right now this may seem a little strange or different to some of you, so I commend you and your courage for coming. While the IV Club may be small right now, I have confidence that over time it will become much bigger and have a social impact that none of us can even imagine. And you will all be able to look back and say that you were the ones who pioneered it! Our mission is to show people that being treated unfairly, or going through difficult experiences, or having been born with disadvantages, *none of this is your fault*. And by learning this, you can *stop* being a victim."

Julia had to admit, the lady had some pretty powerful charisma, plus her words were spoken with such passion and conviction. She thought of some experiences she'd had in the past – being caught as a child between her now-divorced parents' brutal arguments, being taken to the police station for egging her teacher's house in 9th grade while her friend Britney who had done all the throwing got away scot-free, being born with a damn unibrow which needed constant tweezing – the idea that these things that had caused her so much inner torment could be gone for good was very seductive, in a way. But something about the woman's words rang hollow, though Julia couldn't quite put a finger on what it was.

"We don't need to live in pain," Ms. Eddy continued. "We are all taught to believe that suffering is a natural part of being human, but it isn't. Pain is unnatural, and undeserved. You are all beautiful and unique beings, and come into this world filled with innocence, but then the world starts to teach you that pain is normal. We grow to believe that we deserve to suffer. Is that fair?"

"No!" came the replies from a couple of brown-nosing students.

"Very sad," deadpanned Julia under her breath, who immediately regretted it as Ms. Eddy's head swung swiftly around, locking on to where she sat, surprise and self-righteous anger hovering just beneath the surface of her perfect smile.

"It is sad," Ms. Eddy replied, somehow both curtly and profoundly. Julia felt her face blossom like a rose. She hadn't really planned to say that aloud, it just sort of came out. "You're new here, right?"

"Umm, yeah."

"And you are?"

"Uhh, Julia."

"Julia," Ms. Eddy drew her name out, letting it hang in the air like a guillotine. Then she grinned. "Glad to have you here, Julia! And all of you, new and old. Sarcasm may be a tool for self defense, but here at the IV Club, we try to create an environment where everyone can feel safe to be themselves. Why don't we take a little time, go around the room, introduce ourselves and share a little something – just something small, like what you like to do for fun. Later, we can take volunteers to share our more personal stories."

Julia subtly sank deeper into her chair, willing herself to disappear. What, she thought, did I get myself into?

ONE EXCRUCIATINGLY PAINFUL hour later, Julia cringed as Kelly raised her hand to speak next. She had already gone through the "breaking the ice" exercise and shared her joys of going on hikes and eating ice cream, which already felt like more than she had wanted to share with this group, and somehow felt inadequate. Next, a guy named Ernie confessed his life-long struggle with overeating, spurred on by an overbearing father and an over-babying mother, shedding profuse tears that rolled down his large cheeks and pooled under the folds of his neck. Afterwards, the whole group was compelled by Ms. Eddy to say to him, "It's not your fault, Ernie," while he sat there grinning as if he had just discovered the joys of playing with his wiener for the first time.

Ms. Eddy chose Kelly to share next, but before she could begin Julia quickly picked up her backpack and apologetically dismissed herself, while trying to avoid meeting Ms. Eddy's accusatory stare. "Piano practice, sorry," she mumbled, as she awkwardly headed for the exit, even though she had never played the piano before – it was just the first lie that came to her mind. Truth was, she just didn't want to see her friend in a new light. She had always liked Kelly just the way she was.

SURE ENOUGH, MS. EDDY WAS RIGHT. The IV Club grew, and it grew fast.

Within a month they had to find a new venue for the meeting, which had quickly outgrown the boundaries of room 304. Now they were gathering in the school gym, with students sitting in the bleachers and Ms. Eddy hooked up to one of those Madonna-style headphone deals with the little microphone sticking out.

And Julia started noticing a change in the day to day life at the school.

People were acting kind of different. Not really in any sort of overt way, in fact it was often so subtle as to make Julia think she was imagining it at first, but they seemed more... more important? And like they were seeing something now that they hadn't seen before, which made them more... more special? Or was it enlightened? Geez, Julia was racking her brain trying to figure out what was going on, and it was making her feel a bit nuts.

For example, her friend Sarah had always been a riot to be around – a snarky, rebellious, playful troublemaker type who enjoyed driving people up the wall with her witty jabs, and despite being slightly annoying was one of the most fun people Julia had ever hung out with. Now Sarah was constantly spouting wise sayings and helpful advice. She seemed to have lost much of her sense of humor and adventure, and in fact one day Julia, in trying to pull some personality out of her, had ribbed her about being a skank for showing so much cleavage. Sarah had just rolled her eyes, told her to "grow up", and walked off. WTF? They had stopped hanging out together much as Sarah had found a new crew from the IV club she went around with.

Jack Noble was the school's star quarterback, and had always been an egotistical asswipe, but Julia hadn't really minded – after all, this was high school and the Jack Nobles of the world came with the territory. He had often approached Julia with a sideways grin, trying to get in her pants with clichéd come-ons, like "Hey Jules, you must work at Subway, cuz you just gave me a Footlong." Stuff like that. She would glare at him, but inside, enjoyed his innocently perverted mind.

Now, what used to be an irritating but playful attraction had turned into something completely different. Jack was intentionally snubbing her, looking straight through her, or catching her eyes then blatantly looking off to the side as if the wall was more interesting to ponder. Yesterday, she had been at her locker and Jack had stood nearby talking to a friend. After looking her way, he spoke in a loud and obvious voice, "Yeah, this new girl is different. It's like we're connected in a deep way I can't explain, like we're meant to be or something."

Oh my God, thought Julia, who talks this way? Let alone Jack the jerk-off?

"It's like we have a soul connection," he continued.

Ew, gross.

Pointedly, Julia turned to Jack and looked him right in the face.

"Don't you mean a *hole* connection, Jack?" she said grinning lewdly, passing her comment off as an insult, but secretly hoping for the old dirty-minded Jack to dig the joke.

Jack just scowled at her. "Whatever, Julia. Like *you'd* even get what I'm talking about." Then he and his friend turned their backs and walked off.

The rebels and goth kids traded in their leather jackets, black eyeliner and trench coats for skinny jeans and geek glasses. Computer nerds and sensitive "emo" boys went from fantasizing over porno to inexplicably hanging out with and even dating cheerleaders. People stopped getting acne. The drama kids started a singing club, which attracted all types of students, even some jocks, who looked ridiculous in their burly physiques performing a choreographed song and dance to Billboard's top hits. Stylish and creative handshakes and "what's up" were replaced with hugs. Everyone smiled at each other in a very caring sort of way. It became cool to cry, as you confessed your deepest and most painful experiences.

Even the teachers were different. Her English teacher, Mrs. Bean, who at the beginning of the year gave them "Brave New World" to read, had led passionate discussions about the repercussions of valuing society's ideals of perfection and perpetual happiness over individuality and life. Julia had felt excited every day going in to class.

Now they were reading "The Fountainhead," and Mrs. Bean had lost her vigor. While she still seemed to recognize the courage of Howard Roark's pioneering spirit and architecture, her discussions were more diplomatic and her enthusiasm had become dulled. "Don't you think there is value in Peter's re-creation of the historical architecture as well?" she said at one point. Julia's heart sank. "I mean, not everyone can be as talented as Howard, or as freely individualistic. Are we to say that he is a better person, or better architect than Peter? In life it is important to appreciate everyone for who they are. No one is innately superior to another." Julia wanted to raise her hand and cry out, "That's not what Ayn Rand is trying to say!" But she felt afraid of being persecuted for it. Meanwhile, the class around her seemed to silently nod in approval of Mrs. Bean's platitudes.

Laughter and raucousness, the normal sounds of a high school hallway, had fallen eerily silent. People talked in low, serene voices, often of things like pity and sympathy for the less fortunate, or criticism of those with less enlightened ways of thinking or behaving. A plethora of new charities and causes began to arise, with a new drive or fundraising event being started nearly every week, each with a new purpose. Anything from the usual breast cancer and HIV awareness, to the more odd and obscure causes like researching Crohn's disease or rescuing abused poodles – they were all game and everyone seemed to get involved.

The whole school seemed very caring and at peace. No more after school brawls, no more bullying, no more cheating or love triangles. The couples in the school behaved less like young lovers and more like pairs of married fifty-year-olds. Everyone was so fucking mature.

THE CHANGE HAD HAPPENED QUICKLY, but not exactly overnight. In the early days of the IV Club, before it had taken over the culture of the school, there had been some dissension. But for the most part, when behavior that wasn't so self-aware had crept up, it had been treated like a noxious weed, and the powerful influence of peer pressure combined with the innate fear of not fitting in seemed to have molded the behavior of most students. Over time, the "transgressions" decreased in number.

There had been one incident that really stood out for Julia, though she wasn't sure anyone else was too fazed by it. A couple of months back, around when the IV Club had really hit its stride, a sophomore named Roger had basically lost his shit. He was one of those artist types, but rather than hanging out with all the art and drama kids, he had generally kept to himself. He was fantastically talented too, working mostly in charcoal to draw still-life portraits of people so vibrant they seemed to pop in motion off the paper.

It was a Wednesday, Julia remembered, because the basketball team had been wearing their letterman's jackets in preparation for the big game that evening, though the usual pregame roughhousing and exuberance was more subdued than it once was. Between third and fourth period, as Julia walked alone – as was the norm by then – to her English class, she caught Roger standing still in the middle of the hallway, watching the students go by with a look of utter confusion and frustration on his face. Suddenly, he yelled out.

"What the fuck is *wrong* with you people?!"

There must have been at least one hundred students in the hall, who suddenly all went quiet, and swiveled their heads in unison to target Roger. Julia thought he looked so alone in that moment, and instinctively wanted to go up to him and comfort him, but common sense told her the damage was already done, and coming to the rescue would only be bad news for her. Little by little, the students turned away and resumed whatever it was they were doing. No one said a word to Roger – it was almost as if he wasn't there at all, and hadn't said a thing. He put his head down and slinked off.

Roger didn't show up to school on Thursday. Julia had a Social Studies class with him, so she knew he was absent. No one said a word about the day before. On Friday, he was back.

He seemed to have recovered quite well from his outburst. In fact, he was all smiles and friendliness, turning to socialize with the students next to him, patting people on their shoulders. He had gotten a haircut, and traded in his disheveled artist clothes for a new wardrobe that looked to have come from the Old Navy collection. The satchel he always carried with him, containing his art supplies and some current pieces he was working on, was missing.

Julia couldn't help it. She tapped him on the shoulder.

"Hey Roger, how are you doing?"

He turned back at her and for a split second she thought she glimpsed a flash of terror in his eyes. Then it was gone, and his eyes crinkled at the corners in a warm and friendly grin.

"Hey Julia! I'm great. How about you?"

"Uhh, I'm good. Thanks."

She bent down and pretended to reach for something in her backpack, in order to hide the goose bumps popping up on her forearms.

YOU COULD FEEL IT IN THE AIR everywhere you went. There was no escaping it, seemingly no pocket of space free from its influence. The weekly meetings of the IV Club had turned into full-on events, with Ms. Eddy leading the charge like a preacher in a cathedral. Julia never attended, though she didn't know of anyone else who didn't.

No more victims.

Julia was starting to feel like a ghost. People she thought she had known before seemed to lack any familiarity when they looked at her or interacted with her.

At first, she had been confronted on a regular basis

by students trying to recruit her into the IV Club. She always responded with a polite "no, thanks" which effectively ended the interaction. They cared only about getting her to join, not about who she was or anything else that wasn't related to the club, and the discomfort people at first showed towards her rejection of membership slowly morphed into thinly veiled hostility.

Over time, she had gradually become an outcast; people avoided getting near her as if she had leprosy or something. She had taken to eating lunch outside most days, by herself on a bench near the library. The big maple tree in the center of the courtyard became her new BFF, and she would telepathically have conversations with it as she ate.

"What is happening?" she thought. "What's happened to me? Have I changed? What is going on in this school? I used to get along with people here just fine. I mean I was never that popular or anything, but I know people liked me for me, and I liked them for them. Now everyone's so different, so weird and self-important. Am I going crazy?"

Mable the Maple never replied, at least not in English. But Julia felt her stoic and solid trunk, her reaching arms and dancing leaves, were silently sending her a message. Don't worry, Julia. You are still you. Stay that way, and the rest will take care of itself. Despite feeling so alone, Julia came to value her solitary lunches with Mable more than any other part of the school day.

The days, weeks, and months went on. Things kept getting stranger, and Julia progressively felt more perplexed. Just beneath that, an insidious fear was gnawing away.

IT WAS MAY, AND THE WINTER CHILL was officially thawed out. They had just gone through a week of bitterly cold rains, and now it was as if Mother Nature had had enough, and with Monday came a pleasantly warm and sunny day. The birds were out in full force, singing cheerfully. New buds were pushing their way from branches, and a light breeze drifted carelessly through the air. Julia was feeling happy to be able to move her solitary lunch from the library back outside, when a shadow fell over her from behind.

"What's up, Loner?" came a brash and deep male voice.

Julia turned to see a somewhat familiar face grinning at her. She felt her cheeks flush, and glared.

"Just kidding. What's up, I'm Andre."

"Yeah, I know. I'm Julia."

"You know? How flattering…" The mocking smile again.

"Well yeah, you're on the basketball team. Plus you're like, you know…"

"The only black kid in school?"

"Right." She smiled tentatively at him. Even though he was giving her a hard time, it was nice to actually be talked to for a change.

"Well, there's Ernie, but kinda hard to mistake me for him." Ernie was a chess whiz with coke bottle glasses and a receding hairline, kind of looked like Urkel, only he had a voice closer to that of Barry White – weird combination. Andre was at least six and half feet tall, and athletic. Not too bad looking either, she thought as her cheeks went an extra shade deeper.

"Good point."

He stood there quietly, awkward, a little anxious. Looked as if he had something to say. Julia wondered if he was going to hit on her, or more likely, try and get her to join the IV Club. But it was neither. He cleared his throat.

"It's bullshit, you know," he whispered.

"Excuse me?"

"All of this. I mean, you know that, right?"

"All of what?"

"You know…" Andre gestured vaguely back toward the school.

Julia scowled. She had grown so suspicious and disconnected from her peers lately, that the first thought she had was that this was some sort of set up. But Andre looked so earnest, and also guilty, as if he had done something wrong, that she began to feel she could trust him. He fidgeted with his nose, glanced around surreptitiously, then checked himself and stuffed his hands into his pockets.

"Yeah," she said finally. "I do know."

Andre breathed an audible sigh of relief.

"Phew," he laughed. "Actually, you're the first person I've said that to."

"I thought I was the only one."

"Yeah, me too."

"Umm, you wanna join me for lunch?"

They spent the next fifty minutes of lunch talking, mostly about the school and how the IV Club had changed it. Occasionally other students would walk by and glare at them.

Andre explained that despite being on the varsity basketball team, he had always felt more like an outsider, largely in part because of his race. Before, people at school had always treated him with a tense courtesy, as if they were afraid he was dangerous, and he had gotten the sense that despite their politeness many of them spoke

81

condescendingly about him behind his back.

"I didn't know race was still an issue these days," Julia had replied.

"Sure it is. I mean it's not like the old days, I don't have to worry about lynch mobs or someone calling me the N-word. But I'm still different from the majority. And people still fear what's outside of the norm."

"Yeah, I guess I've noticed."

But strangely, since the IV Club had come along, he had become sort of a celebrity. People were always inviting him to come hang out with them, wanting to sit with him at lunch, competing with their friends over who was tighter with him.

"Honestly, it's all fake," he said to her. "These are the same people who just a few months ago would cross to the other side of the hallway to avoid me. Now, they're calling me 'Bro'." He shrugged. "Guess nowadays having a black friend is proof of what an enlightened person you are. I used to think life would be so much easier if I lived somewhere else, somewhere I belonged. Now that I do belong, I wonder why I wasted so much time wishing for it." He laughed cynically.

Julia couldn't help it, she felt a little pang of jealousy. "At least people talk to you," she said.

"Nah, they don't. They don't really see me. They're just talking to themselves, to the ideas in their heads."

"Well, you're welcome to join me and Mable out here any time."

"Mable?" Andre looked around for another person, confused.

Julia pointed to the big tree and grinned. "Yeah! Mable the Maple."

Andre gave her a sideways glance, and Julia wanted to crawl into her backpack and hide. Then he burst out laughing, and despite feeling like a total dork, Julia laughed right along with him. It felt like she hadn't laughed in a thousand years.

"Sure, definitely. I'll do that."

Julia felt a glow of warmth deep inside her stomach, a familiar flame that had lain dormant for so long, now slowly melting through heavy layers of ice.

"Just to warn you though, hanging around me isn't too good for your social status. I'm like a contagious disease around this place."

Andre suddenly became serious.

"No, you're not. It's not you that's got a disease around here."

ON TUESDAY, THE IV CLUB blossomed beyond the confines of extracurricular activity and invaded the school assembly. The principal, Rich Mossberry, enthusiastically introduced Ms. Eddy as the leader of what he described as "an enlightened venture of goodwill and good spirit." Whatever that meant.

Julia sat with her chin in her hands and felt her own spirit fading. The movement was too big, too powerful to do anything to change it, and she had gradually resigned herself to long days of invisibility and silence.

After thanking the principal, Ms. Eddy cut right to the point.

"Humanity has come a long way, but we still have a long way to go." She paused for effect. "Intolerance and inequality are still rampant, people are still looking out only for themselves, hurtful and critical behavior is far too prominent in the way people relate to each other and to themselves. We are cruel toward each other. Our goal is to change that, and I believe we can." Applause erupted from the stands. Ms. Eddy beamed with conviction.

"True change can't happen in isolation, on an island. It has to happen together, as one. Real strength and courage can only come from our bonding together, through a collective effort towards promoting life and the welfare of everyone equally and without prejudice. Selfishness is a sickness. Only by giving yourself to something more important than yourself, can your life be truly significant. Suffering is a disease. To fully live we must stop existing in pain and inflicting it on others.

"Today, I would like to ask all of you to commit yourself wholly to this idea, to making a positive difference in the world. I'm so proud of how far we've come. I see this school as a shining example not only to other schools, but to society as a whole. In fact, I have some very exciting news…"

The whole auditorium buzzed. "ABC's 20/20 has contacted us, and would like to do a special on the IV Club sometime at the end of the month. I'll be asking for volunteers later on this week to be part of the interviews they'll be conducting." The audience went crazy.

"Now calm down, calm down," Ms. Eddy laughed. "Remember this isn't about us getting famous, it is about us spreading our message the best we can, and this kind of exposure will surely help us do that. This is ongoing work, and it won't be easy. Now, I know the school year is coming to a close soon, but you can be sure the work of the IV Club will continue through the summer and into next year, and for many years to come. I'd like to go over some of the ideas I have to keep progressing in our mission…"

Ms. Eddy pulled up a Powerpoint presentation on a huge projector screen, and for the next twenty minutes expounded on her lofty goals, such as improving non-judgmental verbal communication, treating every individual as an equal, growing networks of inter-connectivity, un-conditioning of selfish thought patterns, adding curriculum to schools which focused on "spiritual education," and so on, with the ultimate goal of creating a world with "no more victims." Despite her articulate ideals, Julia just couldn't shake the feeling that Ms. Eddy was a fraud, and even worse, dangerous.

IT WAS COMING TOGETHER NICELY. Okay, nicely was an understatement – it was coming together perfectly. Like a finely aged wine – no, more like a meeting of low and high pressure fronts to create a swirling tornado. After all, in a sense, destruction was what this was all about. In order to rebuild, things must be broken down first. That was the way of the world, the way of change.

The past felt so far behind, another lifetime ago lived by a different, far lesser, person. The hard mattress, the ratty second-hand clothes, the taunting, the cruel and unjust punishments, the impotent rage boiling inside but never set free. Being different, being wrong. The ugliness. Most of all, she was glad to be free of that. In her new skin, she was beautiful, whole, and radiant.

That fated day so long ago, she had begun her long journey towards burying the past and embracing the future. She had started with a literal burial, could still remember vividly the rough handle of the shovel burning blisters in the palms of her hands, the thump of the dead weights falling unceremoniously into the empty ground, the finality of returning the soil to its home, the world now absent the two people who had brought her into the world, the two who she held most at fault. It was a beginning, but her journey was far from over.

She played the victim well, and when it was over and the authorities could find no leads, she moved on. Finished high school, put herself through college. She ended up digging a few more holes in those early years for a couple of people who deserved it, until she found herself realizing that the physical act of eradication was tedious and somewhat infantile. She was destined for bigger things. She got her degree in Education. She wanted to make a difference on a grander scale.

The world had changed, and not for the better. It used to be about sacrifice, but now everyone wanted to have their cake and eat it too. She had sacrificed so much – her youth, her dreams, her desires. She had become a better person because of it, and she saw the larger picture and understood that without sacrifice, the world was an empty, meaningless place. As a teacher, she could do more than just educate, she could show her students the true value and meaning of sacrifice.

AT THE END OF FIFTH PERIOD, the classrooms emptied and everyone headed to their next and final class of the day. Julia had forgotten to put her shop project in her backpack, a wooden box which she was earnestly attempting to engrave with a picture of Mable. It wasn't going so well, so Julia wanted to take the project home with her to try and remedy the situation. She stopped and put her backpack in her locker, since her last class was Drama, and she didn't need anything out of it.

On her way back to the shop classroom, she passed

by Room 304, Ms. Eddy's classroom and the original site of the IV Club. The door was open a crack, and she heard a voice coming from inside. Julia pasted herself against the wall next to the door, and listened.

"Thank you for taking the time to come." It sounded like Ms. Eddy's voice.

"No problem." The other voice was hesitant, suspicious, a girl's voice. Julia tried to place it, but couldn't.

"I wanted to talk to you about some things I've heard that are a little concerning to me."

"Umm, okay..." came the reply.

Julia peeked through the crack in the door to see a slightly chubby brunette girl, sitting at a desk in the front row. She recognized her as the girl who had once been pegged in the face during P.E. class with a kickball. Paige? Or was it Paula? No, it was definitely Paige. Her expression was pinched with the effort of forced friendliness.

"Some of your peers, friends of yours actually, have told me you don't think so highly of the IV Club and what we are trying to accomplish here. I was wondering if you could tell me why that is."

"Well, uhh..," Paige struggled for words, clearly uncomfortable. "It's not that I don't approve, I mean a lot of people are really into it and you know, good for them, it's just not, well, I don't know, not really for me..." She trailed off.

"Okay, that's fine. Do you mind telling me why not? Some of your friends told me you thought the club was 'filled with a bunch of fakers,' that you used the words, let me see here... 'hypocritical do-gooders' and 'self-important assholes' to describe us? Is that fairly accurate?"

"I don't see how my opinion really matters, Ms. Eddy." Paige was getting irritated, but sounded a little guilty too.

"Oh, but it does! Everyone's opinion matters, as do their thoughts, and of course their feelings. That's what the IV Club is all about. Which is why I'm a little concerned about you."

"You're concerned about me? Don't worry, I'm fine."

"I'm sure you think you are, but you're also very young, and the youth tend to have a chip on their shoulders. I'm just trying to help you see beyond your small world, that there are bigger and more important things than just yourself."

"So let me try and understand this. My opinion matters, how I feel and think matters – but only if I think and feel how you say I ought to. Is that right?"

"Young lady, it's clear I'm not getting through to you here." Julia could hear the tension in Ms. Eddy's voice. She was thrilled to hear someone stand up to Ms. Eddy's bullshit and get under her skin, but also a little worried about Paige.

"No, you're not."

Suddenly the charming Ms. Eddy was back.

"Okay Paige, that's alright. I just wanted to see if we could sit down and have a civil discussion about this, but I don't want to force anything on to you."

"Great. Can I go now?"

"Of course."

Julia heard the scraping of a chair, the rustle of a coat being put on.

"Would you perhaps be open to one more thing? It'll only take a minute."

Paige sighed.

"What?"

"I can't really just tell you. I have to show you. I think after seeing this, you may change your mind about what good work the IV Club is doing not just for this school, but even perhaps for humanity as a whole."

"I've got to get to Geometry, Ms. Eddy."

"It'll take five minutes, ten tops. I'll give you a pass for your teacher. And if after you see what I have to show you, you still feel the way you do, I promise to never bother you again."

Ten seconds of silence as Paige wavered.

"Fine."

"Fantastic," replied Ms. Eddy. "Follow me, then." Julia heard the sound of another chair scraping back. Shit.

She scurried down the hall as quickly and quietly as she could, and threw herself around the corner, out of sight. With her back against the wall, she stood there breathing in short, shallow spurts, wondering why it was she was hiding, and why she felt so afraid. She heard a pair of footsteps, and the classroom door opened. She had a sudden jolt of paranoia that Ms. Eddy had sensed her presence.

The footsteps began again and Julia prayed they weren't coming her way, until she realized they were getting quieter. They were heading the other direction. She waited a little longer, then peeked her head around the wall. Ms. Eddy and Paige turned right at the end of the hall. Julia stealthily tiptoed after them.

She came around the corner just in time to see a door closing on the left side of the hallway. She went up to it, reading the sign marked "Basement" pasted on in black block letters. Wasn't the basement usually locked? And why in the world would they be going down there?

Julia could hear them faintly, talking from behind the door. Echoing her own thoughts, Paige asked, "Why are we going down here?"

"You'll see," Ms. Eddy responded. "A lot of what we accomplish in the IV Club is kept down here. I want you to see the proof for yourself."

Julia waited a good thirty seconds until she was sure she couldn't hear them anymore, then put her hand on the knob. With sweaty palms, she softly turned the handle to the basement door, and carefully descended the stairs.

THE STAIRWELL WAS DARK, but there was light glowing from below. A group of pipes ran along the ceiling and walls, and Julia could hear an occasional drip of water on metal. Other than that, it was silent. The temperature seemed to have dropped at least ten degrees.

Julia crept tentatively downwards, listening for the sound of people talking. As she got closer to the bottom of the stairs, a large room opened up in front of her. It was a typical basement – shelves filled with odds and ends, janitorial supplies, a large metal furnace humming softly, a set of fluorescent lights buzzing from the ceiling. No one was there.

She listened carefully, and thought she could hear voices coming from the far end of the room. Crossing the basement floor and around a large shelf, Julia looked to her left and saw a dark corridor that had been hidden from view. There was no light coming from it, its entrance so black it almost looked like a dark rectangle painted on the concrete wall. She heard the voices again, and it sounded as if they were coming from somewhere within.

Julia crossed into the darkness. Feeling along the wall with her hands, she eventually took a right angle to the left, and saw a doorway outlined by light shining through the cracks around the frame. She crept closer.

"Ouch, what was that?! What did you do to me?" Paige's voice.

"Nothing. Just a little poke in your arm to calm you down. Keep your voice down." Ms. Eddy.

"Wait, what are you doing?" Paige sounded sleepy all of a sudden, frightened but out of it.

"It's for your own good, I promise you. You'll see shortly. Now hold still."

"Oh my god, what are you doing to me? What are you putting in my arm?"

"It's an IV."

There was silence, then Paige chuckled, a bitter, despairing laugh. "Oh, IV Club, huh? Now I get it." Her words were starting to slur together.

"Smart girl. I thought the double meaning was pretty clever myself."

"Why are you doing this?"

"Why? To help you learn of course. I'm a teacher, aren't I?"

"What's in it?"

"It's my own special cocktail, sweetie. Anectine, chloryl hydrate, and sodium pentathol. Creates the perfect combination of hypnosis and fear. Now we wait. In a few minutes, the lesson begins."

"Oh my God… you're insane."

Julia was bathed in sweat, trembling as she held her ear up to the door, uncertain as to what she should do. She considered running for help. But if she took too long, what would happen to Paige in the meantime? She couldn't bear to imagine it. Plus, who would believe her in time, that the virtuous and selfless Ms. Eddy was actually a dangerous psychopath? Steeling her resolve, she gripped the door handle and swung it back.

The look on Ms. Eddy's face was one of pure surprise, but nowhere near the shock that Julia registered at the twisted sight before her. Paige was bound to a chair, an IV bag hung from a pole next to her and inserted into her right arm. Her head lolled back, but she was conscious, struggling to fight the effects of the drugs coursing through her system. Ms. Eddy recovered quickly, and her mouth curled up into a smile of horrible malice.

"You meddling little bitch," she spat. From a metal table next to her, Ms. Eddy picked up a filled syringe.

As much as Julia wanted to come to Paige's rescue, her desire to live was stronger. Instinct took over and she ran, shutting the door behind her and slamming into the wall in the darkness, turning back toward the main room of the basement and doing her best to keep her feet underneath her. She heard the door open soon after, and the footfalls of Ms. Eddy's shoes not far behind. A voice in the back of her mind fought to deny the reality of her situation. This could not really be happening – she was at school, this was a place of books, classrooms, boring teachers, gum-chewing and gossip. Not a place where almost an entire student population was being lobotomized by a maniac masquerading as a hero.

As she rounded a long shelf in the middle of the room, she slipped, landing on her bottom and sliding across the floor. She glanced back at the corridor, but Ms. Eddy hadn't come through yet, so rather than get up, she crawled along the floor to the corner, and pulled herself back as far as she could between a large gray garbage can and a hamper of some sort filled with dirty towels. At the last moment, she pulled a few of the towels over her head, hiding her body but leaving a small gap so she could see.

Seconds later, Ms. Eddy emerged into view. Her face looked crazed, hair wild and disheveled, bright burning blue eyes scanning the basement like laser beams seeking a kill. Julia didn't dare to breathe as Ms. Eddy's gaze hovered over the place where she hid. Julia was certain she'd been spotted, was already imagining the tiny syringe piercing her neck. She would pass out and probably die on this very floor, and no one would ever know what happened to her.

Just as Julia couldn't take it anymore and was about to burst out of her hiding spot, Ms. Eddy's eyes moved on. Abruptly, she dropped the syringe from her hand, then turned and ran up the stairs. Julia heard the door open and close behind her and finally let out the breath she had been holding. Still, she didn't move. Ms. Eddy could be bluffing, so she waited a good five minutes, listening intently for even the smallest of sounds. Finally, convinced that she had gone, Julia pulled the towels off of her and tiptoed back toward the corridor to help Paige. Unfortunately, she had left her cell phone in her backpack, which was of course sitting in her locker.

She found Paige still conscious, though barely. Her skin was pale and covered in clammy sweat, her eyes open but not registering anything.

"Paige."

"Mmmm."

"Paige, are you okay?"

"Who are you?" she managed, her voice barely a whisper.

"Julia. We had P.E. together last year."

"Oh yeah… Julia. I think I'm dead, Julia."

"You're not dead, Paige." She pulled the IV needle from Paige's arm. A thin spray of the poisonous fluid, tinged with Paige's blood, squirted onto the concrete floor. "Come on, we gotta get out of here. Do you have a phone on you?"

"No, in my locker."

Damn. Julia lifted her out of the chair, pulled one of Paige's arms across her shoulders, and awkwardly half-dragged her back into the main room of the basement. "Here, hold on to this." Julia draped her like an old coat over a janitor's cart at the bottom of the stairs, then ran up to the top and opened the door a crack. The hallway was empty, so she went back down, then practically carried Paige up the steps.

The hallway was eerily silent. Even though sixth period had started, she should at least be hearing the muffled voices of teachers and students. But she heard nothing. Where was everyone?

"Hey!"

Julia almost jumped out of her shoes.

"What's up, Loner! Why aren't you at the assembly?"

It was Andre. Julia turned as he walked towards them from down the hall, his easy grin gradually transforming into confusion, then worry.

"What the hell happened to her?" Andre asked, looking at Paige's limp and listless body.

"Andre, oh my God, I'm so glad you're here. I can't believe what happened this is so fucked up Ms. Eddy was down there with Paige and holy shit we've gotta get help gotta stop her –"

"Whoa. Hold on. What? What happened?" Andre was starting to look genuinely afraid.

"She's a fucking psycho, Andre. She was doing something to Paige down there, had her hooked up to some IV drug, was going to brainwash her or something, I don't know. Lemme see your phone, I need to call the cops."

Andre opened his mouth to talk, but no words came out. He fumbled in his pants for his cell phone.

"Wait a sec," Julia said. "What assembly?"

Andre handed her his phone and said, "Uh, Ms. Eddy called some sort of emergency assembly or something. I figured it was about that 20/20 thing… wait – are you fucking kidding me?"

"No. I'm not."

"Oh, damn. I knew that lady was messed up, but I never would have imagined she was this bad."

"Me neither." Julia felt a wave of relief wash over her. Andre believed her.

"Andre, I'm afraid she's gonna do something. She knows I saw her, Paige and I can testify to what she was doing. I bet she thinks she's got nothing left to lose and is going to do something crazy."

"Let's go."

They both helped Paige into the nearest classroom and sat her down at one of the empty desks.

"Paige, we've gotta leave you here," she said. "Ms. Eddy is gone, so you're safe. I'm calling the cops right now, I'll tell them where you are. But we have to go stop her."

Paige managed a nod, and for a brief moment some clarity came back into her eyes.

"Get that bitch."

Julia dialed 911 and told the dispatcher what was happening and where to find Paige. The woman on the phone sounded incredulous, but informed her that officers were on the way, and that she should stay exactly where she was until they arrived.

Julia and Andre ran outside and across the high school campus toward the gymnasium.

IT WAS RUINED. Her whole plan had depended on illusion and secrecy. That rebellious troublemaker had destroyed everything. No doubt she was on her way to blabbing to the authorities, portraying her as some sort of monster. Ah, the burden of being a pioneer in this world.

She despised strong-willed, independent people like Julia, especially in the youth who should be more obedient and respectful of their superiors. She hated their unwillingness to give up their petty and egocentric ways for the greater good, hated their arrogance and ignorant ways of thinking.

If it weren't for brave and insightful people like her, the world would go down the toilet.

Fortunately, she had a backup plan. The chemist who had provided her with the IV elixir she used for persuading the more stubborn souls to her point of view had also had little issue with obtaining another product for her, for the right price of course.

It was time the school learned firsthand the depths of her sincerity to her cause.

"SACRIFICE."

Both doors to the gym had been locked, and strangely chained as well. Julia opened a side window, and as she and Andre climbed through they heard that one word echo through the high rafters, settling like a blanket of snow over the huge assembly of students and faculty seated on the floor and bleachers. She knew the voice, of course. She would know it until the day she died.

"Sacrifice is a lost art. All peaceful societies in the history of humankind have had at their core a deep seated belief in the value of sacrifice. The IV Club, I'm happy to see, has taught all of you the benefit of sacrifice, of putting aside a self-centered way of thinking for the sake of connection and the good of others. Sacrifice of the past, of the person you used to be, of the victim inside of you. Sacrifice of selfish desires, so that we can come together as a community of one, as equals. The lesson is spreading, not just among us, but outwardly, and it will continue to do so even after we are gone.

"Unfortunately, because of the way the world is and the improper way we have all been taught to live, not everyone will be able to come to understand our mission. Some people will oppose what we are doing, and I'm sorry to say that today, someone has done just that, and now all of our hard work and sacrifice is in danger of being ruined."

Gasps came from the crowd. Julia and Andre crouched behind the corner of a set of bleachers, watching Ms. Eddy, trying to determine what she was up to.

"I cannot, *we* cannot, let that happen!" Ms. Eddy proclaimed.

A rumble of agreement rolled through the auditorium, a few shouts of "No!"

"What is she going to do?" whispered Julia.

"I have no idea," Andre replied. "But I don't like the looks of where this is going."

"Me neither."

Ms. Eddy continued. "In order to stop this saboteur and keep our progress going forward, we must make a strong, unbreakable statement, here today. We must come together as one, and demonstrate fully what we stand for, the commitment to our cause, and show the world that we will not back down from anyone. Our mission is sacred. We must make a great sacrifice to ensure that it continues."

Murmurs echoed throughout the crowd, a mixture of excitement, and some confusion. From a table on the stage, Ms. Eddy pulled a sheet that had covered a large object hidden underneath. Upon its unveiling, it appeared to be a tank of some sort, similar to a propane tank but much bigger, and attached to the top of it was a funnel-shaped object that looked like a giant megaphone. Ms. Eddy pulled a small object out of her pocket and held it up to the crowd. It was a grey rectangle, with a single button on its surface.

The students became uneasy. Doubt began to ripple like waves through the audience, though nobody moved. Someone yelled out, "What is that?"

Ms. Eddy smiled, a grotesque thing to behold.

"This? This is my gift to all of you."

Julia turned to Andre, gripped in fear. Ms. Eddy was about to do something terrible.

"What are we going to do?" she cried.

Andre looked back at her, in shock and at a loss for words. Out of the corner of her eye, to the side behind Andre, Julia caught a glimpse of an orange, circular object that had rolled behind the bleachers. A basketball. Brushing past Andre, she picked it up, and handed it to him. He held it in his hands, confused.

"What am I supposed…" he trailed off. "Oh."

"I want to thank you all for your commitment," Ms. Eddy continued. "We are the pioneers of a new and better world."

"Do it," Julia said. "Quick."

The distance was about 90 feet, approximately the same length of a basketball court. Andre liked to stay late after practice sometimes and work on his full court shots, just in case it ever happened that a game was on the line and he had to make a Hail Mary shot to win it.

He leaned back with the ball in his right hand, his long muscular arm extended behind him, his well-honed athletic body coiled with every bit of potential energy he could muster. Then, with a grunt he unleashed, just as Ms. Eddy raised the remote control over her head with both hands and poised her thumb over the button.

Julia held her breath. Time stopped. The only motion was the smooth trajectory of the ball flying toward the stage. Andre had thrown it with such force it appeared to have no arc whatsoever, traveling in a straight line directly toward Ms. Eddy like a giant orange bullet. Though in reality it was mere seconds, to Julia its flight seemed to take an eternity. Out of the corner of her eye, Ms. Eddy caught the ball's movement heading her way, and faltered.

The ball nailed her right in the face with a solid *whump,* breaking her nose with a loud crack that resounded through the gym like a gunshot.

Ms. Eddy fell to the ground like a dead weight, the remote falling harmlessly from her hands, bright red blood gushing out of her shattered nose and onto the floor of the stage. She lay there, unmoving.

A loud bang sounded from one of the entrances to the gymnasium. Suddenly the doors burst open and a pair of young police officers ran in, bewildered looks on their faces as they took in the scene. By now, the audience seemed to have snapped out of their trance, and while most were still sitting there stunned, many were yelling and getting up to head for the doors. Total chaos was starting to ensue.

The cops pushed through the panicked students and made their way up to the stage and the unconscious form of Ms. Eddy.

"Can someone tell me what the hell is going on here?!" one of them yelled.

Andre and Julia struggled through the crowd and eventually reached the stage.

"I can tell you," she said, breathless. "But you're not gonna believe it."

"LEWISITE." THE DETECTIVE, a large walrus-shaped man with a paintbrush mustache, looked as if he hadn't slept in weeks. Apparently Ms. Eddy, after being driven by ambulance to the hospital and treated for a broken nose and a concussion, was now also being charged with attempted mass murder and lay handcuffed to her bed, watched over by a couple of armed guards.

"What's that?" Andre asked him.

"It's a chemical agent used in biological weapons, causes immediate and severe burns to the skin and respiratory system. With the doors chained no one could've escaped, and there was enough lewisite in that tank to kill every person in that gym ten times over. Ms. Eddy had rigged a garage door opener to trigger the valve on the tank, and one push of that button would have released the gas over all of you."

"Jesus," Julia replied.

"Yeah. It would've been real bad." He turned to Andre. "Nice shot, young man."

Andre shuffled his feet. "Thanks. Good thing I've been working on it. Though I never expected to hit a game winning shot like that one."

"Interestingly enough," the detective continued, "we've also done a little background research on Ms. Eddy. Her parents disappeared into thin air when she was a junior in high school, and were never heard from again. It was assumed they had been murdered. She was never an official suspect because there was no evidence, but the reports of the detective in charge described her as behaving strangely, and that she seemed emotionally detached from the whole situation."

"Whoa," Julia replied.

"And when she was in college, two students also mysteriously disappeared, both of them revealed to have had some sort of conflict with Ms. Eddy. She was questioned, but never charged with anything because again, there was no evidence. The police strongly believed she was behind it though."

Julia felt chills running up and down her spine.

"We'll get your official statements tomorrow. I know you both probably want to get home to your parents and get some rest after all that happened today. Can you be at the station tomorrow at eight o'clock?"

Julia nodded. "We'll be there."

Andre and Julia went out the back door of the gym onto the football field. Most of the students had cleared out and left by now, though there was still an army of news reporters and vans out front. Luckily, the field was empty. Julia and Andre walked together to the fifty-yard line.

"Damn Julia, if it wasn't for you the whole school

would have become a bunch of brainwashed zombies."

"Me? What about you? If you didn't have a rifle for an arm everyone would have been gassed to death."

"Yeah, well." Andre shrugged. "Let's just say, I'm glad you are who you are."

Julia smiled.

"Thanks," she said. "About time someone noticed. Same to you, Andre."

He put his arm around her and they kept walking.

PILL

"JUST TAKE ONE OF THESE in the morning and one in the afternoon. We'll follow up in a month, okay?" Dr. Spangler produced a yellow capsule with a small numerical imprint. Lacey always wondered what those numbers meant and if it was important that her medicine bear a name almost like a prisoner would. Lacey had been through three medications so far with Dr. Spangler and none of them had done the trick, whatever the trick was supposed to be. Had Dr. Spangler tried this medicine herself? Lacey stopped herself from asking.

"What's this one for?"she asked instead. Dr. Spangler frowned, though she tried to disguise it as something else. It was doctorly detachment at the end of the day, healthy for both the patient and healer alike.

"It's just a sample, like those you tried before. Try it out and see how you like it." Lacey nodded at Dr. Spangler's answer, noticing at the same time that it was no answer at all. This didn't look like a typical sample, like of cheese cake in the baking department or of lotion from The Body Shop. This sample had the potential to adversely affect her sleep pattern, appetite, heart rhythm, nerve conduction, or bowel movements. All of this she would probably learn from doing her own research on the internet after the visit.

Dr. Spangler suddenly placed her hands in her lap and stiffly crossed her legs. The office was super posh with a thick decorative carpet and cushy couches, but neither Lacey nor the doc ever seemed at ease during their weekly sessions. Lacey wondered more than once if she made the doctor uncomfortable since Dr. Spangler was always talking about her excellent rapport with other patients.

"If you try and look up this medicine, you probably won't find much because it's new. Whatever else I learn I'll pass on to you, but I can assure you it's safe and many patients have benefited from it." Dr. Spangler, now a mind reader, handed Lacey the capsule along with a small tinted bottle containing another handful. The capsule contained tiny blue beads that shook as Lacey jiggled it.

"Are there any side effects? . . . I mean, I have important exams tomorrow. My anxiety's really been getting in the way of studying, so I'm hoping taking this will help," Lacey tried as a last ditch effort to learn more. Visiting the doctor always made her feel queasy, like she wasn't getting all the info. Seeing Dr. Spangler for counseling had been no different even though she'd assumed it would be more relaxing than sitting on an exam table with a tongue depressor in her mouth. Although in her psychology classes at school, she'd never imagined that sitting in Dr. Freud's office back in the 1880's sounded that relaxing either. Reclining couch or not.

Dr. Spangler smiled and shook her head. "What?" Lacey blurted out. She always felt like she was misbehaving there for some reason, no matter what she did or didn't do.

"It's just—I think you're trying to find a reason not to deal with what you're going through." Dr. Spangler let her words hang in the air as her expression changed to one of softness and caring. "Lacey, I know this transition to college life has felt challenging for you. I also know from our sessions that you feel like there's nowhere to turn to for help. I'm trying to help you, and it isn't always possible to do that without prescribing some form of medication. This medicine should help you feel calmer, less anxious, and definitely aid you in preparation for your exams tomorrow."

The atmosphere seemed to have changed in the room, or Lacey's eyes were playing tricks on her. As Dr. Spangler spoke, her face first loomed large in Lacey's visual field and then drifted far away as if to an unreachable planet. Part of the experience tickled Lacey's wonder about human interaction and communication. She was a Psychology major after all. She wondered whether something physical happens in a room when people are near each other, something invisible to the eye but still felt on some level. Unfortunately, this wasn't a classroom lesson and it was actually happening *to her*.

Dr. Spangler's face suddenly returned to a natural distance from Lacey's visual field. Her wedding ring sparkled from the room's sky light as she extended a box of tissues. But Lacey hadn't shed a tear. It seemed like the gesture used up the rest of Dr. Spangler's energy for the session and she just managed to get out the words, "Unfortunately, we're out of time for today. I'll see you next time, Lacey." Dr. Spangler rose and walked toward the door. She had done everything she could possibly do, her manner indicated.

Lacey noticed her reflection in the office mirror on the way out. She looked tired and discombobulated. Her dark brown hair had managed to get frazzled and was now sticking out from the barrettes behind her ears. Even her barrettes were betraying her these days. Her eyes were shaded by a wary haze that she'd never seen on herself before. Her naturally curious mind asked whether a drug could start exerting its effects before you even took it. Maybe her personality was anticipating what was to come with this sample, but the change didn't feel that good so far.

She turned one last time to look into Dr. Spangler's office, but the door was already shut. Funny, she hadn't even heard it creak or the knob's latch click into place. It was almost like she'd never been in there. The receptionist smiled, her red lipstick slightly smeared onto one tooth. "Would you like to reschedule?" she asked, turning toward her computer. Lacey shook her head and said she'd call instead. The receptionist looked disappointed, but she still managed a courtesy smile. This lady has to be on drugs, Lacey jokingly thought to herself. But she probably wasn't and that's what made it scarier.

The spring air caught her by surprise in its freshness after leaving Dr. Spangler's stuffy office. A soft wind lapped at her back and led her down a small path to her car in the parking lot. "Hi car," she greeted, patting the driver's side door for a second before getting in.

Sometimes she felt like inanimate objects and animals were her best friends in the world, including her car. It's time to get back to the campus apartment and take these drugs, Lacey accepted. Dr. Spangler may be a bitch, but Lacey didn't know what other choice she had right now. End of semester finals were around the corner and she could hardly call herself functioning right now. She popped one pill in her mouth as an appetizer and dry swallowed it. Here we go, she thought, bringing her car to life with a key. A new feeling felt imminent in her body. She didn't know yet where it would take her, but hopefully through straight A's on her finals. She felt nice, like good things were heading her way.

LACEY HAD EXPERIENCED HER SHARE of prescription drugs in life, but none had felt like this one. There was the good old nitrous when she had her wisdom teeth taken out. It was her first experience with mind altering substances. The Adderall had been for her ADHD, attention deficit hyperactivity disorder. It had been helpful to make her more attentive in school, but ultimately the root of her inattention had less to do with her brain and more to do with something else.

Lacey didn't want to psychoanalyze her background, but it had been the opposite of calming. With multiple siblings, a watchful mom, a dad with an addictive personality, and even live-in grandparents several times during the year, she never felt the luxury of privacy. She knew a lot of kids grew up that way in New York, but her mom's desire for her to go to Cornell made it impossible to get by without the meds. She took them for as long as she could before the sleep issues became a bigger problem than the attention deficit. She was slowly weaned off the drugs by her doctor. Not a biggie, her grades had already been bred for excellence and she mainly felt fine without medication. She was a bit slower, but she studied harder to make up for it.

Then she had that bad skiing accident in the Catskills. Ended up in a couple casts and some rounds of oxycodone. It made her feel nauseous at first. With the motion sickness pills added in, she had quite a nice semester in high school. The social phobias weren't a problem for a change and she learned to see people in a new, softer light. Lacey's mom, a pharmacist, was experienced with prescription pills both personally and professionally and she knew when to start weaning her daughter off them. By that time, the meds never got her that high anyway. Coming down from them was hardly memorable. She almost felt relieved when life went back to normal and the casts came off.

Of course there was an array of other anti-anxiety medications prescribed by Dr. Spangler. Those had certainly felt weird, but not this bizarre. They were fast-acting and seemed to help her out with anxiety in the moment, but ultimately Lacey felt her moods getting worse over time because of them. She had stopped taking them recently and lived with the anxiety instead.

This new drug had kicked in by the time Lacey got back to her apartment. She felt...she couldn't quite describe it. She didn't even know if she had a word for it. It was different than sparking a doobie, which she had done a couple of times at parties. The marijuana was instant and predictable, while this drug felt like it was developing inside her somehow. It created a softness around the rough edges of life like the oxycodone did, but the effect was more insistent than with pain meds. Lacey got out of the car and realized she didn't remember anything about the drive over to her place. It must have been that good. She patted her car on the head and walked with her backpack, purse, and a few extra books toward the entrance of her apartment. Students have to carry too many things, she thought out loud.

Lacey stood in front of the door to her place and felt like she'd forgotten something. That feeling haunted her menacingly these days since school started. But this time it was different. It felt very important, yet somehow trivial all at the same time. What was it? Oh well. She opened the door and dropped her stuff to the carpet, relieved. Her gray and white cat, Cleo, took her usual walk toward her as if stalking prey. It was her way of saying that she was glad Lacey was finally home, but she had all day to show it.

"What's up dude?" Lacey heard her roommate, Brad, yell out from the kitchen. His mouth sounded like it was sloshing around something he'd just pulled out of the refrigerator. It was most likely an item he didn't stock there himself. Lacey lived in the apartment with three roommates total, as if to satisfy her familiar need for a chaotic household full of mismatched people who didn't respect each other's space or privacy. It felt nice at times to have the distraction and background noises, but on certain days such as this one she couldn't bear the thought of having to interact with someone she hardly knew. At least her two female roomies stayed out a lot. She wondered if she should preempt further conversation by quickly sticking her head in the kitchen to say hi, or if she should wait for Brad to come to her.

She didn't have to wait long because he soon entered the living room all sweaty and proud from a recent workout. He stood there a moment to give Lacey a chance to admire his physique and pit stains before continuing his inquiries. "So, you start studying for finals yet?" Brad threw himself with mock exhaustion onto the couch, reclining his body onto all the cushions which would soon absorb his moisture. Lacey cringed internally and picked up her cat so he wouldn't be tempted to dry himself with her fur once the couch was saturated.

"Not yet, pretty soon though." Cleo wriggled around in her arms, not being the type of cat that liked being held much. Lacey put her down and the cat scampered off toward wherever she liked to hang out. It was just her and

Brad now. It was also time for her to follow up her comment with some kind of chaser, like a question back to Brad about his life. That, she was learning, was how young strangers in college got to know one another better. The back and forth play of questions and answers, sometimes ricocheting around without real interest backing whatever was said. It felt new to her, and she couldn't remember meeting new people in this fashion during elementary or high school. But this style appeared so easy and natural to a lot of people she met in college, as if they'd been doing it for years. Extracurricular chit chat about testing and finals was popular too.

"What about you?" It felt so unoriginal, but it's all Lacey could think of. It was hard to be interesting and interested all the time, as college life seemed to demand. Professors and students were addicted to it like cigarettes.

"Eh, you know, I work out my mind and body at the gym. I don't like to study too hard." Brad winked at her. Lacey couldn't tell if he was joking, insecure, boasting, hitting on her, or all of the above. And for some reason he chose to ask her about studying when, according to him, he didn't do any of it. During her time so far at this institution of higher learning, Lacey found herself wondering at times about Darwin's theory of natural selection and where it was headed for humans. Brad, for one, looked like he was at risk of procreating anytime the opportunity arose.

Lacey tried to back her mind off the cynicism which her family and recently Dr. Spangler had told her she was prone to. She'd be meeting a lot of new people in college and in life, and she supposed now was the time to learn to get used to that. She liked meeting people, but sometimes it was challenging like in this moment with Brad. She quickly searched her mind for a friendly response to

Brad's quip and couldn't find a good one. "Cool," she finally picked.

Brad smiled, taking her response as a compliment. "Hey, you wanna go 'study' together later on at a coffee shop, or maybe that bar everyone keeps talking about?" He made exaggerated quote marks with his fingers as he said the word "study." Lacey had managed to swerve his flirtation for most of the semester up until now, but at least her next response was easy to find.

"Thanks for the invite, but I'm not as skilled as you. I have to work my brain outside of the gym to pass finals. See you later." Lacey picked up her backpack in a swift motion to get going and failed to notice that the side pocket's zipper was open. Her bottle of pills fell out and rolled a few feet on the floor toward Brad.

"Hey, let me get that for you," Brad said as he jumped off the couch to scoop up the pills, even though they were lying closer to Lacey.

"That's okay, I got it," Lacey tried to squeeze in before Brad could execute his favor. But it was too late, his gym prowess had given him a speed advantage.

Brad held the bottle up to his face and tried to read the label. "What have you got here?" he asked Lacey, a stupid smile on his face. Lacey really wished her other two roommates hadn't asked Brad to move in to help with rent.

"It's nothing. Just something to help me focus when I study…I have ADD." Lacey's lie drifted into the background as Brad was too busy x-raying the pills with his eyes. Was this guy just waiting to discover a new type of roid or something?

"ADD, huh…?" Brad's synapses were chaotically firing, but he had still managed to hear what she'd said. "Can I try one?"

Lacey tried to grab the bottle back from his fiendish hands. Drugs definitely did seem to exert their effects even before they entered the body. Brad's behavior right now was stranger than she'd ever seen. He was jiggling the bottle around, mesmerized by the capsule's tiny blue beads. "Brad, they're prescribed for me. Just give them back, okay? I have to get going."

It was too late. He'd already managed to escape her grab attempts, open the child proof bottle cap, and swallow a pill.

"Brad! What the heck? That's not going to help you with hockey, or with studying, which you don't seem to do anyway." Lacey found herself scolding Brad like he was a child and he actually looked for a moment like a kid caught red-handed.

"Sorry...I just wanted to try one, you know. They look kind of interesting. Try anything once—that's my motto." Brad flopped back onto the couch as if he hadn't disturbed anyone's day and was back in jock mode. He actually was a top player for the university's ice hockey team, which rightfully earned him his stereotypical status.

"Well, go try studying for once instead of bothering me." Lacey felt foolish since it looked like Brad was already bored with bothering her. The whole world seemed to have ADD these days, not just individual people. Lacey got all her stuff together and went straight to her room, not offering Brad a goodbye, which he didn't seem interested in anyway. He had flipped on the T.V. to watch football and Lacey no longer existed.

Back in her room, Lacey found Cleo curled up at the foot of her bed in a state of peace seemingly unattainable for humans. She shut the door on the world the best she could and changed into something more comfortable, turning on some music to drown out the monotonous clamor of the football game on T.V.

The next few hours were strange. Lacey emptied out her back pack, stacking her books on her desk and lining up highlighters and all the accessories that came with studying. She felt almost exhilarated to get started and was building up confidence that she would pass her exams with flying colors and little stress. The momentum was naturally propelling her toward her best. For once, maybe this wouldn't be such an arduous process, with the help of that pill.

Time passed. She fingered the spine of each book and stared at the stack for half an hour without opening to a single page. She finally opened to a bookmark and stared at the foreign lines of type. When had she studied any of this? She couldn't recall. Lacey looked up at the clock, which seemed to be playing tricks on her. The ticking of the second hand sounded like it was fishing for something, something from her. The seconds passing by tugged at her mind with the promise of pure potential as much as for utter waste.

Lacey wasn't the least bit distraught by her inertia and the passing time, and that's what surprised her more than anything. Normally, she would become frustrated with her lack of focus. She'd will herself to open a book as she dredged her mind for alert brain cells. The drug was kicking in, she was sure of that because she felt different. Just how, she couldn't explain. Instead of exerting a limited effect for an hour or two, the drug's effects were sprouting slowly as if from a seed inside her. Each moment felt new but also somehow long forgotten.

She wondered if Brad was feeling these things after the theft of one of her pills. The T.V was off now, so maybe he'd wandered off somewhere to procreate instead of sitting in one spot like her. What a motivated young

113

man, she joked to herself dryly.

Cleo turned her head and sleepily winked at Lacey. The cat's eyes opened wider as she yawned and simultaneously stretched out all paws, her body shivering for a moment in release of sleep. She emitted a small but satisfied high pitched purr. More alert now, Cleo turned back to her human master. A moment passed between them that transcended language and Cleo seemed to be using her instinctive feline probe on Lacey. The cat was seeing something, and it made Lacey feel momentarily uncomfortable. She felt the sudden need to get out of the house.

Cleo didn't object as Lacey gathered her purse and a couple books, quickly changing out of her comfy clothes and into standard college fare, which didn't look much different. The sun was still obeying the clock, even if Lacey wasn't, as it sank lower toward the horizon. The late afternoon light filtered in through the slanted window blinds, casting broken shadows on the walls. Lacey marveled at how much time had passed by while she'd been busy doing nothing. She didn't know where to go next. Her heart suddenly skipped a beat, which seldom happened. She felt a pang of anxiety start to surface in reaction, but then it was gone.

She suddenly found herself standing on the other side of her door, observing Brad sitting on the couch. His eyes were wide, staring at his computer screen in amazement. Funny, she couldn't remember having opened her door or even petting Cleo goodbye in her usual style. Cleo wouldn't care either way, but still. Brad looked up at Lacey as if he'd never seen her before and was trying to place her face. Or maybe her presence was nowhere near as exciting as his website surfing, and he was inconvenienced by her interruption of it.

"What's up?" Lacey asked, hoping to break his confused expression.

"Oh, it's just…there are lots of websites that show you how to make a peanut butter and jelly sandwich the right way. Did you know that?" Brad was acting like he'd made the biggest discovery of all time. He waited for Lacey's response.

"I know how to make a peanut butter and jelly sandwich, Brad." Lacey rolled her eyes.

"Yeah, but there are a lot of websites that show you how." Brad was fixated on this point, for some reason. "Do you wanna see?" He pointed at his screen.

"I'll pass for now. What have you been doing this whole time?" Lacey thought he'd left the house.

"Stuff, online…I feel great, can I have another one of those things?" Obviously he meant the pills and was becoming increasingly lazier in his speech.

"Don't you have hockey practice, Brad?" Lacey seemed to remember that Brad headed to practice after his workout most Tuesdays. And she wanted to sidestep his question.

"Yeah, I'll head out in a bit," Brad muttered, Lacey only half believing him. After the nothing that she'd been doing in her room for hours, she wondered if Brad would still be here when she got home. She ducked out of the house quickly while Brad continued to teach himself how to make peanut butter and jelly sandwiches using the videos online. His eyes glistened in a fiendish way, as if the very knowledge entering his mind would elevate him toward enlightenment. Lacey shook her head.

Outside, the birds seemed to chirp with more meaning than she could muster for her own day. She had to return to herself after watching Brad and admit that she felt pretty off too. She couldn't remember where she'd just been or where she was going. *Where was she going?*

Lacey sat in her car for a moment, taking deep breaths. Of course she couldn't even remember having opened the car door or throwing her stuff in the back seat. No matter, somehow her car offered comfort as the seat cushion slowly sank beneath her and the steering wheel grew warmer and almost malleable in the sun's rays. Her fingers clutched the wheel, searching for an answer in the feel of the material. That's right, she thought to herself, remembering now. Going places. Going somewhere. Why was moving so hard right now?

On top of everything, Lacey didn't know how she was feeling at all right now. She fumbled around in her purse for her phone, pressed the "on" button, and stared at the screen. A bunch of apps were lined in rows on the screen's menu. Stupid screen, she thought. It acted like it knew so much, like it had its shit all figured out. It seemed to be mocking her bewilderment.

Lacey's brain cells connected just enough so she could find Dr. Spangler's number in the address book and press the green dial button. She had to let the good ol' doc know what effects this medication was having on her, sooner rather than later.

"Hello Dr. Spangler's office, Dana speaking." The receptionist sounded about as inviting as a prison warden.

"Hi, my name is Lacey and I saw Dr. Spangler earlier. I just have a question about the medication she prescribed me . . . or gave me samples of, actually." It occurred to Lacey that she didn't even know what the name of the medication was with all the samples Dr. Spangler had flying around in her office.

"Dr. Spangler isn't available. Do you want to leave a message?" Dana's voice was growing in annoyance value with each passing word. It was as if by Dana's association with the doctor, patients were expected to bow down to her supposed authority as well.

"Sure, I think I'm having side effects from the medication I started. If she could please call me back as soon as possible, I'd really appreciate it. I'm kind of concerned and I have important exams tomorrow."

"I see, exams," Dana repeated, and snorted with mockery that was barely audible. "I'll let her know that you called. Have a good day."

Lacey thanked her, though she didn't want to, and pressed the foreboding red icon on her phone that disconnected her call. The icon was shaped like old rotary phone receivers used to be, devices that people had stopped using years ago. Lacey hadn't noticed this useless detail before, and she certainly didn't know why she was hanging on to it like a lifeline in that moment. She also didn't know when or if she'd be hearing back from Dr. Spangler, but she had to head out into the world and at least try to study again. If her earlier attempt could be called studying.

Her mouth did feel dry, the one side effect Dr. Spangler had warned Lacey about. But she felt other sensations too that didn't strike her as normal or therapeutic. She felt out of her body, but not her brain specifically. On the contrary, she felt like her brain was constantly trying to deliver a message that held the promise of deep meaning. This message felt irretrievable so far, tucked teasingly into an envelope that had been sealed with herculean glue so Lacey couldn't pry it open. She was trying, she really was.

She felt smart, but also so dumb. Basically like a brain without a body, she thought to herself. She wondered if she was about to hallucinate in some strange way. She almost craved the company of Brad right now, but she was scared to trip out to peanut butter and jelly YouTube videos with him. What was happening to them, and would it be reversible? Fear allowed a small jolt of sensation to travel through Lacey's belly and then it was gone. It quickly turned into a wormy worry inside her head and then her brain quickly stitched that up too. It suddenly occurred to Lacey that she could one day be famous. For what, she couldn't imagine.

Lacey eyed her house, parked in front of the car. Then she turned her gaze to the sky and the rest of the universe outside her driver's side window. Which one presented more danger right now? Lacey's natural courage, which she'd always drawn on during tough times despite any battling anxieties, was turning its back on her and the world felt very unsteady and uncertain. She was scared to even see her reflection in Cleo's eyes.

She was downright more paranoid than she'd ever felt in her life. Yet it was all happening secretly inside her brain, her body showing none of her usual signs of anxiety. The cold hands. A growing and sickening warmth in her head and chest. A menacing free fall in the pit of her stomach. Tightness in her neck and shoulders. She was always wishing these symptoms gone when she had experienced them in the past, but now she found herself missing them in their absence. Yet, a part of her didn't miss them. Maybe no one would be able to detect her anxieties, fears, or awkward moments ever again. Maybe over time she wouldn't have to deal with them either.

All of this was starting to sound crazy and the pills were even calling to her from inside her bag. She, like Brad, was wondering what a second dose of those tiny blue beads would feel like if she downed another capsule. It would be so easy and maybe the extra medicine would kick in and help her study. After all, Spangler had told her to take two a day. It was about time for her next helping.

Lacey's reverie was interrupted by Brad. She must have missed him exiting the house a few moments earlier and now he was running down the driveway toward her car. He had a look of crazed excitement in his eyes and was desperately trying to mouth something to her through the rolled up car window. Before Lacey could figure out what he was communicating, she noticed him clutching a peanut butter and jelly sandwich in his right hand. From all the commotion, you would have thought Brad the inventor of the first PBJ.

I can't take this right now, Lacey thought to herself. She just couldn't wait around to see what Brad wanted. In that moment, her actions kicked in to gear just enough to start the car's ignition and pull out the drive. As she drove off, in her rearview she could see Brad standing where her car was a moment earlier, nibbling on his perfect sandwich with shear amazement. Apparently, he had needed no real audience for his new "invention."

WHAT HAD GOTTEN INTO BRAD, Lacey wondered. And was it also happening to her?

As Lacey reached her local library, an obnoxious wailing erupted from her bag and it took her a moment to realize it was her phone. She pulled into the first parking space she saw and wrestled with the contents of her bag until her phone fell out onto the seat. She pressed the old school phone icon, this time green in color, and held the device up to her ear as she answered, "Hello?" Lacey wondered if people had always been half scared to pick up the telephone since Alexander Graham Bell had invented it. That might be why people, including herself, often answered with a questioning greeting.

"Lacey, this is Dr. Spangler returning your message. Is this a good time to talk?"

"Yes, definitely, thank you for calling me back." Lacey prepared herself to explain to Dr. Spangler how she'd been feeling and what she had noticed since taking the drug.

"Great. So Dana told me that you're not responding well to the sample medication. Can you tell me more?" Lacey may have just been imagining it, but Spangler's voice sounded a bit terse and defensive. Regardless, she'd have to tell Dr. Spangler the truth. This was her health, after all.

"Sure. So, I took the pill after our session and started feeling very strange. I felt good at first, like I'd have a ton of energy to hit the books. In the end, though, I couldn't do anything, much less study. My brain didn't feel right."

"Mmm hmm," Dr. Spangler sympathized through the phone waves, "and what else?"

"Um, that's about it. The medication makes me feel really out of it." Lacey didn't know what else to say.

"Yes, go back to the part about how you felt good at first. What changed after that?" Lacey thought back in time for a moment, trying to figure out what exactly had changed.

"Nothing changed, really. I thought I could study, based on the increased energy and the positive thoughts I was experiencing. I felt like I could accomplish a lot! But it was hard to actually do something about it."

"Hmmm . . ." Dr. Spangler emoted through the phone, as if she had figured something out and because of the truth of it, felt an enhanced and pitiful concern for Lacey. A disconcerting silence lingered, and Lacey supposed Dr. Spangler wanted her to ask for more advice before she would offer it. Getting health care from this lady was like pulling teeth.

"So, what could this mean?" Lacey ventured, never knowing the right question or answer with people like this.

"Well, Lacey," Spangler continued, happy to be prodded on by Lacey's interest in her expertise, "it seems to me that the medicine is trying to help you, and you're resisting its effects."

"And how is it trying to help me?" Lacey asked, getting a bit frustrated at the deficiency this woman kept trying to make her feel. "At this rate, I'm not going to get a single thing done before my exams tomorrow."

"Lacey, the medication is helping you live more in the moment and to feel positive emotions about your potential . . . and about what you can accomplish with it. Can't you tell that from what you experienced?"

"Okay . . . but what's the point of feeling positive about all this stuff in the moment if I can't actively use that energy? I feel it, mentally, but other than that— nothing. It's never been this hard to get down to studying before." Lacey knew that Spangler would start getting pissed at any indication that Lacey actually had a brain and was trying to use it. The added questioning of her expertise as a doctor wouldn't help either.

"Hun, you can use that energy if you stop fighting the medication and let it help you. It's obviously bringing you more into the moment, from what you yourself described. That's its purpose, and research has been done to show that it can help in this way. The feeling that you *can do* anything, be anything—take advantage of it!" Had Spangler ever called her "hun" before?

"Alright . . . but, not to sound doubting, I don't just

want a mental high. I hope that I'll be able to pass my exams tomorrow too."

"And that's just what I'm explaining to you, Lacey. Let the medicine act, and you'll be able to do just that. In fact—now that you already took the first dose, you should follow up with the second dose like I recommended at your visit. Without the full treatment, you may have some trouble concentrating tomorrow. But you'll see after you take the second dose, you'll be good to go for exams."

Lacey didn't want to risk doing badly on her exams the next day. She supposed Spangler was right, maybe it was time for her to take a second dose to get the full effect.

"Alright, I'll take a second one. Hopefully it'll help like you said."

"Don't worry, you'll be fine. But do call if you have any other questions. Good luck on your exams!" Weird, Dr. Spangler was being nice for a change. Very uncharacteristic of her, but in this moment Lacey didn't mind. She'd been pretty freaked out about her new meds and the reassurance was welcome.

"Thanks, bye." Lacey pressed the red phone icon and sat back in her seat, exhaling with relief. She felt like she hadn't been breathing naturally for a while as the air escaped from her whole body. Her chest muscles loosened a bit. Lacey suddenly felt like someone was sitting in the car with her, and she knew it was the presence of the pills. It was time for a second dose.

Her phone rang again and the caller I.D. showed Brad's name. What did he want now? Lacey silenced the ringer and shook her head. She couldn't shake the feeling that the effects of this pill were different than others she'd taken. She just couldn't explain how. Brad was weird, but he usually wasn't *this weird*. As annoying as he was, she hoped he was okay. Another part of her wished he was here so that she wouldn't have to experiment with a second dose on her own.

Lacey fished out the pill bottle from her overcrowded bag with both fear and anticipation. This medicine made her feel like she could do more than just pass silly old exams. Maybe if she took the second dose and got her exams out of the way, she could see just what else she was capable of.

She took the capsule between her fingers and shook it a bit. This was part of her ritual now with this unknown drug. She watched the little blue beads inside shake around fluidly as if they were suspended in liquid mercury. At the same time, each bead seemed to repel off the ones around it. She felt the temptation to break the capsule open and touch what was inside, but instead she swallowed it with a small gulp of water from her water bottle. Lacey leaned back in her seat and looked up at the library's sturdy brick structure. After a few minutes her vision softly zoomed in and out around her. Time pleasantly stood still and the second time around, her panic regarding this phenomenon was less.

Lacey grabbed her books and seemingly floated through the library's entrance. Even her movements felt fluid, like mercury. She saw her friend, Mariah, sitting at one of the long tables nearby the magazine shelves.

"Hey Mariah," she greeted her friend, while staring over her shoulder at some psychology notes that were scattered on the table as if ravaged by a tornado.

"Geez, Lacey! Where did you come from? You scared me." Mariah must have been deep in thought studying. If only she knew how easy it could feel after one of the blue beaded capsules.

"Sorry about that. Looks like you need a break from studying. How long you been at it?" Lacey felt a tad jealous that Mariah seemed to be progressing through her study materials, but any moment now she herself would be leafing through all that with flying colors. Who needed blood, sweat, and tears? No pain, no gain was just a motto that people used when they had no choice but to try so hard. She had harbored doubts about her new medication, but now she felt sure that it was increasing her self-confidence and abilities.

Mariah squinted her eyes at her, almost suspiciously. "Have you started studying at all, Lacey? Exams are tomorrow, you know."

Lacey laughed with uncharacteristic light-heartedness. Normally, she'd be fretting about all this same stuff. But not today. "Yeah, I know that. I'll get around to it. Right after you and I take a break and get in a Frappuccino at the mall. You down?"

Mariah seemed confused about Lacey's behavior, and it was starting to make Lacey nervous too. "You have to start studying before you can take a real break, right? Maybe I'll take one with you in an hour or so, after I'm done with Psych. Are you okay, by the way?"

Lacey shrugged. "Yeah, better than ever. Why?"

Mariah was in a hurry to get back to her studies, but was also slightly concerned about Lacey. She put her pencil down for a second and appeared in thought. "You're usually uber prepared when it comes to studying for exams. I mean, it's cool that you're feeling more relaxed about it too. It's just . . . there's so much to do and it looks like you haven't started yet."

Lacey needed to make an exit soon. This was getting weird, and obviously Mariah should notice how confident she was this time around for exams. That was a good thing, not a bad thing.

"I mean, I'm usually more anxious. But my doc gave me something to take the edge off. It'll help me study better. Anyway, I'll check you later and good luck on exams tomorrow." Lacey turned her shoulder and made a step toward the interior of the library.

"Wait—Lacey. Do you want to study together? We've been doing that for quizzes and it's helped me a lot. I'm down for a study buddy if you're interested."

Lacey smiled, she almost felt sorry for the poor girl. It was going to take Mariah so long to get through everything, and Lacey didn't want her friend holding her back. "Thanks, Mariah, but it sounds like you're ahead of me today. Next time."

Mariah watched as Lacey walked away. Lacey's walk was different, Mariah felt sure of it. It was a little more—pompous? And floaty, if a walk could be described that way. Strange, but it must just be her imagination. She picked her pencil back up again and returned to work.

Lacey glided over to a solitary table around the corner and put her bag and books down on it. She had made sure her study area was out of view of Mariah's. She and Mariah had been getting to know each other better, but apparently Mariah wasn't always a supportive friend. She must be jealous of how easy this will be for me, thought Lacey.

Lacey's phone flashed a display of an incoming text. Luckily she had silenced it before entering the library. Since she hadn't started studying yet, she was curious to see who was trying to reach her. She opened the text, and it was from Brad. It read, "Lacey—could I have just one more of those blue pills?" Lacey shut off her phone, with a small twinge of irritation that was gone before it had even started. Brad was useless. Of all the things he could be doing with this new feeling and its heightened potential, he was choosing to perfect the art of a peanut butter and jelly sandwich.

She brought all the books out of her bag, lined up her study accessories, and felt good that she had more sense than Brad. She was going to kick butt with her exams the next day, she knew it. She felt fearless for the first time in her life. And she was going to make it in this world, in a big way.

MARIAH PUT HER HEAD DOWN on the library table and wished that it was cushioned for naps during study breaks. As the hardness of the wood began to deepen her headache, she got up and stretched instead. Studying never seemed to end, but Mariah felt proud of herself for how much she'd accomplished so far. With enough educational prowess, she hoped to become a doctor one day. Not just a "doctor" in title. She wanted to be a critical thinker in the field of medicine and bring some badly needed healing to what seemed like a broken and stuck system. The focus in her own health, and one she wanted to pursue in profession, was preventive medicine. Teach people how to live healthily enough to avoid preventable illnesses—and who knew what else the world would be capable of?

The library was open late to accommodate the gaggles of students who were cramming as much information as they could before the start of finals. Mariah felt like she'd been hanging out there three days straight and her sweats had become a sort of uniform, just like for many other students. She shook her head while noticing spatters of old coffee stains on her sleeves. She had no idea how those got there.

Mariah's mind shifted to her earlier encounter with Lacey, one that had been quite strange. Was it true Lacey hadn't started studying yet? Her new friend was usually the alarm bell to those around her indicating that it was time to study. During midterms, Lacey had wasted no time in making herself an expert in each class's material. Her binders and notes would be organized and laid out in the library like soldiers preparing for battle. She wasn't even a coffee drinker and somehow she had propelled herself through that week with flying colors. Sure, she could be a bit neurotic and over-anxious about school, maybe even over-preparing half the time, but the girl knew how to hunker down and get things done.

Today was a different story. Lacey looked confident, but she seemed to imply that she would pass her exams just fine without any effort. The meds that Lacey's doctor prescribed for anxiety must be some pretty good stuff, Mariah pondered. But what anxiety medication made people feel superhuman? It was unlikely that Lacey's I.Q. points could surge that much just from decreased anxiety, to the point where she could skip most of her studying. Mariah was confused. Maybe she would take Lacey up on the Frappuccino break before returning to her books. Maybe she would investigate a bit too.

Mariah searched the library floor, unable to find Lacey. Lacey must have picked a table pretty far from her own. Was she trying to avoid her? Just as Mariah rounded a bookshelf, she spotted her friend at a nearby table. Mariah inched back slowly behind the shelf and watched Lacey's "studying." Lacey had a book open and her finger was pointing to the center of the page. As Mariah watched for five, ten, and then fifteen minutes, Lacey's finger didn't budge. Her body was transfixed in one position as if under a spell. Frozen. Mariah didn't know what to make of it. Out of curiosity, she watched a little longer. Still no change. Yikes, she knew something bizarre was going on. Mariah took a deep breath and left her hiding spot to approach Lacey, if her friend was still alive.

"Hey Lacey, how's it going?" Mariah greeted. Lacey's head jerked suddenly as if falling from a reverie.

"Oh, hey. I'm fine. Just studying you know . . ." Lacey seemed slightly uncomfortable and extremely out of it.

"Cool—how much did you get done?" Mariah looked at the page Lacey had been pointing at seconds earlier. There were no diagrams, graphs, or figures to study. Just boring old text. It was the beginning of a chapter in fact. Mariah knew from taking the class herself, and from studying for its exam, that the specific chapter was only the tip of the iceberg of what would be on the final the next day. Lacey hadn't started studying yet, had she?

"Oh you know . . . I'm pretty much done here. Just reviewing everything one more time before I move on." Lacey waited, as if for Mariah to leave.

"Really? Well, I just finished this same section too. Do you want to quiz each other on the material? I can go grab my stuff . . ." Mariah studied Lacey's face, trying to gauge her response. Lacey looked irritated.

"Mariah, I think I'm ahead of you for this class. I don't need the extra quizzing, thanks." Lacey's eyes had grown deep under-eye bags and they were sagging more with each passing minute.

"Please, Lacey. I just watched you for twenty minutes from over there." Mariah pointed behind them. "You were staring at this one page the whole time. You expect me to believe that, at this rate, you're ahead of me for this class?"

Lacey's eyes flared. "You were spying on me? Why the heck would you do that?"

Mariah shook her head slightly. "Lacey, I'm sorry. I'm just trying to look out for you, that's all. You haven't studied much, and then I saw you staring at your book this whole time. What's going on?"

Lacey stood up from her seat and assumed an oddly confrontational stance for a library setting. A couple months ago, this space was almost sacred for a student like Lacey. Now she looked like she was ready to brawl in it. "What's going on? I'll tell you what. Nothing, except you standing there accusing me of stupid things for no reason. How would you know how much I've accomplished? I can achieve anything, you know."

Mariah took a couple steps back. "I know Lacey, I know you can do anything. You're really smart, obviously. I'm just telling you what I saw. You didn't move at all for at least half an hour. Not to flip a page, not to highlight, not to take notes. You say that you've studied everything, but how did you do it all while staring at one spot in your book? This just isn't like you."

Lacey admitted grudgingly to herself that coming from Mariah's mouth, the argument made sense. She supposed that she hadn't done much for the past hour or two. But overall, she felt like she'd done so much, achieved so much. It couldn't simply be her imagination that she felt well-prepared for exams.

"You've known me for a few months, how would you know what I'm really like? I'm someone who can achieve anything." Lacey's face was getting red.

"Yeah, you mentioned that already. Why do you keep repeating it . . . that you can achieve anything? No one said you couldn't." Mariah tried to see what was going on behind Lacey's eyes, see what she might be hiding. At times, she was talented at detecting flashes of expression beneath the surface of people's outward demeanor. She was having no such luck with Lacey. Her friend seemed convinced that she could achieve anything, by simply doing—nothing.

Lacey seemed frozen again. In time, in space, and in conversation. Mariah gave up. "Listen, you're probably right. It's better we do our own studying this time around. You're ahead of me, and I don't want to slow you down. Good luck with exams tomorrow." Mariah waited for Lacey to say something in kind, or at least wave goodbye. Nothing happened, so Mariah turned to leave with an eye roll. College seemed like a place that might break her habit of being nice and helpful to people.

Lacey stared after Mariah, stunned. She wanted to form thoughts around what had just happened, but everything in her head seemed out of reach. Wow, she must have studied more than she thought, she felt so burnt out. Maybe it was time to head home to finish the rest. She'd have to swerve around Brad, but she couldn't handle friends spying on her at the library and flinging strange accusations toward her. Some people were going to be jealous of her potential, and she'd have to learn to accept that.

On her way out, Lacey caught a glimpse of Mariah studying at her table. Books and notes covered every inch of table space and Mariah looked like she hadn't changed clothes in three days. Lacey shook her head to herself. The whole scene seemed familiar to her, but so unnecessary now. There were higher things to strive for.

Mariah subtly caught Lacey walking toward the exit from underneath her eyelashes. Lacey still held that strange gait, floating along as if without a care in the world. Her face displayed a half-smile expression that wasn't rubbing off, even though no one was looking at her. And she hadn't decided to say bye to Mariah, passing right by her table without a single gesture. Something was off, Mariah felt sure of it.

WERE PEOPLE LOOKING AT HER? Lacey sensed it. She felt grander than she'd ever felt and part of her wanted to be seen. Another part of her wanted to run home and hide. Though she felt light outwardly, she was starting to feel a pressure building up inside of her as the drug started to wear off. Pretty soon that pressure might come to the surface and throw her off her game, that was her fear. Energy was swirling around in her and she felt restless for some reason. She couldn't even pinpoint why.

Arriving home, Lacey hoped Brad had calmed down some. She peeked into her foyer and listened for sounds. The coast seemed clear. She was looking forward to her third dose of medicine. Wait, was there supposed to be a third dose? She couldn't remember, but one more dose couldn't hurt given how much was required of her the next day. She'd make her family proud and stand out of the crowd for once.

Lacey sat down in the living room and rummaged through her purse for the pill bottle. She was feeling quite jittery now and almost screamed as Brad plopped down on the cushion beside her. He had appeared so silently. He was grinning at her and also seemed to be bounding with restless energy.

"What do you want, Brad?" Lacey asked him, simultaneously irritated but also somehow relieved by his company.

"Just one more, Lace. Please. Finals and stuff, you know." Finals, yeah right. Brad didn't have any intention of studying. But if she gave Brad one more, then she wouldn't have to be alone in this new experience.

"Alright, one more, but that's it." Lacey expertly flipped the cap off the bottle and dispensed two pills into her palm. She handed one to Brad.

"Wow, just like that? Not going to give me a hard time?" Brad's eyebrow rose but he couldn't muster much suspicion as he rolled the pill between two fingers and hopped up to get water in the kitchen. Lacey took a swig from her own water bottle and swallowed the pill. She sat on the couch, wondering what life held for her. Then she flipped on the T.V. for a little entertainment before studying.

Commercials, commercials, on every channel. She wished networks would stagger their show times better. Lacey settled for the sales pitches until something better came on. A car commercial talked about how many great adventures were possible—in that particularly sleek and audacious car. Was she brave enough? Next was a commercial for electronic devices, including tablets, phones, and interactive watches. It beckoned her to contribute her talents to the world, leaving a unique mark in her wake. What would her special contribution be? Lacey sank deeper into the couch, wondering what she had to offer the world that was special. Next came a commercial for an energy drink that featured people doing back flips, jumping out of planes, and scaling mountains. Maybe it was time for her to take life more seriously too and really apply herself, thought Lacey.

Brad sat down next to her, a peanut butter and jelly sandwich in his hands. He was grinning again. He gestured for Lacey to eat it and Lacey shushed him to be quiet as the next commercial came on. It was a beer commercial. Light, airy, and ageless people clinked dark beer bottles together while spreading contagious laughter among one another. They had all turned into carbonated bubbles of joy just by drinking the magical beer. What was the joke, Lacey wondered, and why didn't she get to laugh effortlessly like that with friends? Maybe that's what she actually needed in her life, to take everything less seriously. She didn't want to be like Mariah—so flippin' serious.

The commercials came to an end and Lacey found Brad still staring at her, holding the sandwich. "Alright, let me try it." Lacey accepted the sandwich from Brad and took a bite. "What's supposed to be so special about it?" Lacey chewed. Brad looked a little hurt but answered anyway.

"I learned how to make peanut butter and jelly the right way, from online cooking videos." Brad seemed really proud of himself and Lacey couldn't deny him a compliment after his having fed her. Each person made a contribution to the world in their own way, after all, and maybe this was Brad's expression of it.

"It's really good Brad, the best peanut butter and jelly sandwich I've ever had!" Brad's face was beaming and in that moment, Lacey felt a twinge of sadness for the two of them. She couldn't explain it because on the surface they both seemed really happy. But they also both seemed so . . . bored. Lacey's thoughts turned inadvertently back to the car, the electronic devices, the back flips, the beer, and the pill. How were all of these things related, and why was she thinking about all of this? Dr. Spangler must have been right about her, Lacey realized. She was resistant to being helped.

"Well, thanks Brad, I have to get back to studying

now." Lacey got up to go, an emptiness growing in the pit of her stomach that wasn't being filled by peanut butter and jelly. Brad's eyes grew as he frantically searched for some way to keep Lacey around.

"Wait . . . um, you want to go study with me somewhere?" Brad didn't look like he'd picked up a book all quarter.

"Thanks Brad, but I'm pretty behind and I need to catch up on my own. I'll see you later." Lacey grabbed her stuff awkwardly as she somehow felt scared to go off on her own too. Brad was a useless anchor for her right now. Not in a personal or offensive way, but Lacey knew that his presence wouldn't normally be something she would seek out. Today just felt—wrong. She wondered to herself how much people used each other for lonely flotation devices these days. Then she felt guilty for thinking that.

As Lacey escaped into her room and started shutting the door, she saw Brad still looking her way. He looked almost terrified. Lacey avoided eye contact and the crack in the door's frame disappeared as she met the privacy of her room. After the third pill, the high-flying effects of the medication felt more fleeting and were quickly dispersed by feelings of doubt and fear. In fact, the doubt and fear were worse than Lacey ever remembered occurring naturally. She could see it in Brad's eyes too. They were starting to need more medication just to cover it up. Just as Lacey came to this realization, there was a knock at her door.

"Lace—do you think you could spare just one more?" Lacey didn't answer and sat very still on her bed. She noticed she had locked her door and breathed a sigh of relief. The knocking went on for a few more minutes along with Brad's imploring, and then there was silence.

She heard the front door to the house open and shut. The strange thing was, she wanted one more too. She took out her pill bottle and shook it around a bit, a strong internal battle happening in her mind. She pictured a scenario of taking the fourth pill, followed by one in which she didn't take it. She couldn't imagine either case too clearly since she still didn't know the effects of this medication well. She had never seen anything strike dependency in her so quickly. And Brad was showing similar effects.

Lacey decided against it. If anything were to happen, it could jeopardize her exams for the next day. It dawned on her, though, that she was just mouthing these sentiments to herself. She barely cared about her exams anymore, she just wanted that feeling back. The feeling that she could do anything, achieve anything, contribute anything—to the world. How could that feeling hurt her potential to ace the exams? Lacey held her bottle a second too long and the next thing she knew she'd swallowed a fourth.

The nice edge came back . . . a soft melty glow in her psyche that said everything was going to be okay. Because she was talented, and she was the best. The world had no idea about her true potential. She was powerful and could really make an impact on the world. She would be recognized, maybe even world-renowned. Her contribution would be felt.

Lacey went through her familiar routine of spreading out study materials and then sat upright in her chair. The twinge of sadness shot through her again, but she zipped it back up and reminded herself she should be willing to take help for once in her life. She began to study as a whirlwind of chapters, notes, and highlighting flashed before her eyes. She had never felt so prepared.

LACEY AWOKE FROM A NAP the next afternoon, clothed and groggy on top of her bed. She yawned, sat up, and noted a bit of nausea after the slew of exams she'd taken earlier in the morning. Cleo glanced up from the foot of the bed, indifferently. Lacey remembered how grueling her exams had been, but she'd been prepared. While other students were fidgety with nerves, sleep-deprived, and on the verge of collapse, she had been calm and in control. She was the first to turn in every final and was met with an approving nod from each of her professors. She felt confident she'd aced them all, but now her body was suffering with the aftermath and it probably didn't help that she'd missed her morning dose of whatever that drug was called.

Lacey looked down at herself. She had stayed up so late studying that she hadn't even bothered to change out of yesterday's clothes before taking exams. Mariah must have thought she looked like a slob, wearing the same clothes she'd worn at the library the day before. Who cares what Mariah thinks, Lacey reassured herself. While Mariah had needed to clock at least three days at the library to pass her exams, Lacey had only needed one night. If the one tradeoff was looking like shit, she'd look and feel brand new again anyway after taking a hot shower and eating something. Plus, she needed her morning dose. Without exams to think about, Lacey pictured all the fun and exciting things she could do with that beautiful feeling the blue pills provided.

Hopefully Brad wasn't hogging the shower after his exams, hockey, or whatever else he was up to. Lacey opened her door a crack and noticed Brad reclined on the living room couch. The T.V. was turned on to the same channel they'd been watching the previous day and Brad had also neglected to switch out of his clothes before taking his exams. Lacey silently admonished herself for displaying habits that resembled those of Brad, but it was okay for just one day. Maybe the drugs had helped Brad fly through his exams too.

Gathering a change of clothes and a towel, Lacey felt prepared to nab the bathroom when her cell phone rang. The incoming display read: Mariah. Lacey rolled her eyes. The girl just couldn't quit with her jealousy issues, could she? Lacey hadn't realized Mariah was so competitive with her until the day before at the library. They hadn't even interacted with each other during exams, but Mariah must have been spying on her yet again. Lacey considered giving her friend one blue pill to try just so she'd shut up. Reluctantly, she answered the call and pressed the phone to her ear with her free hand.

"Hey Mariah, what's going on?" Lacey's air blew out audibly in exasperation, which she wanted Mariah to hear. She didn't have time for stupid shenanigans after such a long day. She figured Mariah would know that already if she was so smart.

"*What's going on?*' I mean, isn't it pretty obvious?" Mariah was acting confrontational again, unfortunately. Lacey didn't have time for this.

"Mariah, it's been a really long day. I worked hard and now I deserve some rest. Okay? If you're calling to accuse me of something or you're still mad at me for yesterday, I don't know what to tell you. I didn't do anything wrong. You don't need to be resentful toward me just because I studied less than you and still aced everything." Lacey waited, there was complete silence on the other end. "Hello, Mariah—are you still there? . . . Geez, she hung up on me."

"I didn't hang up on you," Mariah filled in. Her voice sounded a bit scared and hesitant all of a sudden.

"Okay then, what do you want?" Lacey made a mental note to steer clear of this psycho from now on after they were done talking.

"Listen, Lacey, I don't know how to tell you this . . . but you never made it to exams."

Lacey had had enough. "What do you mean I didn't make it to exams, what are you talking about? Have you utterly lost it?"

"Lacey, please don't hang up, I'm serious. I looked all over for you, and a couple teachers even asked me where you were. You didn't show up for a single exam."

Lacey sat down on her bed, almost on top of Cleo who issued a fed up yelp and hopped to the floor. The cat glared at her from across the room. From this angle, Lacey got her first glimpse of the table against the wall. All her study materials were still spread out, almost as if she'd never touched them after emptying them from her backpack. The bag itself was propped up against the wall, next to the desk. It was open and gaping at her, letting her know that she'd never left the room after returning home last night. She looked down at her clothes, completely rumpled as she had slept the whole day away. Her hair looked like a bird's nest in the mirror, and one side of her face was flattened and imprinted with her sheet's pattern. She hadn't left her room at all. She had missed all her exams. And this wasn't the usual nightmare people had about missing exams.

But why did she clearly remember taking them? What had happened?

Mariah's voice jostled Lacey back to reality, the reality in which she was about to flunk all her college courses.

"Where were you today?"

"I thought I was taking exams, Mariah. Honest. I

remember it as if it happened, I can't believe it didn't." Both of them fell silent for a moment, thinking.

"Lacey, what's that drug called that you're taking?"

Lacey flinched. The drug. She had forgotten all about it and yet it had also been everything to her lately. "I have no idea. Dr. Spangler gave me a sample of it in a bottle. I don't even know the name, there's no label. Why?" Lacey knew exactly why but decided to ask anyway.

"Lacey, I think the new drug you tried is related to what happened to you today. When I saw you at the library yesterday, you seemed different."

"Different how?"

"You just didn't seem to care, about anything."

"Not care? I cared a lot, Mariah! I wanted to accomplish so much and ace my exams. To be the greatest . . ."

"Yeah, that stuff again. Be the greatest at what, Lacey? Do you even hear what you're saying?"

Lacey's cheeks flushed and she felt embarrassed. Mariah was right, what was she saying? Her words sounded so—grandiose. Greatest, accomplished, world-renowned, can do anything. These words were like a flamboyant merry-go-round in her head, moving with such flair but heading nowhere. Until this moment, Lacey hadn't noticed how much time she'd spent simply thinking about the words and the ideas they represented. *Being seen* for what she could do. But what had she done lately? Nothing.

"I'm not trying to be hard on you, Lacey. I don't even think it's you talking—it's the drug. Did Dr. Spangler tell you *anything* about it?"

"No. She said it's just like the samples I've taken before."

"And what did the samples help you with in the

past?"

"Anxiety, I guess. Yeah, pretty much that. I would get performance anxiety before tests, quizzes even. The meds helped a little, but nothing felt as strong as this one."

"Do you know for sure that this sample's for anxiety?"

"Spangler didn't really answer when I asked her that question. Actually, she seemed kind of uncomfortable with me asking. She did say that it's new, it's safe, and many patients have benefited from it."

"Hmm . . . somehow I doubt that. If she's still giving out samples of a "new" drug, it hasn't helped as many people as she claims. She didn't give you a brochure, handout, anything with a drug name or information?"

"No. I was feeling pretty desperate in her office yesterday. I'd been trying to study for days and my anxiety was too strong, so I was more trusting than usual. I just took it."

"How do you feel now?"

Lacey had no idea. She started to remember that she had a body, a mind, and real feelings that lived down off the pedestal she'd been placing herself on. She hadn't experienced anxiety lately, but she also hadn't been feeling much of anything.

"I'm just so confused. After I took the drug, I felt incredibly confident. It's like all the stuff I was saying to you yesterday—I felt I could do anything, accomplish anything. Not just like I could, but that I *already had* in a way. It was as if I truly lived in the moment, and actually time seemed to freeze too. Everything felt so . . . easy. So effortless. Rewarding."

"How many did you take?"

"Well, the prescription said to take two, but I ended

up taking three total. Brad took two of them."

"And . . . ?"

"And he was acting like a whack job, to be honest." An image of Brad running down the driveway with his peanut butter and jelly sandwich flashed across her mind and she cringed. She must have seemed that crazy too. "I just saw him lying on the couch in the living room, and he's wearing the same clothes he wore yesterday. I think he missed both his finals and his hockey game."

"Yikes, that means even with the prescribed dose, this stuff sounds dangerous. Lacey, I think that what your doctor did yesterday was really messed up. What's even more messed up is that this drug exists and is being passed out to people. We have to find out more about this new drug and what it does. Do you think Spangler would tell you more about it if you called her?"

"I'll give her a call and a piece of my mind! What am I going to do, Mariah? I'm going to flunk all my exams." Lacey felt like crying, and the one person she could talk to was the friend she'd been so rude to yesterday.

"Try and stay calm, I have a plan . . . okay? Don't tell Spangler that you're angry and want an explanation. But definitely give her a call. Let's figure out what you can say."

Mariah and Lacey laid out a whole plan, one that could get them more information about the drug and possibly save Lacey's grades too . . . if done right. In order to do it, Lacey would have to use a little psychology of her own outside of what she'd learned in class that quarter. Lacey felt better afterward.

"Hey Mariah, I'm really sorry about how I acted yesterday. That's not how I really feel."

"I know, don't worry. We'll make this right. I know it was just the drugs talking, but don't let other people be the judge of who you are and what you're capable of. It's easier said than done, I go through this same dilemma too. But you get what I'm saying, right?"

"I do. Do you think the drug was tapping into a tendency I already have to worry about what others think of me?"

"Everyone has that tendency, that must be why they created this drug in the first place. Whoever made it knew it would work because we all struggle with the fear of how other people see us. Doubting and questioning ourselves along the way. We seek out approval, recognition, and acceptance that never really comes. But there's always the empty promise of it, and the pursuit of that feeling can become everything. It can override what we really want in life. This drug seems to convince the mind that it has already attained a sort of ultimate achievement and recognition."

"Yeah, that's what it felt like! Everything seemed so easy. It was like a feeling of accomplishment without enduring what it takes to get there. But I felt sure that everyone could see how awesome I was. I know this sounds crazy . . ."

"You're not crazy, Lacey. Dr. Spangler is the crazy one for handing out this drug so freely. Hey . . . if the drug taps into our natural tendencies, maybe you can use that to your advantage when you talk to Spangler."

Lacey fleshed her script out in more detail for what she would say. There was no guarantee this plan would work, but they had to try. Not just to save Lacey's grades, but to stop the careless spread of this drug.

"Thanks for your help, Mariah. I really appreciate it."

"Hey—I want to be a doctor someday, so I might as well start learning what this medicine stuff is about, right? To be honest, so far it seems kind of creepy."

Despite all the strange events surrounding them, the two college students enjoyed a laugh together. Once the girls were off the phone, Lacey rested for a bit and prepared herself to break the bad news to Brad.

"BRAD, I'M BEING SERIOUS." Lacey waited as Brad processed what she had just told him, his initial response one of disbelief.

"But how is that even possible?"

"Well basically, the drug that made us feel so awesome yesterday was tricking our minds into somehow believing that we were invincible superstars who didn't need to do anything to earn our kudos."

Brad's eyes were glazed over. Lacey had no idea what he was thinking.

"So . . . what did we do yesterday?"

"Honestly, I don't even remember much of it. I sat in my room for a while, tried to study. You were having too much fun making peanut butter and jelly sandwiches. Do you remember that?"

"Kinda . . ." Brad looked like a sad little dude lost at the fair. Unfortunately, Lacey didn't have time to console him.

"Okay, why don't you think on that for now. We have to do something about our missed exams. I have a plan that will help us recover from this disaster—if it works. Gotta' get going." Brad opened his mouth to speak, but nothing came out.

Lacey went into her room and sat on the bed. She had a choice. She could either visit Spangler in person and carry out her plan or she could call her on the phone. She and Mariah had discussed the pros and cons of each, but

Lacey felt very undecided now that she was left on her own. The cobwebs in her brain needed clearing out, it felt like she hadn't used that organ for so long. Whose brain had she been thinking with anyway? That was the strangest part about the drug, its ability to inspire such wild aspirations about the future without any part of the mind engaging in actual action.

Lacey had to find out more about the drug. If she were to meet Spangler in person, it might be a mistake. She was a bad liar and Spangler was probably trained to read clients' facial expressions and body language. In some ways, she wished she had never met Spangler. But another part of her wondered if all this was happening to her for a reason. She picked up her phone and dialed.

Her heartbeats thudded along to the dial tone until Spangler's receptionist answered.

"Good morning, Dr. Spangler's office, Dana speaking, how can I help you?" The voice was so official it could have been an answering machine.

"Hi—I was wondering if I could talk to Dr. Spangler?"

"Can I tell her who's calling?" Lacey cursed in her mind. It sounded like Spangler might be available to talk. Since taking the pills the day before, Lacey felt her anxiety spiraling out of control and she knew she'd have to somehow get a grip.

"It's Lacey."

"Okay Lacey, just a moment." The way Dana relayed that simple sentence made Lacey wonder if she and Spangler had talked about her. Or maybe she was just being paranoid, it was hard to tell these days.

"Hello Lacey, what can I do for you?"

Lacey was startled to get the doctor on the phone so quickly.

144

"Hi Dr. Spangler, I was calling to give you an update on how I'm doing on this new medication."

"Yes—so how have you been feeling?" The words were devoid of any real curiosity or care.

Lacey took a deep breath and launched into her script. "Dr. Spangler, you have literally saved my life!" She knew how much doctors loved it when patients said stuff like that. Now she just had to wait and see if Spangler took the bait.

The wheels were spinning in the doctor's mind as she registered the compliment that she had originally assumed would be a complaint. She had probably labeled Lacey as a whiny patient, and now Lacey was switching places in Spangler's mind. It was hard not to hear Dr. Spangler's mental grinning as she continued.

"That's lovely, Lacey! I'm so happy to hear that. How did your exams go?" Dr. Spangler had, in the blink of an eye, turned into a very compassionate soul.

"It's not just my exams, Dr. Spangler. Those went way better than I expected. But I just feel like . . . like a brand new person! I'm more confident, less anxious, and it's like I can do anything. Like I can conquer anything."

"I had a feeling this medication would do the trick," Dr. Spangler reaffirmed. "You're lucky, you know, to be one of the first ones to use it." Funny, Lacey thought to herself. Earlier, Spangler had said that many patients had benefited from the pill. The pill probably hadn't even been approved for patient use yet. Hence the unlabeled "samples."

"You were right. Everyone around me notices the difference too and it's like I've gained a new respect from the people I know."

"Mmm hmm, go on . . ."

"Before, I hardly felt anyone recognized me for what

145

I did. Now, they're more aware of my potential and what I'm made of—they see me. I don't feel so small out in the world. I feel like I'm standing on the top of a mountain where I belong. It's nice to finally feel so valuable in my own life. Sorry, I guess I'm getting kind of carried away, I'm just so excited about this new feeling."

"Don't be sorry, Lacey. I love to get updates from my patients and to hear how they're doing. More than anything, I like helping people." I'm sure you do, Lacey thought to herself. But she continued.

"It's just my opinion, but I think everyone should be on this medication. I know a lot of students who would benefit from it. The world really needs this type of positivity and go-getter attitude right now."

"You may be on to something there, Lacey. Without anxiety and depression, people could achieve their highest potential."

"Have you tried it?"

Spangler's voice hitched for a second as she tried to come up with a professional response. "I'm afraid I can't discuss my own health with a patient, but I have had many other patients benefit from the medication." There was that lie again. Dr. Spangler had managed to contradict herself within a span of two minutes.

"Oh, I understand. The only reason I ask is because my psychology professor wants to learn more about the medication. She found my performance so stellar that she actually wants to meet you and discuss the wonderful work you're doing. I wasn't sure if doctors tried out their own samples or not, for first-hand experience I mean. Anyway, would you be able to meet with my professor? If it goes well, she'd like to invite you to do a department-wide talk."

Wow, Spangler thought to herself. Recognition and

acclaim at Cornell University. She was rejected by the school back in her day when applying for college. Now she could be a key speaker there and maybe even get certain teaching privileges and acclaim in her field. Lacey was on to something.

"Please, Dr. Spangler? You're the best doctor I've ever had and even though a part of me wants to keep this all to myself, I know so many people who would benefit from meeting you."

"Why, sure Lacey. I would be honored to meet with your professor and do a talk at Cornell." Spangler was almost purring now. Lacey had apparently nailed it with the "best doctor" bit.

"Awesome, thanks Dr. Spangler!" Lacey switched to a more clueless, unassuming college student tone to secure the last piece of the plan. "I'm so excited and I know everyone else will be too. If I were you and I had samples, I'd try one out for some insider knowledge before the talk! I'm just kidding . . ." Lacey started laughing like a dingbat and flaunting like she had the confidence to act that stupid. "By the way, Dr. Spangler, how does this medicine work again?"

Dr. Spangler was nearly salivating over the phone, ready to put her expertise in action. "Well, Lacey . . . research from renowned neurobiologists over the past few years has shown that different neurotransmitters turn on in the brain when you tune into 'the now.'"

"Uh huh . . ." Lacey chimed in. It made sense now why she couldn't study at all the day before. Lacey had no problem with living in the present, but the drug made Lacey's brain unable to escape "the now." Each moment had felt too heightened with meaning, and yet she was unable to access any part of her true self while on the drug. Looking back, it was the most self-conscious she had ever felt in her life. The other problem with the drug was that it didn't even allow you to admit the insecurities that it was designed to trigger. Real anxiety paled in comparison to the dangers of this "now" feeling.

"Neurotransmitters are the brain's chemical messengers, and they play a part in directing how we think, feel, and act. Typically, people obsess too much on the past or the future. Why have a past at all when this new pill can eradicate the torturous feelings it evokes? Why have a future when it only conjures feelings of dread for most people? Instead you can have the feeling of freedom and immortality each and every moment. Research involving brain scans demonstrated that different areas of the brain light up, or are stimulated in people who live in the moment. These people also tend to have higher ideals and the feeling that they can do great, powerful things and thereby impact the world. They are rewarded for what they can offer to us all. In fact, one of the neurotransmitters that the medication affects is dopamine, the main chemical involved in the brain's reward and pleasure centers. The pharmaceutical company who made this drug, NeuroLife, had an aim to help people live more meaningful lives, embrace higher ideals, and essentially be like Mike."

"Excuse me? . . ." Communicating with this lady was like speaking to a lunatic, Lacey heard echoing in the back of her mind.

"To be like Michael Jordan—you know, the greatest basketball player of all time? To experience greatness itself. To be known for exceptional skill and talent. To impact the world and those around you. To have the feeling of being able to accomplish anything and be recognized for it."

Wow, Lacey thought, Spangler couldn't be more

wrong about what the phrase "I wanna be like Mike" really meant. She didn't have a clue, but she sure was star-struck by this drug's potential to help everyone be like Mike. Oh by the way, Lacey wanted to scream: You can't accomplish shit while taking this drug! She calmed down her inner response and focused on her outward acting instead.

"Mmm hmm, I get it . . ." Lacey agreed with feigned earnestness. She found herself wondering why Dr. Spangler had given her this drug for anxiety in the first place. She didn't want to ask accusingly though, so she settled on a different approach. "How was the drug able to treat my anxiety so effectively?"

"Well, Lacey, what you kept calling anxiety I felt was really a lack of self-confidence with an excess of insecurity. I could tell that you're a unique individual in your response to life, but the only eyes that can see us clearly are possessed by those around us. I wanted you to be able to feel more powerful around other people and like you could truly be admired by them. Make a better impression, you know? That would help your confidence really soar and resolve the insecurity problem. And then, ta-da! No more anxious Lacey. Did you enjoy that effect?"

Lacey's blood was boiling now. If Spangler wasn't high on the drug already, then she was even more of a sorry excuse for a healer than Lacey had thought.

"Oh yes, I loved it! I took three of the pills, by the way. I hope that's okay since it was more than prescribed. I think the extra dose helped me to study better and really gave me an advantage toward exams."

"No worries Lacey, it sounds like that did the trick for you. Now, when would be the best time for me to get together with your professor at Cornell? I'm very much looking forward to it." I am too, thought Lacey.

"How about tomorrow afternoon at 2 pm, does that work okay for you? That's when my professor, Dr. Daniels, has office hours and she said it would be a good time. I might join too, if you don't mind, to learn more from you."

"Perfect, Lacey. Of course you're welcome to partake! I want to thank you for calling. It's so important for me to get feedback from my patients and I'm very happy that I was able to help you."

"I should be the one thanking you, Dr. Spangler. I'll see you tomorrow." Lacey waited until Spangler hung up and then smiled.

"Hey Mariah, did you catch all of that?" Mariah had been on a three-way call with them during the conversation.

"I sure did. Had it on speaker at the highest volume, and recorded it too."

"Awesome. Are you ready for tomorrow? The script may not be as tight, but I have a feeling that something will come out of it."

"I'm ready, and I already got the meeting prepared. Are *you* ready? Your doctor's pretty insane."

"You know what—I'm finally ready to take that lady on. And not with the help of any drug, but instead by offering her a dose of my own medicine. Time to be like Mike."

YVETTE SPANGLER WAS NEARLY SHAKING with excitement. She lounged back in her therapist chair and tried to take in the moment more fully. The sun was winking at her through slits in the window blinds. The patient charts on her desk seemed perfectly stacked. Her diploma shined down to her from its prominent position on the wall. Nothing was out of place, the environment in tune with her feeling of inner control. The clock was ticking louder as if to mark the occasion. Her whole office just felt more important now.

This was the opportunity she'd been waiting for all her life and she was finally going to get the recognition she had always deserved. Lacey was definitely a pain-in-the-ass patient, but Yvette was glad she'd stuck with the case and was going to get rewarded for once in her life.

In her past, Yvette had never felt that she was good enough . . . yet. She was patient, though, and she knew that it would come one day. While spending time with her family during her youth, she felt completely misunderstood by them. They were never able to see her for who she was. College was supposed to be different, and even though alcohol could make it feel that way sometimes, it really wasn't.

She went straight to grad school, attended even more school after that. She had been proud of her dissertations along the way, but the pride dissipated because no one else cared about her work. Opened up an office and saw her patients. Over time, what she grew to want most was to be seen and yearned for in her field. Lacey was proof that Yvette had patients' best interests in mind, even when they were resistant to getting help. Even more than that, Yvette was positive she should be a leader and an expert in her profession, as she'd always known.

Dana knocked on the door and ruined the moment. She opened the door just enough to peek through the crack and launched into her agenda. Yvette hated that Dana felt it was her right to just barge in and start talking.

"Yvette, your three o'clock patient cancelled and I

rescheduled her for next week. Also, are you able to take a new patient at five today?" Dana popped her gum and waited for an answer. Yvette simply stared back at her, her face reflecting a new expression. Could it be even more condescending than usual, Dana pondered. While Yvette's look was supposed to exude intelligence and confidence, it seemed strangely bovine and hostile instead. She appeared more powerful and more stupid all at once.

"Dana, please don't intrude on my time in this fashion from here on out." Yvette took a deep breath tainted with irritation, and proceeded. "Call me from your desk instead, and start referring to me as Dr. Spangler, as it's more professional. I want you to stop chewing gum, and don't bother me about every patient that reschedules or needs an appointment. Make those decisions for yourself because I'm going to have less time in the future. Soon, I'll be accepting a prestigious teaching position at Cornell, and I'll need you to step up your level of work to keep up with that. If you can't, I have no problem seeking a replacement. Thank you, and please close the door on your way out. Oh, by the way—I want my time blocked off for the rest of today and tomorrow. Cancel all patient appointments."

Dana had no idea how to respond. She pulled a strand of loose hair behind her ear and tucked her shocked and hurt feelings inside, quickly shutting the door. She had worked for Spangler for five years and had never seen this side of the doctor. Dana's mind filled with worries for the patients, and she happily cancelled the appointments as Yvette had requested. She didn't want the patients seeing the doctor in her current state. It might be time to search for a new job too, she noted to herself. It didn't look like Spangler would miss her a bit.

Back on the other side of the door, Yvette stood up and walked to her desk. She fingered the top drawer and an unsettling wave of guilt washed over her. She wasn't even supposed to have them, yet alone dispense them to patients.

Earlier that year, NeuroLife had performed a research study on a new drug and a select few of her patients had been chosen to participate. The medication was originally for patients with weakened senses, a new condition that had been popping up in the therapy world from people spending increased time on computers or tablets. Screens in general. People weren't interacting with their environments very much and even young men and women were starting to lose both interest in and responsiveness of their five senses. They were also losing track of "the moment" and of time in general. Previous research studies supported the development of a drug that could help by putting these patients back in "the now." Spangler had three such cases in her practice.

The drug worked. Patients in the study reported not only heightened senses, but also remarkable relief from any existing sadness and depression. They also reported increased levels of motivation and the feeling that they could accomplish more.

The drug was then tweaked into a different form to specifically bring out these anti-depressant effects, a new medication tentatively called Amplus. NeuroLife hadn't even created a label for it yet. Spangler was very curious about this new class of drugs after speaking to her patients who had participated in the study. It sounded like a miracle to her.

One day, during a personal tour of NeuroLife's research facilities, Yvette managed to steal a couple bottles of the newest version of the drug. She couldn't believe her luck, as she was always so nervous about doing quote unquote bad things! But she told herself it was for her patients. What could go wrong with a few harmless samples anyway? Doctors did it all the time.

Lacey was the first and only of her patients to try Amplus so far. And the positive results had been beyond what Spangler had imagined. NeuroLife would surely put the medication on the market soon, and Spangler's experiment would be no big deal. In fact, she'd be one of the front-runners in promoting it. And of course, she'd be flexing her muscles over at Cornell too. No one messed with experts.

Yvette slowly pulled open her drawer and stared in wonder at the two pill bottles. The little blue beads sparkled attractively from inside the capsules. She had only dispensed a total of ten pills to Lacey, and her own private supply was still very lush. Hmm, maybe Lacey was right. Perhaps doctors should try out their own medicine. Yvette pictured the confidence, power, and intrigue that the pills could boost in her for the meeting at Cornell the next day. She was already a very confident woman, but the pills would just give her that extra edge.

Lacey had taken three, and she had performed well on them. Yvette figured she could take about four while preparing for her presentation. She popped open the cap and dry swallowed a couple. She could take more in a bit when she needed it.

Yvette got out her clipboard, a notepad, and a pencil. She turned on her computer and opened a blank PowerPoint presentation. Good to go. She then smiled to herself with satisfaction, looked at the clock, and opened up to her true brilliance.

WHEN YVETTE OPENED HER EYES the next day, she lifted her head to a blinking cursor on the computer screen. She watched the thin vertical black line appear and disappear against the contrasting brightness of the white page. She found herself wondering whether she could catch the exact transition between there and not there.

For some reason she couldn't trace back how she'd ended up in her office again. The previous day had been amazing with the news about Cornell's interest in her. She'd spent the rest of the afternoon working on her presentation until it was complete. During her preparation, she'd come up with her own innovative treatment protocol for prescribing Amplus. At the presentation earlier, she'd wowed everyone with her expertise and had been offered a teaching position at Cornell. So far, this was one of the best days of her life. Maybe *the* best.

Why in the world was she back at her office again? She should be out celebrating, Yvette thought. She didn't know who she could share her important news with, but still. Maybe Dana could join her for some drinks later that night.

As if reading Yvette's thoughts, Dana knocked on the door timidly. She waited for a few moments before knocking again. "Um, Yvette . . . I mean, Dr. Spangler? You have a number of messages from Cornell. I didn't want to bother you, but they sound important."

Wow, Yvette couldn't believe how much Cornell wanted her. She would make them wait for a little bit before responding. Now she was the one with leverage, for a change, and it felt good to use it.

"Hey Dana, would you like to join me for drinks later tonight? We can celebrate my new position at Cornell."

Dana hung back away from the door, as if Yvette's

threshold had become radioactive and could suck her in if she got too close. She couldn't understand what this lady was about anymore and she was unsure if she ever really had known her boss. One second she's threatening to fire her, and the next second she wants to hang out like best friends and share some drinks. Whatever, Dana concluded. Her synapses fired as quick as they could to find a valid excuse.

"Thanks for the invite, Dr. Spangler, but I have dinner plans with my mom tonight." Yvette probably didn't know that her mom lived two states over, that's how little effort she had put into getting to know her over the past five years.

"Okay, well maybe next time." Yvette couldn't think of who else to invite, but she'd figure it out later. "Can you buzz me through to Cornell, please?"

Dana rushed back to her desk and connected Spangler to Cornell.

Yvette sat at her desk and prepared for some major butt kissing—directed toward her for once. "Hello, Yvette Spangler speaking." She waited for it.

"Hi, this is Dr. Daniels' assistant, Lisa, calling from Cornell University. Dr. Daniels finds it unfortunate that you didn't make your appointment today at two. Are you still interested in meeting with her?"

The blood rushed out of Yvette's face.

"NICE OF YOU TO FINALLY JOIN US, Dr. Spangler. And to what do I owe your late arrival?" Dr. Daniels sat back comfortably in her chair as Yvette rushed into the professor's office at Cornell, out of breath. Though still light out, it was nearly six in the evening.

"Nice to finally meet you Dr. Daniels. I'm so terribly sorry . . . my car had some troubles . . . and I . . ." Yvette looked around the room in shock. Not only was Lacey there, but so was a group of students and professors she had never met. Why were so many people waiting here for her? Yvette uneasily noted a man and woman who stood by the door. She recognized their faces from somewhere.

"Yes, and in the meantime did it occur to you to let us know?"

Yvette felt very watched all of a sudden, as if not just these pairs of eyes but every stare in the world was directed at her.

"Did I what?" Her attention snapped back reluctantly to Dr. Daniels. Yvette felt out of it in a way that she had never experienced.

"Never mind. Now that you have our full attention, please go ahead with your presentation. We've been eagerly awaiting it."

Spangler looked over at Lacey. Lacey seemed to know something, that ungrateful bitch. She then put her bag down on a chair and made a show of searching for her presentation. "Oh my gosh, it seems that in all the chaos with my car, I've misplaced my presentation." Spangler looked up at Dr. Daniels with her best "good guy" look. Everyone always forgave her after seeing it.

"Yvette, you seem really out of it. If you don't mind my asking—are you on drugs?"

Spangler felt drenched with sweat, her armpits soggy and emanating fear. "What do you mean?"

"I mean exactly what I asked."

Yvette turned toward Lacey. Sheer panic filled her words so she was almost incomprehensible. "I don't know what Lacey has told you about me, but as her doctor, I can tell you she is a pathological liar . . ."

"Dr. Spangler, Yvette—let's cut the bullshit." Dr. Daniels' voice barred Yvette's entry into further conversation. "I'll tell you what's really going on. Lacey is one of my best students in class, and it's been obvious this quarter that she cares about her quality of work. Somehow, she missed a full day of finals, as did her roommate, Brad. Nobody even knew where they were. In fact, they were at home, conked out in bed. When they awoke, they were both convinced that they'd already taken their exams. Not only completed them, but aced them. Can you explain that?"

Yvette stared dumbly at the air.

"No, of course you can't. Well, it turns out that the drug samples you gave Lacey for 'anxiety' are not anti-anxiety medications after all. Did you know that?"

Yvette said nothing and gulped.

"These drugs are not even approved for patient use and are still being researched at NeuroLife, an important point we suspected after listening to your recent phone conversation with Lacey. Luckily, we have two NeuroLife reps who were willing to donate their time to come down here and test both Lacey and Brad for Amplus, the drug they're currently researching. What d'you know—both students tested positive. They were nice enough to stay a little longer so they can test you as well after this meeting."

Yvette's body felt on the verge of collapse, her spine barely able to hold her up.

"Now, based on your recent actions, I don't expect you to care about the welfare of these students. But they do care about passing their exams. And it turns out that even more than passing exams, they care to make sure that no other students are subjected to the dangers of your medical negligence and lack of ethics. To help them out, I'm going to give you one opportunity to tell the truth. Did you illegally dispense stolen, experimental, and dangerous medication to Lacey while claiming it was for the treatment of her anxiety?"

"Yes." A tiny gust of air propelled the word out of Yvette's now deflated body.

"Well, there we have it! I won't be sharing my opinions today about the risks of pharmaceutical drugs and how they're marketed to young people." Dr. Daniels turned toward the NeuroLife reps with a pointed look on her face.

"I do have a lot to say on that matter, but it's for another time. There are more important points to make anyway. Today I'm going to sit back, be an old fogey, and invite the youth to do a brief presentation for you since you've misplaced yours."

Dr. Daniels leaned back in her seat and gestured toward Lacey. "Thanks, Dr. Daniels." Brad and Mariah stood on either side of Lacey for moral support.

"Despite what you may think, Dr. Spangler, I'm very happy I met you. Through your example, I learned what not to do in my life." Lacey's voice felt shaky for a moment as she faced her doctor. With each word that came out, it then smoothed out into a unique rhythm, as if she was hearing herself speak for the first time.

"I told you that the drug made me feel like I could do anything. I felt uneasy about that though, because I wasn't able to *actually do anything* while on it. Do you remember what you told me when I expressed my concerns?"

Spangler blinked a few times, unable to speak.

"You told me that I was resistant to being helped. Do you know what I learned instead?"

Spangler's cow-like eyes locked onto a spot on the

wall behind Lacey, as if she were about to start grazing.

"I learned that I'd rather earn a reward after doing something I'm really proud of . . . instead of only having *the feeling* of being rewarded. See the difference?"

Spangler dumbly sat down in a chair.

"Today, it seems like left and right people want to be known 'out there' for impacting the world." Lacey gestured with her hands. "People aren't taught to do anything for themselves anymore and they want everything to look and feel easy. And that's the feeling that this drug gloms on to. But it starts with the individual first, not the drug. Dr. Spangler, is your greatest dream to be world-renowned for what you do?"

Spangler waited a beat and then nodded.

"You know . . . I've felt that way too. I wanted to do well in school, but I wanted to show everyone that I did it. I don't even know who 'everyone' is! The drug just enhanced what I had already been feeling. It made me think that I could do anything, but you can't just think about things in your head and make them happen. You have to face the real world, which is not simply made up of your brain. It's not easy, but the challenge is more exciting than simply staring at the clock—thinking. Wouldn't you agree, Dr. Spangler?"

Spangler appeared as if she'd turned to stone.

"Don't worry—we already know that you took the drug too. After I took it, I was paralyzed with the idea that I was incredibly special and superior. I stared at the clock, doing nothing and waiting for my accolades. In my mind, I didn't need to work for anything anymore because I was entitled. I was even mean to my friend who was trying to help me.

"I stopped listening to myself, and I stopped learning. I slept through all my exams, and I thought I'd still aced them without any preparation. The same thing happened to my roommate, Brad, who took a couple pills himself. We know that's why you missed the meeting today, Spangler, and why you don't have your presentation prepared. There was no presentation in the first place. You just wanted to prove to us how awesome you are . . . for nothing.

"You told me that I was weak. You encouraged me to look to others to verify my self-worth . . . look at myself through their eyes, is what you said. And finally you said that the pill is what will help me be 'like Mike.' You want the truth? Michael Jordan didn't play basketball for everyone else. He didn't sit around all day thinking about how he could be great in everyone's eyes. If he had, like you've been telling me to do, he wouldn't have played ball the way he did. Greatness doesn't come from the thought of greatness. It takes guts. It takes honesty. It takes hard work. It demands that you be real and that you care about what you do—stuff you'll never find in a pill. That's how you can be like Mike. Do you have what it takes?"

Lacey's challenge was met with a frozen expression from Dr. Spangler. Everyone else had been glued to Lacey's words and were now asking themselves the question she had posed.

"That's the end of my presentation," Lacey concluded. Immediately, a couple of men who had appeared to be random spectators by the door took out a pair of handcuffs and started to read Dr. Spangler her rights. A dazed and speechless Spangler was arrested and led out of the office for drug testing by the NeuroLife staff.

The three students thanked Dr. Daniels and the other professors for their help. The professors were more than happy to grant Lacey and Brad another chance to take their exams once the drug had detoxified out of their systems. Everyone agreed that Dr. Spangler was in a lot of trouble.

"Lacey, you kicked butt. I'm never messing with you again!" Brad joked and shuffled his feet, his manner suddenly shy around his roommate. "Seriously though, thank you." Brad said his goodbyes and headed off to hockey practice, a note in hand to explain his previous absence.

Lacey and Mariah walked out of the office and down the stairs of the building to the fresh out-of-school air. The campus was thinning by the minute as students headed home for break after exams. The whole atmosphere seemed relieved as the adrenaline rush went with them.

"So, any plans now that the quarter's over?" Mariah asked Lacey.

"Well, I do have some exams to study for . . . but first there is a good friend of mine, who helped save my butt, that I'd like to treat to a Frappuccino at the mall. You down?"

Mariah smiled. "We definitely earned it! Let's go."

PRECIPICE

I WATCH HIM INHALE, the orange embers glowing ominously in the darkness of the stairwell under Kipling Hall. In the flame of the lighter, with clarity as if in a photograph, I see the dark circles underneath his eyes, the unkempt and greasy hair, the week old beard growing like an infectious moss on his chin and neck. Youth has left us in a rapid and brutal fashion.

He smiles at me. Once upon a time, that smile held a delightful mischief, a bold promise of adventure and freedom. Now it is mostly muscle movement. I see fear in his eyes, and something worse, something like apathy. It unnerves me. I reach out for the pipe, take it and light up.

College had come and gone, a debt accumulating adventure within the confines of a bubble, mostly pointless class work mingled together with drinking and partying, our lame attempt at holding the inevitable future at bay. Kevin had gone to the middle of the state to farm country, to Central University, home of the frat houses, beer kegs, and cow manure. I had gone a mere thirty minutes up the interstate, to Western, land of the hippies, weed, and evergreen trees. The result was mostly the same, four years gone with the wind and a piece of paper entitling us to a Bachelor's degree, tens of thousands in the hole, and no gainful employment. Hi Ma, hi Dad, I'm back! Fuck my life.

You follow the rules of life, I suppose, because that's what you're expected to do. Maybe some people do it better than others, and probably those are the ones who are off somewhere new, making salaries and building their IRAs, taking out a loan for a new home, saving up for an even bigger home somewhere down the line. I am not one of those people.

"Are we the only fuck-ups on the planet?" I ask, laughing emptily.

"Feels that way," Kevin says to me. "Though I hear Josh and his brother are both back with their parents too."

"Yeah, but they're morons. This bites, man."

"Yeah, tell me about it."

We had ended up driving north back to my old university. Originally, we had planned to go relax at the rock quarry, our old haunt, the place we had discovered hidden away in the woods and had turned into *the* spot to go in high school to party. But when we got there it had been filled with, of course, a bunch of high schoolers.

"This was *our* place, Jake," Kevin had said bitterly.

"Yup. *Was* being the key word there."

"Let's go. I'm not hanging around with a bunch of kids."

WE WALK THE GROUNDS of the university for a while, the laughter and bass coming from the dormitories like sounds of wildlife in a foreign jungle. They talk about culture shock, when you go somewhere new and everything feels weird and different, and maybe I had been through that to some extent when I started college four years ago. But this feeling was much worse, it was some sort of twisted reverse culture shock, like you're part of something one minute and the next minute you're just like, *out*.

"Wanna see if we can get into the dorms, maybe find a party to hang out at?" Kevin asks hopefully.

"Nah. I don't want to feel like a douche."

He looks disappointed, but fuck it, I don't want to. College was the last safe haven in life, and when your time is up, it spits you out like a used up piece of gum. Unless you're living in a dream world, you know that the moment you graduate your life changes for good, there is no going back. Whether you like it or not.

The truth is, I probably could look a little harder for a career, and maybe if I did I wouldn't be living in my old bedroom, sleeping on the same sorry twin bed I had when I was ten, my feet hanging off the mattress. But something in me was resisting it, and I didn't know exactly what it was I was afraid of.

"What's your plan, Kev? I mean, we can't live like this for long, you know?" I ask.

"I know, I know. I'd have to go samurai on myself if I did, you know honorable death by katana blade." He mimes the suicide by self-impalement for emphasis. "I guess I'm probably gonna go work with Rick at the auto shop. My dad talked to him, says he can hook me up."

"Rick the Dick?" In a small town, everyone knows just about everyone.

"Yeah, he's not so bad, really. Plus, a job's a job."

"Right, not so bad." Rick the Dick had a son a year younger than we were, had played on the high school baseball team with us. When his kid would strike out, he would always yell from the stands and call him a pussy.

Very encouraging in that way. "Well, anyway, I guess you're right. It's a job."

"What about you, man?"

"I dunno yet."

I don't know how to say to him that when I close my eyes I see my future as a huge monster with a gaping mouth full of gears and cogs, burning oil and grinding metal, driving up from the depths closer and closer to swallow me up. I see myself standing on the edge of a cliff looking down at it, and the whole world is behind me telling me to jump, to let it eat me, that's the way life works and don't be a loser, don't be a failure, just do it already. I hear my father's scathing recriminations, my mom's concerned worries, and all I want to do is run. But there is nowhere to go.

I LEARNED FROM A YOUNG AGE how to GTL, aka Get Through Life. I did enough to get by, to stay under the radar, but never enough to excel at anything – I didn't want to stand out. I had always felt like I was on the outside looking in at my peers. I had broken them into three different types, the Achievers, the Coasters, and the Strugglers. It was pretty obvious where most everyone fit in, though there was some overlap of course – the Achievers were mostly high IQ, high expectation types who performed well in school and whatever else they put their minds to, the Coasters got by with passing grades, made friends easily and were destined to become paramedics or realtors or something, and the Strugglers, well they're pretty self explanatory. In a way, I had always wished to fit in to one of those categories, so at least I knew where I stood in life, at least I could feel I had a place.

But in another more real way, they were all the same to me, defined by the system – success or failure, line-walker or rebel, normal or outcast, in the end the outward differences were almost insignificant. It seemed that life was defined by a code of values superimposed upon individual identity that categorized who you are based on criteria *outside* of the person. I watched as the people around me slowly but inevitably became further entrenched in the gears of society, some being chewed up, others turning fluidly and in harmony. While I gradually became more of an outlier, a strange detached observer of humanity with nowhere to go and nothing to do with my life.

On a Tuesday night, the campus is relatively empty. It is autumn, and the crisp air is biting and still. The season of death always makes me feel more alive somehow – there is a thirst in the back of my throat and the cells of my body seem to tingle with anticipation.

Orange sodium lights line the brick pathway we walk on, cutting through a courtyard strewn with random abstract statue art and old oak trees, creating a surreal environment where I half expect to see a cluster of hooded druids chanting in a circle nearby.

"Creeeepy," Kevin says, half sarcastic, half serious. I laugh, but he's right, the air is buzzing with strangeness.

While passing a particularly unusual piece of art which looks to be three metal sheets placed on end in a triangle shape, lit from within so it glows like some alien relic, we hear a voice drift out to us from inside of the triangle.

"Hey," it whispers, soft yet commanding.

I jump a little and feel the blood course through my body to the ends of my hands and feet. Goosebumps jump up along my neck and arms. "Did you hear that?" I ask Kevin.

"Yeah, what the hell was-"

"*Hey.*" Louder this time.

I glance over at the sculpture while simultaneously veering away from it, ready to bolt if anyone or anything pops out that looks suspicious or dangerous.

There are cracks between the sheets of metal which widen toward the bottom, and I see a head peeking out through one of them, at first just a shadow but as my eyes focus I can see it's a young man about our age wearing a black hooded sweatshirt.

"Woah man, what the hell?" I ask. "What are you doing down there?"

"Look," he says, "I don't have much time to explain. They're after me, okay? They know what I have and they know how to find me and I can't keep running from them because eventually I'm going to get caught and then -" he pauses for breath – "then what'll happen? You have to take this."

The man's eyes burn with a mixture of adrenaline and fear, but also something else – conviction. His longish blond hair pokes out from beneath his hood, framing sharp, angular features wearing a grim and determined expression. He looks exhausted. From behind the sheet of metal, he slides a black pack.

"Take it."

Kevin, the strange circumstances perhaps rekindling his old sense of spontaneity and thirst for danger, automatically reaches for it. The man shakes his head and puts his palm out to stop him.

"Not you. Him," he says, pointing to me. Kevin looks at him like, what the fuck? I'm equally surprised.

"Me? Why me?"

"I don't have time to explain it."

"Who are *they*?"

"No time. Let's just say they want this for a different reason than you or I do."

"What is it?"

"I can't tell you that either." He looks around anxiously. "Look, there's no time. You take it or you don't."

Fuck it. I can't explain why, but I reach for it, with a strange dreamlike, underwater sensation, as if my arm isn't my own but some detached appendage acting of its own accord. I look questioningly into the eyes of the odd man crouched on the ground. He nods at me. The pack has two slits on either side and straps hanging from it, so I assume it is like a backpack, and run my arms through the loops to wear it like one. Again, the man nods.

"Good. Now get out of here. They're looking for it. For you."

The pack feels solid on my back, not heavy or light, but substantial. Almost as if it has molded into my body and become a part of me. Weird, I know. We take one last look at the man, and start jogging.

"WHERE ARE WE GOING?" Kevin asks between breaths, both of us out of shape and laboring. I remember when I used to be able to run for miles, no problem. Too much weed and cigarettes, pizza and late night TV.

"Let's get off campus, head back to the car ..." deep breath, "drive away somewhere ... see what this is."

"Do you really think ... people are after us? Or after this thing... whatever it is?"

"Dunno. Don't want to find out."

We keep going for a few more minutes. Western's campus is carved out of a hillside, large and long, and we had started on the opposite end from where my car was. But we were almost there. I can see the lot where I had parked just a quarter mile up ahead.

"Dude, I need a break," Kevin says.

"Ok, let's walk."

I scan the trees and surrounding buildings for movement. A couple is walking together near the Psychology building, clearly drunk and happily groping each other, paying us no mind. A group of guys and girls is cheering from one of the houses on sorority row across the street. Seems like a normal college night. I start to relax a little bit, my mind rationalizing the fear away. The guy was probably some freak tripping on acid, just handing me a backpack filled with his used socks and underwear. Top secret stuff, my ass.

"He kinda looked like you, did you notice?" Kevin asks.

"What? No way, he looked crazy. Plus he had blond hair."

"Yeah, but the face was kind of the same. Yours is fatter though."

"Whatever." Though come to think of it, there was something familiar about him.

"Plus, what's with him wanting you to take the thing, not me?"

"I dunno, maybe he thinks I'm sexy. How the hell should I know?"

"Weird, that's all."

"Yeah, weird. As in he is a *weirdo*. Fuck it, this is stupid. Let's just open the damn thing and see what's in it."

As I start to swing the pack off of my back a group of three young men seem to materialize from behind the corner of a building ahead. Nothing stands out about their appearance, their clothes are unremarkable, bland and clean, their ages similar to ours. But it is the way they move that puts me on immediate alert, stiff yet efficient, purposeful and aggressive though not in a macho sort of way. One of them, a brown-haired man with a green button-up shirt, points in our direction, and they start to walk towards us, the other two spreading out to flank us on either side. Their expressions are not friendly, though not exactly hostile either... rather they are just, well, blank. I have an idea what they want, thinking of the mystery man's cryptic warning, but I'm not about to stick around and find out for sure.

"Shit. Run."

We run back the way we came. Though tired from our earlier jog, the threat of danger puts an extra gear in our legs, and we move like the teenagers we were not so long ago, wind in our faces, the landscape tearing by in a blur. I glance back, and sure enough, the men are running too. They still have yet to make a sound or say a word, which scares me even more.

"This way."

I cut through a path between the Biology building and Steadman's Hall where the pre-law students study, heading towards Red Square, hoping to find a place where there are more people. But when we get there the square is empty, the huge fountain which dominates its center blooming for no one to see.

"Where the hell is everyone?" Kevin asks. It's true, I think, suddenly the campus feels very deserted. The sounds of post-adolescent, pre-adult revelry reverberating through the air are gone. The only noise is the rough rushing of water coming from the fountain.

And now, footsteps. From behind us.

We turn and see the three men walking towards us and I'm shocked they were able to keep up so easily as we had been on quite a tear. My lungs are burning, yet our pursuers look inexplicably fresh and not the least bit winded. What the hell is going on?

"Listen," the green shirt guy says, and I assume he is the leader of the three. He is wearing those geek glasses which are all the rage now, and his brown hair is slicked perfectly off to the side. His eyes are wide, but his expression is flat and closed. He smiles, and the eyes don't change at all. "It isn't what you think. We're trying to help you here."

"Help us, huh?" I say as both Kevin and I walk slowly backward. The three men, about ten feet away, match us step for step.

"Yes, help you," he replies. "You don't know what you're doing here. What that man gave you is dangerous."

"What is it?" I ask him. The obvious question.

"That's not important. What is important is that you give it to us."

I feel a strong sense of possessiveness over the pack that I can't explain.

"I don't think so."

His mouth tightens. Something in me snaps.

"Kev, fuck these guys. Let's take 'em. I'm done running."

I close my fists and feel that familiar sensation of tightening in my chest as I look over at Kevin. We'd had our share of brawls in our day, at parties or on the playground, and knew how to fight and back each other up, but my courage dips a little at seeing Kevin's doubtful expression.

"I don't know, Jake. Why don't we just give it to them. Then we can go home."

I'd known Kevin for seventeen years and never seen him back down from a confrontation. That he was doing so now bothered me even more than the fact that these weird fucks outnumbered us three to two.

"Good call, Kev," comes a voice from behind the corner of a building.

A familiar figure steps out.

"Rick the Dick?" I say, the surprise at seeing him overriding my common sense to not call him his nickname to his face.

"That's Mr. Bradford to you, boy."

My mind starts to short circuit. This is all too strange. I open my mouth to say something but no sound comes out. I look over to Kevin, and he similarly appears to be at a loss for words.

"Kevin," he says, "you're coming with me. This has gone on long enough. You know I've been waiting for you to call me for over a week. Your dad told me you would. Now get your shit together and stop being a pussy."

Kevin is frozen, his face a mask of confusion and fear.

"Kevin!" I yell to him. No response. "Kev!" He doesn't look my way or even register he's heard me.

"Kevin," Rick the Dick commands. "Time to come along now."

For a split second, I swear I see a flash of rage in Kevin's face, a pure and holy spirit of defiance. I ready myself for battle. Then suddenly, like a duck shot-gunned from the sky, the muscles in his face drop and sag, leaving only resignation. He nods.

"Yeah. Right. Okay."

Kevin starts to walk towards the group, eyes downcast, shoulders slumped forward. But for the briefest moment, his eyes catch mine and in them, a flash of lightning. Quietly, so only I can hear, he whispers just one word to me: "Run."

"Kevin!" I call to him. He continues to walk.

Torn between wanting to help my friend, and feeling a strong need to get out of there as fast as possible, I stand frozen for a few seconds as time slows to a crawl. The moon casts a silver glow over all of us, the buildings surrounding the square silhouetted from behind, looking more like ominous cathedrals than lecture halls or libraries. The men stare at me, and the leader with glasses gives me a half-cocked smile. He winks.

My heart kicks back into gear, and then the moment is over, time rushing back in like a tidal wave. I take Kevin's advice.

I run.

NOT LOOKING BEHIND ME, I sprint across the square and take a circuitous route toward a place of familiarity, Jackson Hall, aka Ye Olde English Building (of course room 40 was our favorite), nestled up against the hill in a clearing surrounded by evergreen trees. As an English major, I had spent a good portion of my time during my Junior and Senior years attending classes and study halls somewhere in the building's many rooms. I knew them well, and thought if I could only get in somehow, I would be able to find a place to hide until this whole thing blew over.

The brick facade of the building, a mixture of Gothic

and Romanesque architecture, had always inspired in me a sense of deep connection to humanity, and many a time I had gazed up at it with my notebook in my backpack and a fresh idea to write about rattling around in my head. Now, that sense of mystery and awe is gone, replaced by a feeling of dread. The building looks more like a haunted mansion than an institution of learning. Most of the lights are off, but a few on the top floor where the professors' offices were stay lit. Maybe I can find a familiar face up there to help me.

As I approach the main front doors, I take a chance to look over my shoulder. Luckily no one is coming. I try the door on the right – locked. Same with the left. Circling around towards the back of the building, I head for a stairwell leading down to the basement floors. I have no idea whether the door will be unlocked or not, but I have to try. It is.

I slow as I enter the dark hallway. Under normal circumstances, this would probably freak me out a little, but given what had happened tonight, I am downright terrified. The moonlight casts its spell through the windows, making shadows where there shouldn't be, creating hidden monsters in the gloom. I expect those three men to appear at any moment from behind every corner, every unopened door. Walking as quietly as I can, my heart racing like a jackhammer, I make my way down the hall to the stairs, then take them two at a time to the fourth floor.

I feel a surge of hope when I get there. From underneath one of the doors shines a light. I know that door, know whose office it is. I've found help, at last. I try the knob but it is locked, so I knock and after a few moments hear footsteps. The door opens and bathes me in light.

"Jake?"

"Dr. Robertson." The sight of his familiar wizened face, bald head and white beard is like finding an oasis in the desert.

"What in the world are you doing here, son? Come in, come in."

Despite the confusion on his face, his eyes hold a glint of merriment I had always loved about him that, along with his unprejudiced passion for unraveling the deeper meaning in all forms of literature, had compelled me to sign up for every one of his classes. Over the years we had developed a sort of friendship, or maybe more realistically a teacher-student bond, though I liked to secretly think of us as friends.

Suddenly the urge to cry like a little kid wells up in my throat, and I have to blink my eyes rapidly to hold back any tears. Then the words come pouring out. "I was here with Kevin, just visiting, and these guys started chasing us, someone gave me this thing, this pack, and they took Kevin, or he went with them, but he wasn't himself, and I don't know what they want but—"

"Hey, slow down, Jake. Come, sit down."

I sit in the chair across from his desk, take a deep breath, then start from the beginning. I tell Dr. Robertson everything. He watches me calmly, nodding at times, understanding. When I finish, he clasps his hands in front of him.

"Wow, now that's quite a story, Jake," he says.

"Story? It's not a story! It's what happened!" I protest.

"No, no, I don't mean it like that. I believe you," Dr. Robertson tells me.

"You do?"

"I do."

I breathe a huge sigh, and an enormous weight lifts off of my body. Thank God. Dr. Robertson will know what to do. He looks at me gently, clearly concerned for my predicament.

"Listen, Jake," he says slowly, softly. "You were always one of my most gifted students, and I enjoyed having you in my classes very much—"

"Uh, thanks but I don't know what that has to do with anything…"

"Just listen. You were one of the best, if not the best writer I had. People who really think about what is going on in this world, who see things on a deep level and genuinely feel, genuinely care, well it's a rare thing these days. And I get where you're coming from, I do. In fact, you remind me much of myself when I was your age."

"Look Dr. Robertson, I appreciate it," I say, and really I would, except for the tiny problem that I was being chased by a group of fucked up robo-men. "But I don't know how to deal with this problem and I need your help!"

He looks me directly in the eyes, and suddenly I'm taken aback. Is easygoing, kind Dr. Robertson actually irritated with me? And that glint, that mischievous, joyful glint – is there an edge to it? I push the thought away. No. Must be my imagination, all the stress I'm feeling.

"What do you think I'm trying to do?" he asks.

"Okay. I'm sorry."

"Jake, here's the thing. You can *see*. I know that about you. More important, *you* know that about you. And it's a good thing, it really is. But there's one thing you don't realize yet, because you're young and you haven't been around long enough to figure it out: You can't change the way this world works. For all you can see – no, *despite* all you can see about how life *could be*, there is nothing you can do about it."

"I'm not trying to change the world, Dr. Robertson," I say, still confused as to what this has to do with the situation, but feeling the need to get through it so he can help me. "I'm having a hard enough time figuring out my own life."

"But don't you see? The world, your life and who you are, it's all the same! You can't live outside of this, you have to learn to adapt. You can't exist on your own, who you are is defined only by the world and what you do in society, by where you belong in the system." As he says this, his face lights up with a sickly sort of fanaticism, causing the hairs on the back of my arms to stand on end.

"Here's how I can help you. I can set you up on the fast track," he continues. "Automatic admission to the Education Department, put in a few more years of school and you can be a teacher, eventually a professor if you want. You will be great at it. With the gift you have, you'll have them eating right out of your hand."

I had never seen this side of him before, and I don't like it at all. Like the man who gave me the pack, his face glows with a certain conviction, but instead of the calm determination the other man had, Dr. Robertson reeks of a cloying desperation and fear. I feel something shift in my mind, like when you're working on a puzzle and a piece randomly falls into place.

"I don't think so," I tell him, parceling each word out as carefully as a baby taking his first steps. He smiles. It is an ugly smile.

"You don't think so?" he says mockingly. "You don't know shit." His demeanor has completely transformed. His eyes burn with a self-righteous venom I can barely believe I'm witnessing. He stands from behind his desk, shaking his head in disappointment. "I tried to help you, Jake, I really did."

Suddenly it is clear to me.

Through all of his classes I felt Dr. Robertson leading us somewhere, his intelligence, his depth and insight a hymn singing songs of a rich life deeply lived. I felt he held the secret keys to a wisdom I craved to uncover for myself - he had been a role model, even a hero to me. But in reality, he was nothing more than the Pied Piper. He used his sight as a siren's song, luring myself and others towards a promise offered but never to be fulfilled. I feel duped, I feel like a fool. But more than that, I am livid.

"You're a fucking fraud."

He looks right through me, shakes his head, and walks to the door and opens it. Standing there are my three pursuers.

I stand and pick up the chair I'd been sitting on. It is heavy, constructed of hard solid wood covered in places by light cloth cushioning. Grasping the backrest on either side, I twist and hurl the chair through the large plate glass window to my left.

We're on the fourth floor, but luckily I'm familiar enough with the building to know that there is a long central outdoor patio connected to many of the upstairs offices. In the darkness of night I can barely see out the window. Before the men can converge on me I jump out of it, ripping my shirt and slicing my arm on a shard of glass, and run past the outdoor chairs and tables set up where students like to go and study on sunny days. Behind me, Dr. Robertson uses his jacket sleeve to brush away shards of broken glass clinging to the window's frame, then he and the three men casually step over the sill and onto the patio.

Casually, because the thing is, there's nowhere else to go, and they can afford to take their time.

I've run out of space, heading straight for the edge of the building and away from the other offices. My instinct wants to keep on running, screw the consequences, but my mind tells me that if I keep going in the same direction, a four story fall will be the last thing I experience on this earth. So I will my feet to stop. I turn and face them.

They're standing in a line, watching me. The moon is bright enough so that I can see them clearly, and even though I am finished running and they know they've got me, it isn't victory I see in their faces. Instead, it's just business as usual, the expressions of people who never doubted the inevitable, who have a job to do and will get it done, sooner or later.

"Give us the pack, Jake," Dr. Robertson says amicably.

I don't reply. Instead, I turn back toward the edge, walking right up to it so that my toes are touching the edge of the patio. There is no railing, only a small lip, empty space and darkness that pulls at me with a magnetic force. Far below, I see the well tended grounds of the campus.

"Jake."

A new voice, female. I know it. I know it well. I turn around slowly.

"Jake, honey, please," my mom pleads with me.

My father is there too. They stand together holding hands, looking worried, and the child in me longs to run to them, to let them take me in their arms as if I were five years old, pick me up and hold me, whisk me away to safety. But the feeling is short-lived.

"Jake," my father says, "Time to be a man. Give us

the pack. You don't have any other choice."

I look at him, and all of the others, and realize something. They believe what they're saying. They don't see anything else. A feeling of overwhelming sadness descends on me, to know with finality that this is the way things are. I cannot join them, yet they cannot let me go, because to do so would shatter their beliefs and the very essence of who they see themselves to be.

I turn back to the edge, and there it is. The thing from my vision is creeping up from the darkness, a gigantic round mouth filled with oil and smoke, turning gears and machinery. It looks like a massive overgrown bullfrog, its yawning gullet opening ever wider, the hole growing deeper and blacker as it rises from below to swallow me. A deep groaning sound interlaced with higher pitched whirring noises emanates from its depths, filling my head so completely that I can't even tell where the sound originates from. It has eyes of halogen lights which hang askew from metal pipes, and they light me from below so that my shadow stretches across the entire patio.

I look back over my shoulder at them all, my parents, Dr. Robertson, the three young men.

"You're wrong, Dad. I do have another choice."

I jump.

A MOMENT OF STILLNESS before gravity takes effect. The look of shock on their faces. My own heartbeat, still audible beneath the roaring of the machine, slowed and rhythmic like the beating of waves on the shore. Then I start to fall.

The pack on my back unfurls with a sudden

whooshing noise. I feel them, extending powerfully outward from my shoulder blades as if tearing from beneath my skin, from the bones themselves. I can see them reaching outward from my body, one on the left, another on my right, long, graceful and bold. The mouth of the giant bullfrog reaches up to swallow me, wholly and completely and finally, but before that happens there is a rush of air, and I am carried by it, lifting up, then higher and beyond, looking down as the forms of the people below grow smaller, and I swear I hear the machine roar in anger. No matter.

I turn with the currents of air, riding them, beautiful speed, wind and motion. It's finished. I am done running.

This time, I fly.

SIDETRACKED

R AJ SETH TOOK A SIP from a grape-flavored
energy drink, before switching to bottled water
and a quick bite of banana. He emulated his idol,
Rafael Nadal, when he played tennis. The Spanish player
"Rafa," as Rafael Nadal's fans affectionately called him,
had this routine he followed during breaks in the matches
he played. Raj had essentially copied the routine but still
found great comfort and calm in it as he rose up through
the ranks of high school, college, and up-and-coming
challenger tours. He also smoothed back his wavy black
hair between plays, like the great Roger Federer.

As a five-year-old, Raj felt he should play tennis
because his Indian parents encouraged well-roundedness
in both academics and athletics. Based on these
Renaissance Man-like experiences, he was to earn easy
entry into Harvard undergraduate studies one day, and
eventually into Harvard Law and Business schools. These
goals felt a long ways off, but seemed very important to
his parents and therefore they were to Raj as well. His
older sister, Sapna, was getting straight A's *and* playing
softball, serving as a natural role model for Raj's future.

It wasn't until Raj was ten years old that he became
less interested in math, science, and nearly every other
school subject and more interested in developing his
forehand topspin, volley, and dynamic serve. His coach,

Bill, saw Raj's natural talent and encouraged him to practice more on these skills to give him an edge over his opponents. Bill's recreational league tennis buddies in their 30's and 40's could stand to learn a thing or two from ten-year-old Raj's creative plays. He didn't dare dream further than that, however, after having met Raj's rather strict parents. But sometimes Bill would accidentally picture the grand tennis arenas of the US Open or Wimbledon, with Raj as a young man duking it out with the best. It was in him.

As Raj entered his teenage years, he felt a strain entering his life and for all his natural intelligence, he could not quite label it. The genes on both his mother's and father's side had made him taller than the average young Indian man. By age 14, he was 6 feet one inch tall, even taller than his dad. His dad, Jay, had always cautioned Raj not to get "too big for his boots." Raj didn't fully know what that meant, but he suspected that his metaphoric boot size was getting larger than his parents were comfortable with.

Raj's grades started slipping from A's to B's and B+'s. Raj's parents sat down with him very gravely one night and laid the report cards out on the kitchen table. "Raj, can you explain this?" was all they asked. Raj searched his thoughts for the correct response and out came the only reasonable explanation he could think of: "You both wanted me to play tennis. I'm doing pretty good at both school and tennis now." Raj's parents looked very sad to hear this, like trust between them and Raj had been irrevocably broken. They said only that his grades would need to improve. Raj went to his room and broke a tennis racket against his desk.

Raj simmered on this new problem, without really arriving at any answer. Sometimes to calm himself, he walked around and around the kitchen table. He felt in a trance, like the circling would lead to his destiny. All he could picture was beating player after player on the tennis court and ruling over that arena. He wanted to be the best, number one. Just not in the way that his parents envisioned. He couldn't find the words to communicate this to them and wondered in what secret vault the words were locked up. Where was the key?

He felt ashamed to admit it, considering both his parents were successful engineers, but he didn't give a darn about math and chemistry. Was that a crime? Out on the court, Raj channeled his feelings into deliberate forehand shots, and his favorite, the Ninja backhand. His backhand on the court, when it was lined up, flew from his racket like arsenal beyond just a single tennis ball. It discombobulated his opponents and sent tingles down Raj's arms and spine. It was as if all the energy in his body, all the frustration, all the confusion at being a brown Indian kid playing tennis could be boiled down to the power in that one beautiful backhand shot. He was a Ninja.

Raj's parents hardly showed up to his matches, but his sister Sapna did occasionally. She had entered college at Northwestern University, which was not far from where she and Raj grew up in Chicago. Of course she was studying to become an engineer. After one of his matches, Sapna ran over and gave Raj a congratulatory hug for his win. "Hey, when did you get so good?! I used to beat you all the time, now I wouldn't stand a chance." Sapna was beaming with pride but she noticed the hesitance Raj showed at being truly happy with his win.

"What's wrong?" Sapna prodded Raj about his moroseness. Raj unloaded, feeling that if anyone could understand where he was coming from it would be Sapna.

After all, "Sapna" did translate to "dream." Raj almost pleaded as he talked, "I've done everything mom and dad asked of me. I didn't mean to get so good at tennis, but they wanted me to play and I'm really good! I like it. Sapna, I really want to do this. I want to play tennis as a career. But they won't listen to me. What do I do?" All the breath had run out of Raj and he knew now that his life depended on this. If he never got a chance to find out how good he was, he'd regret it forever. He was only sixteen years old, but he felt this certainty in his bones.

Sapna mulled over what Raj had told her. She had always wondered why the stands at tennis tournaments were full of Indian families watching and loving the sport, while there were so few, or rather no Indian-Americans to root for among the contenders. It couldn't all be because Indian kids were short. Raj, at least, was tall enough to play professionally. Sapna leapfrogged beyond the dutiful sisterly advice that her parents expected of her and landed on what she really felt in this moment. "Go for it, bro."

Both Sapna and Raj knew that to "go for it" did not serve as a guarantee that a dream would pan out in reality. But to have one person behind him, and two counting his coach Bill, Raj felt more confident to flaunt his talent as enough evidence to fight for his dream. One night after dinner, a couple months before high school graduation, Raj mustered up all his courage to sit down with his parents and relay his goal to them. "Mom and dad, I want to pursue tennis as a career." These words were uttered softly, but they seemed to fall as explosive bombs on his parents' heads. They stared at him as if he were crazy.

"Raj," his mom, Ranjeeta, began, "I know you like tennis. But you cannot expect to go far in that field. There are no Indians who play." Ranjeeta turned toward her husband, Jay, for the next line. "Yes, Raj, your mother is right. Indian people don't play tennis professionally. Your teachers have told us that you have a very analytical and sharp mind for the sciences. Your cousin, Bobby, is becoming a biomedical engineer. And your other cousin, Nick, is a lawyer. You need to start preparing toward advanced education and a respectable career. Do not distract yourself with this tennis. You are in good shape and health because of it, so that is enough."

The more the family talked, the more the chasm between Raj and his parents deepened. The words he expressed plummeted down into the abyss, never to fully pass from human to human. Raj pleaded some more, cried a little. His mom told him that he had broken her heart, and that she had told all her friends what a wonderful lawyer he was going to be one day. Raj's dad sealed up into silence and looked off at the wall. Damage had been done according to Jay, and any compromise would be an insult to his culture, his heritage, and his role as a father.

Raj went on to graduate from high school and entered his undergraduate studies with Sapna at Northwestern University. He entered pre-law because that's what his cousin, Nick, had studied and he knew it would make his parents happy. He learned to forget tennis like something he had only dreamt of in his sleep and could barely grasp remnants of. In the dormitory and lecture hallways, he was surrounded by other Indian teens studying pre-med, pre-law, and pre-engineering, so it was not too weird to picture himself like the rest of them. He must have only imagined his athletic strength and it was best to forget foolish thinking.

One day, he met with Sapna for lunch and she caught his lost eyes. It felt as if he wasn't fully sitting there with her. "Where are you?" She asked. Raj wearily glanced up from his sandwich. He replied, "I guess I didn't score too well on my chemistry quiz." Sapna rolled her eyes. "Come on, Raj. Really, what is it?" Raj slowly felt blood return to his fingers, to his toes, down to his knees, and around his shoulders. Maybe he hadn't dreamt it. "Sapna, I still want to play tennis. I don't want to be a normal Indian boy!"

College was a world away from home. Raj joined the college's tennis club and quickly showed the coach how good he was. His grades not only didn't slip, they got better as he re-honed his Ninja backhand and his slightly rickety serve. Though not recruited to the school for tennis, his teammates and coach caught on to his infectious spirit and readily welcomed him. His coach, Joe, approached him one day after practice. "Hey Raj—what else are you doing here at Northwestern? Ever thought of shooting for pro tennis?"

Raj told Joe the full story of his ambitions and how they were being thwarted by pre-law. "To tell you the truth, I don't even know what pre-law is," he admitted to Joe. Joe smiled. "Listen, Raj, you're not the first brown kid I've talked to about tennis. Have you ever seen the movie, 'Bend it Like Beckham'? You're brown too just like the character in that movie...so what? These days there are Indian actors, comedians, dancers, chefs, models, surfers—you name it. Don't let Indian or American culture define for you what you can or should do in this country. You might see some other Indian guy playing pro tennis one day, and you'll realize it was actually possible."

Raj took one more sip from his grape energy drink and looked up at the giant scoreboard. People say life flashes before your eyes during a near-death experience. For Raj, there were many other times it did so as well, and this was one of them. Joe's words preceded the continuation of a path that led Raj here. To New York. To five sets of play in the first round of the U.S. Open. It wasn't his imagination. He hopped up from his seat, stretched out his calves quickly, and jumped in place to regain some energy and momentum against his opponent—Rafael Nadal. As the point started and Nadal served, Raj leaned in to his Ninja backhand and looked piercingly at the topspin of the ball into his future.

REDEMPTION

MIKE HURLEY KISSED THE PALM of his hand and put it up to the window of the taxi cab containing his wife and five-year-old daughter. As they departed toward the hotel for Ali's afternoon nap, he felt a surge of affection for his family. He was a lucky man.

He strolled along the boardwalk with no real purpose in mind. They were already two weeks into their vacation, with only three days remaining here at their last destination of Barcelona, and he wasn't about to waste any of his limited time left watching TV in a hotel room. So far, they had rode to the top of the Eiffel Tower, taken a train through the Swiss Alps, visited the site of the torn down Berlin Wall, wandered the maze of canals in Venice, and seen some of the world's greatest art in the museums of Rome. In addition to the more traditional tourist attractions, they had explored hidden villages and castles, crossed paths with an array of interesting people of various ethnicities and languages, and in Mike's case, taken a day to learn to paraglide in the hills outside a small village in France called Mieussy. Even though he'd had to be strapped to another dude all day, it was still pretty incredible.

At the age of 33, Mike was 15 or so years past the time where most people do their whole backpack across

Europe thing to see the world and sow their wild oats. Being married, of course his oats would be staying in his pants, but Mike wouldn't have it any other way. He could think of no two people he'd rather share this experience with than his wife Ariela and their adorable little girl.

Mike found an empty bench and rested his aching feet. From behind his sunglasses, he admired some of the most exotic and beautiful women he'd ever laid eyes on. Not to knock the girls in Tennessee where he lived, but they sure didn't make 'em like this back home. A striking young lady with unruly jet-black hair flowing wildly down her back walked not three feet in front of him across the sand, wearing nothing but an olive bikini bottom that clung to her rear end like cellophane. Her naked breasts bounced happily in the sun, nipples perked at attention. She smiled at him, not seductively or anything, just a warm grin hello, like she wasn't giving him a free show he'd remember for the rest of his life. Ahhh, Barcelona. American girls could make you feel like some sort of lascivious creep just for looking, but here it was A-OK. Not to mention there was the whole topless thing.

Mike wished he could stay forever.

After sitting for an hour or so, he felt the sun baking its way through his SPF 30, and headed to a nearby tapas bar for some of the most delicious appetizers he'd ever eaten. It was running on five o'clock by now, so after downing the last of his sangria and paying his bill, he started the three mile trek back to the hotel, where he'd shower and change, then head out to dinner with Ariela and Ali. Tonight he had decided they would splurge, and had made reservations at a 5-star restaurant called Els Pescadors.

Ten minutes into his walk, he heard someone cry out. A female voice. Down on the beach, near where the water met the sand, a large man wearing a straw sun hat held a much smaller woman by the hair. She was struggling to free herself, but he had a firm grip and to try and run would leave her with half her hair torn out in a clump. She raised her hands up to try and pry his fingers open, but he was too strong. His expression was angry, but also amused, as if the whole incident was just a mild form of afternoon entertainment. At this point, a small group of bystanders had accumulated on the rail of the boardwalk, Mike among them.

"Help!" cried the woman.

No one made a move to go down there, though an elderly British lady suggested to her husband that he call the cops, so he pulled out his phone and started dialing. Mike felt the muscles of his body tensing, fear and adrenaline mixing around in his bloodstream, and he quickly cycled through his mind the pros and cons of intervening. Pros: this lady needs help and that guy is an asshole. Cons: I could get my butt kicked or worse, and I'm in a foreign country and have a family to take care of. Mike stayed frozen in his indecision.

Realizing that no immediate assistance was coming, the woman on the beach picked up a handful of sand and hurled it at the man's face. Like an enraged bull, he started snorting and stomping his feet, rubbing his eyes with his free hand and trying to get his vision back. As he struggled, he was yanking her hair this way and that, which eventually caused her to fall to her knees where she broke out in tears. At this point a strange thing seemed to be happening, where the spectators' mindset collectively started turning from deciding what should be done, to becoming more entranced by the scene unfolding before them. The man who had called the cops had put his phone away and was watching with rapt attention. Mike was filled with a mixed sense of horror and fascination, his feet rooted to the concrete, eyes locked on the horrific scene unfolding on the beach.

"Why won't someone help me?" the woman sobbed. The man had managed to get the majority of the sand out of his eyes. Mike could see that what had once been more of a cruel game had quickly escalated toward something more violent and dangerous. He was about to do something bad. The man stared directly at Mike and the rest of the group watching him, insolent and malicious, daring anyone with his hateful gaze to try and stop him. No one did.

Mike glanced questioningly to the others around him, and caught many of them doing the same to each other. Everyone was wondering if someone else, especially one of the men, was going to make a move and alleviate the others of the burden of responsibility.

The woman must have sensed the heightened volatility of the situation, and perhaps found some resolve in accepting the sad reality that no one was coming to her aid. A medium-sized stick was lying half buried in the sand, and as the man was busy mocking his audience, she grabbed it, holding it at one end with both hands like a baseball bat. In one fluid motion and with more power than her small frame suggested, she rose to her feet, channeled the energy from her legs and torso like a whirlwind, and launched a brutal swing that connected squarely to the man's left temple. The crack of contact caused Mike to wince, but he felt a surge of triumph as well, and immediately a river of blood poured down the man's face, soaking his t-shirt and shorts. He roared in pain and let go of her hair, putting his hands to his head. The woman began to run.

Mike let out the breath he'd been holding. She was

going to get away – no way the guy could recover from a blow of that magnitude, no matter how strong he was.

But, he did. With blood still streaming from his head, the man shook it to clear the cobwebs, and took off after her. She had a good twenty foot head start, but it was clear that his long legs and athleticism outmatched her. The distance closed quickly. Mike's heart sank. The man tackled her from behind, and flipped her over. He raised his fist and dropped it like a massive hammer to the center of her face with a sickening crunch. Droplets of blood from his head wound splattered over her body. He did it again. And again. And again.

Suddenly, two police officers came out of nowhere and tore across the beach, guns raised in front of them, yelling for the man to stop and pulling him off of the now unconscious and bloodied woman. He tried to fight them off, so one of them pulled a night stick from his belt and slammed it across the man's kneecap. He buckled and the officer hit him again across the back, where he crashed headlong into the sand. The other officer deftly cuffed the man's hands behind his back, while his partner radioed for immediate ambulance assistance. As the officer was talking he glanced around the scene, and noticed the group of spectators watching. A look of disgust passed across his face.

Mike felt the tapas he had eaten begin to rise up in his throat. There was no denying he was a coward. The woman could be dead, or at the very least, severely injured with a number of broken bones. He had done nothing, watching helplessly as if caught in a nightmare, or watching a horror movie on TV. While the rest of the group talked amongst themselves, Mike looked down at the ground, then shoved his hands in his pockets and briskly walked off in the direction of his hotel, cold trickles of sweat snaking from his armpits down his sides.

His cell phone rang. His wife. "Hi, honey." Doing his best to sound unperturbed.

"Hi, you on your way? Ali's awake and we're getting hungry."

"Yup, walking now. Should be there in about thirty minutes."

"Okay." She paused. "Everything ok?"

"Yeah, everything's good. See you soon."

Mike said goodbye and tried to shake what he had just seen and done – or rather, not done – from his mind. Shame was gnawing away at his insides like a gigantic tapeworm. A few minutes later, he heard the scream of an ambulance siren start up from the direction he'd come. At least the woman was getting medical attention. Not a religious man, still, Mike said a small prayer for her safety, and couldn't help but wonder if he was praying more for her, or for his own soul.

We've all had intense or traumatic experiences that have the power to take us away from the reality around us. Sounds become muffled, objects lose their definition and become a nonsensical collage of random colors. Our bodies go through motions like automatons, while our brains try and process whatever it is we've been through. Life takes on a dreamlike, surreal quality.

In this state, Mike began to cross the street, oblivious to the red hand on the other side signaling him not to. His ears registered, but did not comprehend, the growing volume of the ambulance siren getting nearer by the second.

The wheels of the ambulance screamed as it took its right hand turn, as Mike stepped off of the curb and directly into its path. He felt an impact, but no pain, and a brief sensation of flying before strangely finding his body lying far away and looking up at a brilliant blue sky. The sounds of skidding tires, horns honking, and people screaming weaved together, and Mike briefly wondered what all the commotion was about before the noise faded out like the end of a bad love song.

"NICE WORK, DOUCHE BAG."

Mike opened his eyes. The lids felt heavy and swollen and his entire body, especially his head, ached terribly. He groaned.

"Ugh. What happened?"

A blast of cold water hit his face, and Mike opened his eyes to see a blurry form holding what appeared to be a bucket standing over him. He wiped the water from his face and tried to focus.

"What the fuck?"

"Wake up, Sleeping Beauty. We need to talk."

Gradually, his vision became clearer and Mike was able to make out his surroundings. He was in what appeared to be a hospital bed, in a hospital room. A window looked out to a grassy courtyard with cement benches and Mike could hear the sounds of traffic in the street beyond. All in all, that wasn't so unusual. It was the face of the man that blew his mind. It was like a trap door suddenly opening beneath his feet.

The man was him. Wearing a white doctor's coat.

He stared bug-eyed at what appeared to be some sort of long lost twin, uncomprehending, incapable of speech.

"Surprised?"

"Uhh, yeah. What is this? Am I dreaming?"

The man laughed. "Kinda, but not really. This is real. But not real in the sense you usually think about."

"What do you mean?" Mike was still trying to wrap his mind around the whole thing, and these were the best questions he could come up with.

"Every once in a while, when someone dies, the way—"

"Wait, am I dead?"

"Kinda, yeah."

"Dang."

"Yeah. But hold on a sec, there's more. Once in a while when someone dies in a way that feels altogether wrong to them, this kind of thing happens. I am you, but I'm you outside of time and space, which is different from the "you" living and getting caught up in the daily events of your human life. You've come to me – or rather, to yourself – because you feel so horrible about the last moments of your life and you don't want to go out like that."

The entire experience before his death flooded back to Mike. The day at the beach by himself, looking forward to dinner with his family, the brutal beating of the woman, his cowardice, the ambulance.

"So am I really in the hospital?"

"No, I just figured that'd be easier for you to process, less of a shock, you know?"

"And the doctor's outfit?"

"Same answer."

"Where exactly am I, then?"

The entire environment changed in the blink of an eye. Now Mike, instead of reclining on a hospital bed, was lying against the trunk of a tree in the middle of a grassy field. Lazy, puffy clouds floated across a crystal blue sky along the horizon and a light breeze gently swayed the stalks of grass. The man claiming to be Mike part two was still there, and he looked quite pleased with himself. He was no longer dressed like a doctor, now just wearing simple khaki shorts and a white t-shirt.

"Wait, let me guess," Mike said, "I'm outside of time and space?"

He cocked a finger and pointed. "Give the man a prize!"

"So you're like my spirit or something?"

"No. I'm just you."

"But you live outside of time and space or whatever, so that sounds kind of like you're a spirit."

"Time and space are manmade concepts. To life, they are irrelevant, and for man they are only useful as tools for reference and measurement. The problem is that humans have taken it too far and defined "reality" using these manmade concepts, and for that reason they learn to view life only within that frame, so their perspective is skewed and limited. The truth is, you, and all of life, exists on a plane that the human mind cannot comprehend."

"And that's you? You exist on that plane?"

"Bingo."

"Or I do, I suppose."

"Same diff. Everyone does. They just aren't able to see it because of the constraints of the mind."

Mike sat there in silence for a bit.

"Okay, so if you're me, and I'm upset about the way I died, what to do? How is any of this stuff even relevant if I'm dead?"

"You want a chance to do it over?"

Mike imagined his wife and beautiful daughter, and the thought of never seeing them again wrung his heart out like a dishrag. He relived that moment of passive paralysis as he watched a defenseless woman being beaten into unconsciousness.

"Hell yeah, I do."

"Cool. So here's the thing. In our concept of time, all events happen in sequence and are basically set in stone and completely linear, right? But considering time is a manmade concept, what happens if you take time out of the equation? In situations like this, where you want it bad enough, people can sometimes break out of the time-centric view of things and play around a bit."

"You mean like time travel?"

"Not really, not like the DeLorean in Back to the Future so much. Think of it more like a record player or a DVD. Sure, you can listen to the album from beginning to end, or watch the movie like normal. But you can also, if you want, skip around to different songs or parts of the movie, right?"

"Yeah. "

"And even though you're playing a specific song or scene, the rest of the album or movie is still there in potential just waiting to be brought to life, right?"

"Yeah."

"So basically all moments in the movie or album still exist even if you're not playing them. Your life is like that, too. Have you ever had a childhood memory so strong that the moment feels as real as if it were happening right now?"

Mike thought about it. In a weird way, this was making a little bit of sense.

"Uh huh."

"It feels real because it is real. For a moment, part of you is simply 'playing' that part of the movie of your life. Briefly, you are stepping out of the prison of time and space, where time is no longer chronological. We just don't see that as real because our minds are taught to think only within a certain framework."

"But it is real."

"Now you're getting it."

"So the moment where all this shit began is still real too."

"Yup."

"And I can go there if I want to?"

The man started to go blurry. The stark hues of the sky and field began to fade. Mike started to panic. He needed an answer.

The last thing Mike heard was, "How bad do you want it?"

He wanted it real bad.

MIKE'S SWEATY PALMS GRIPPED the railing overlooking the beach. He felt like he was going to vomit his heart right out of his throat, it was jumping around so fast. The man on the beach glared condescendingly up at Mike and the group he was standing in. It was the same scene all over again. Mike had only a brief moment to question whether what had happened before was even real – his inaction, his death, his meeting with himself. He came up with no answers, and this time, he had more important things to worry about anyway.

Palming the railing with both hands, he vaulted, drawing his knees up to his chest and gliding over the railing. It was a good eight foot drop to the sand and he hit with an "oomph," gathered himself up and ran toward the couple on the beach. As he approached the man, still holding the woman by her hair, he slowed. The corner of the man's mouth turned upward. It was clear he enjoyed the challenge. Mike felt like some sort of cowboy in the Wild West, a beach cowboy, he thought. He smiled coolly back at the man, doing his best Clint Eastwood impersonation, feeling anything but.

"Let her go," Mike said. "Asshole." He threw that last part in for good measure, though the truth was, he had no idea how to go about being a badass. His voice sounded like it was coming from far away, in some sort of echo chamber.

"Make me." Up close, Mike could see the man was older than he had originally thought, probably in his forties. His hair was graying at the temples. But he was huge. Underneath the rolls of fat padding, there was clearly a very powerful build. Mike weighed only 175 pounds on a good day, and that was with all his clothes on. He had never been in a fist fight in his life. Okay, now what?

"How about this?" Mike said. "You let her go, first. Then, I kick the shit out of you."

The guy burst out laughing. Oh boy.

"Ok, buddy. Sounds like a plan." He released the woman's hair and she scrambled crab-like away from him, then got to her feet and ran away to a safe distance before turning around to watch.

"Leave him alone, Mario!" she screamed.

"Shut up, bitch. Just be glad it's him I'm going to kill now instead of you." Mike gulped. The much larger man walked casually toward him. Mike put up his fists, and the guy started laughing again.

"Oh boy, you have got to be kidding me." Strangely, that's exactly what Mike was thinking too.

As the man closed the distance and the moment of action got ever nearer, Mike thought back to a night a few years back where he had been up late due to his recurrent bouts of insomnia. He was watching one of those obscure channels, and they had a half hour low budget show on self-defense tactics. He didn't recall too many of the details, but he did remember one thing the dorky military guy wearing fatigues had taught his audience – the body has points of vulnerability. Also, Mike knew his opponent was much stronger, but he thought that in all likelihood, he was quicker than the guy. He decided to put these two pieces of information to use.

He feigned as if to take the man head on, blow for blow, which is of course what the guy wanted. But when they got within punching distance, and the man pulled back his right fist to pound Mike's head into ground beef, Mike dropped his hands and ducked down underneath where the swing would fly, bending his legs, keeping his eyes locked right on the guy's Adam's apple. He made a blade out of his right hand, straightened his legs and came up with all the force he had in him, using the crook between his thumb and index finger to land a vicious strike that luckily found its target. Like a snake bite.

The man made some funny choking sounds, like he couldn't breathe. His punching hand stalled in its trajectory and went with his other hand to cover his throat, while his body fell to its knees. Spurred on by some cheers he heard coming from back up on the boardwalk, Mike reached his right leg back, and sent a field goal kick straight into the guy's nuts. The man let out an agonized groan, and fell face first into the sand. The cheering erupted full force from the bystanders now, and Mike felt tingles dancing all along his body. He also felt like he was about to pass out.

He made his way over to the woman, who was crouched nearby in the sand. He was suddenly aware of the strong scent of the ocean filling his nostrils.

"You okay?" was all he could think to say.

"Yeah," she replied, a look of shock on her face.

Mike guessed she didn't expect he would come out the victor. He hadn't thought so either.

"Did he hurt you?"

"No, I'm good. He just pulled my hair a little." Up close, Mike could see that the woman was quite pretty, a lot younger than the man. Her auburn hair was a tangled mess, and mascara streaked down her cheeks, but the fierce anger in her eyes made her even more beautiful. "Thank you," she said.

"Sure, no problem. I think I got a little lucky there," he said, smiling sheepishly.

Mike reached down to help her up.

"Watch out!" came a cry from the boardwalk.

Mike turned just in time to see a huge stick – the same one the woman had used to hit the man before – flying toward his face. He felt his skull crack open like a watermelon, and a second later, everything went black.

"WAS IT WORTH IT?"

Mike looked at the questioner, who was of course himself, and saw both pity and pride in his own eyes looking back at him. He thought about his family, and felt a profound sorrow knowing he would never get to see them again.

"Yeah," he answered. "It was."

MIKE OPENED HIS EYES. As before, the lids felt heavy, and as his vision went from blurry to clear, he found himself in a hospital room once again. He looked around for his doppelganger in the doctor getup.

"Mike?" Not his own voice this time. A female voice. Familiar, too.

Ariela's face appeared before him like a vision straight from the land of angels. The concern in her expression, combined with his relief at seeing her when he thought he'd never get a chance to again, was too much for Mike to bear. Tears began to roll down his face.

"Hi," he managed to say.

"It's okay, honey. I'm here. You're gonna be okay."

"What happened?"

"They told me you saved a woman from getting beat up by some guy." Gradually, the whole scene trickled back into Mike's memory, until he had it mostly put back together.

"Oh, yeah. That's right. I'm alive?"

"You're alive. They say you kicked his ass, too," Ariela said, smiling proudly. "But then he snuck up behind you like a coward and hit a homerun on your head with a stick. He's in jail now, and the lady's doing fine. The doctor says it's a pretty bad concussion, and your skull was fractured a little, but you'll be alright in a few weeks."

"Oh okay, no biggie. As long as it was only a little fracture." He gave her his best sarcastic grin, which amounted to little more than a twitch of his mouth.

"Always the smartass."

"Are you sure I'm not dead?"

"I'm sure. And I'm very happy you're not."

Mike felt himself fading out, and his wife kissed him on the forehead.

"Get some rest. Ali's outside and she wants to see you too, but we'll let you recover a bit first." She got up and headed for the door.

"Honey?" he called to her. Ariela turned back to look at him. "I was scared that saying bye to you in the taxi was the last time I'd ever get to see you."

"Oh, Mike. No way. Not a chance." She winked at him. "There is no last time for us."

SPIRITUAL CONNECTION

"JUST BECAUSE EVERYONE SAYS her book is good, doesn't mean it is good." Janie Day-Smith smiled inwardly for having pronounced a truth. Her eyes skirted past the shoulders of her chatty book agent to a polished mahogany shelf lined with her own glossy book covers, her airbrushed face glistening there with blue eyes and a caring smile. The most recent one published, "Doctor of Spirituality," headed the pack as its leader and offered solutions to many of life's problems. It was for anyone, everyone.

"Janie?" Veronica ventured. As Janie's agent, Veronica Benson had gotten used to the renowned yogini slash shaman's reveries during their conversations. Just recently, a prominent philanthropist and collaborator of Janie's, Sara McGrath, had gotten in touch regarding a joint book venture she wished to pursue. Sara was also a yogini who lived in India during her thirties before returning to America to write a special book on how to integrate Eastern and Western yogic philosophy into a well-rounded spiritual art form. The book had topped the New York Times best seller list for the past month. "Doctor of Spirituality" was bumped in return, but Janie said she wasn't fazed.

Veronica watched as Janie sat on the carpet and wrapped her legs into a pretzel shape. "Sure, I'll participate. I'm familiar with the advanced yogic forms Sara teaches. Hopefully she'll ask some celebrities to help boost our project. Hey, call up Priyanka Chopra for that. She's Indian and somewhat attractive, so that's a plus too."

Veronica fitted the words "Priyanka Chopra" into a cluttered space in her notebook. This was turning out to be a busy month, and the momentum was growing in Janie's world. She had already agreed to co-host the next Cultural Yoga Symposium with Sara, to be held in San Francisco. There were a couple of the usual blips, though. The media was asking questions these days on how Janie felt about Sara's book. "Janie," Veronica broached, "what are you planning to say during tomorrow's 'Today Show' interview?"

Janie un-wrapped her limbs as if she could control every molecule of her matter and glared at Veronica. "What the hell do you mean?" She felt her chest heaving all of a sudden and realized she had betrayed some feelings of irritation and insecurity. "Sorry," Janie explained to the air, "I just meant to say, why prepare when I have nothing to say about Sara's new book? I'm quite happy for her, she is a dear friend. I will appear on tomorrow's show and plug our joint Cultural Yoga Symposium. That is all."

She got up from the floor and handed Veronica a printout with some travel preferences for her next trip to New York. Janie then retired wordlessly to her meditation room. Sitting on a papasan chair, she fingered the spine of her pride and joy, "Doctor of Spirituality." People wanted so badly to copy her level of wisdom; it had become tedious to hear of others' spin-offs on her talents. Janie appreciated open enthusiasm for spirituality, yet the growing number of copy-cats was beginning to pose a threat to the teachings she wished to impart upon the masses. A lot of people wouldn't have access to these truths without her help, and she couldn't let fame whores muddy the lessons she worked so hard to deliver.

Janie allowed her intuitive tingle to guide her finger to a specific passage in her book. She asked the universe for gentle advice before resting her fingernail confidently on the perfect spot. She opened her eyes, and began to read out loud to the audience of her shaggy Persian cat, Shakti, who was rubbing attention-starved against her skirt's tie-dyed blobs. Janie took a deep breath and read:

"Doctor is as teacher, and the spiritual shaman being the most ancient form of doctor, he or she has the most to teach us. During my training as shaman, I learned to trust that a simple walk through nature could call to my spirit the most sublime truth in my being. I learned to listen to the dog as it howls. I entreat to you, listen to every soul you encounter in this way, every soul you meet has something to teach you which you have not yet thought of. Each soul outside of you has a secret, the sacred and generously given ability to save your own soul and help it to expand to the fullest in every way.

"If you cannot feel the throbbing from the hearts of your brothers, sisters, and neighbors as you walk through the streets just as strongly as you feel your own heartbeat, yogic and shamanic practices can help you tap into the spiritual vibrations that underlie these connections. If you don't feel this humble connection to your fellow human being, this is the illness to which you must first attend. Now let's enter a guided meditation I developed during my journeys through India."

Janie felt an unexpected surge of anxiety. That bitch Sara couldn't shut up about her travels to India, did her own words sound like that too? Janie shut the book despondently. She wasn't taking her own advice at the moment. Sara was a beautiful human being from whom she could learn a lot, or so her own book said. What was it that people liked about Sara? She was obviously just a knock-off of Janie.

Shakti mewled affectionately and stared up at Janie, waiting for a little pat on the head or a satisfying scratch under her chin. Janie got up from the papasan and accidentally stepped on the cat's tail, eliciting a sharp squeal of pain. "Stupid cat!" Janie scolded. Without thinking, her foot shot out abruptly at the cat's head. Shakti zipped away under a table. Janie's nerves felt fried, and maybe some yoga would help with that. The whole world should do yoga, she thought to herself. It was the true way to achieve world peace.

JANIE WASN'T BROUGHT UP in a spiritual way. In fact, her family had seemed to lack any religion or connection to a larger purpose in life. Her father was a teacher who liked to drink beer and ride a motorcycle in his spare time. Almost anything seemed more interesting to him than spending time with Janie. Janie's mom, Kathryn, was a counselor who worked with teenagers. Kathryn liked counseling Janie from a young age and during these pseudo-sessions, Janie became familiar with all her weaknesses and problems under a heavy magnifying glass. Her parents were okay, and they seemed smart enough. But Janie always felt smarter. Once she escaped to college, she longed to meet those with a higher purpose in life.

The theology department helped her start the journey. So many religions to choose from all around the world, and these religions felt more parental to her than her family ever was. She didn't totally agree with the philosophies and didn't completely disagree either. But they all offered a way out of the maze of mundane. Janie hated the mundane. There had to be more to life than raising a family and working a nine-to-five. She wanted an in to all the secrets the universe had to offer.

She met Sara during one of the theology courses, Taoist Thought and Philosophy. They were both the prettiest girls in the class and gravitated toward one another, sharing a common love of both the great creator and their own perfectly flouncy curls. It was one of those moments where famous met famous early on, each one sensing the potential to be known in the world. They didn't quite talk about seeking fame, but they fed each other's competitive spirit. Who dressed the best, who had the most connections at school, who was more intimately tied to the divine, who went on more dates and with the hottest guys.

Religion, the divine, spirituality, or whatever you wanted to call it was wrapped up with popularity to Janie and Sara—best friends, forever. They never took their eyes off each other, always wanting to know what the other was up to. After a year, they moved into an apartment together and eventually started a Spirituality Club, their first foray into leadership as co-founders.

The club went okay at first. That is, until Sara started to date Joe. Joe was not enlightened at all, and Janie wouldn't have been surprised if he spent the majority of his time watching internet porn. After Joe came along, Sara was less open about the club, spirituality, and her life in general. She seemed busy with…other things. Janie couldn't believe it, and she started to view Sara in a different light. What could be more important than what they had started together?

Sara moved out, and in with Joe. The best friends lost touch over time and ended up in different cities. Sara followed Joe to New York while Janie carved her niche near Hollywood. Janie eventually stopped thinking about Sara and her betrayal. If it wasn't important to Sara, it wasn't interesting to Janie either. Janie no longer had any close friends, family, or romantic relationships. But she had become the widely televised Doctor of Spirituality. Her name and brand grew as she opened a spiritual center near all the celebrities, held symposiums, gave talks, wrote books, and even hooked her own show. "Spiritual Day" was her true platform to fame, and it was the first of its kind on a major T.V. network. Janie's attractiveness and personality, along with her commitment to spirituality, helped build an army of devoted fans. The celebrity connections didn't hurt either.

"She changed my life, in two weeks," a supermodel would say. "Janie—she's the most warm and compassionate woman I've ever met. She accepts everyone," a talk show host declared. "Janie…wow, there aren't enough words to describe her open heart and her devotion. Meeting her was a turning point for me," said the president of the United States. A Golden Globe winner publicly dedicated her award to Janie (and fifteen other people) as the time cues signaled for her to shut up. She had shed tears while saying Janie's name, and that outpouring boosted Janie's brand instantly. Business CEO's flocked to Janie for guidance, and business magazines advertised her services.

Janie Day-Smith (no one knew how she got a hyphenated last name, but it sounded good) was happy with her life. She was satisfied beyond her wildest expectations. Until Sara came back into her awareness after ten years. Unbeknownst to Janie, Sara had never stopped pursuing her own form of spirituality, and her brand had started spreading on the opposite coast. In New York City in fact. Janie was shocked she had never heard of any of this before. What good was that damn Veronica unless she could keep up with important news like this?

Sara didn't officially walk back into Janie's life. It was happenstance. Sara was giving a talk in Hollywood five years ago and a number of celebrities were attending. It was called, "Finding the Divine You—in Five Steps." It was going to be a big old gala, complete with sponsorship and catering. Judging from the flyers, Sara hadn't aged a day since Janie last saw her. Apparently, Sara had used her spiritual skills to tame two middle-aged Hollywood men who had become more famous for their public tantrums than their acting. Sara, who now went by Joe's last name of McGrath, was very surprised to run into Janie after her talk. She hadn't intimately kept up with her former best friend's whereabouts, though of course she knew of her overall success.

Janie acted as amicably as could be, as if nothing had happened between them during the previous ten years. For Sara, nothing really had. Her life had moved on, and the thought didn't occur that she had ever owed Janie an explanation. She was married, with two kids, two dogs and a cat, two houses and one deluxe apartment, and a beautiful network of family and friends. "Wow Janie, long time no see. What are you doing here?" Sara asked, giving her friend a warm hug.

Janie wanted to puke. "I heard you were visiting my turf and I wanted to welcome you," she said with a hyper neon smile. She patted Sara on the back, as if giving her condolences for something. "Your talk was great, it really was."

Truth is, the talk had been a hit. A cheesy title, yes. But the lady was a good speaker and she seemed to have a charming way about her that was popular with the men. Guys often became confused while looking at her just where the spiritual inspiration was coming from. Making use of her goodies all these years had kept Sara looking a bit more spry, womanly, and shapely than Janie—even after two pregnancies. Janie couldn't even remember the last time she'd had sex. Why was she thinking about this anyway?

"Thanks, Janie. I really appreciate it. What are you up to these days? You live here?" Janie laughed off the assumed innocence and re-capped her life in a nutshell for Sara. Obviously, Sara was feeling super intimidated by Janie if she was pretending so hard to be ignorant of Janie's established fame and spiritual brand.

"Well, great to see you again Janie! Hey, maybe we can partner up for a talk or something in the future. Here's my card." Sara nervously handed Janie an elegantly designed business card and motioned that she had to go as her family was waiting for her. Something had changed in Janie since ten years ago, but Sara couldn't pinpoint what it was. She wasn't interested in finding out at the moment.

Next week, after her monthly appointment with spiritual healer and psychic, Helena Heart, Janie knew what she would do next. She had felt out of sorts since seeing Sara. She hadn't named it to herself, but she felt jealousy toward Sara despite all the fame and wealth she herself had amassed in Hollywood. Helena told her the best path was to invite Sara for collaborations so they could combine their talents and give to the world. Helena saw their partnership affecting great change in ways yet unimagined. It was the answer, indeed.

SARA WAS SURPRISED TO HEAR FROM Janie so soon. As they spoke over the phone, Janie explained how she was so excited to work together in the future. She wanted to take Sara up on her recent proposal to collaborate. Imagine the things they could accomplish together, the healing they could offer society!

Sara felt silly now toward her apprehension for meeting up with Janie again. Her old friend was being so friendly and sincere, and she even offered to open up Hollywood to their combined spiritual projects. This could be a terrific way to grow and spread her work beyond the East Coast.

Sara had to talk to her agent first, but she definitely looked forward to meeting up the next time she was in town. It would be during the summer. The two women hung up with a tentative plan in place. "Who was that?" asked Joe.

"Oh, you remember Janie? She came to my talk in Hollywood. She wants to work together on some stuff, it could really help me grow. Want to come next time I visit there?"

Joe shook his head. "No thanks, I'll pass on Hollywood and on Janie. She still ultra-competitive with you?"

"Competitive?" Sara asked, confused. Sara liked to think the best of everyone. She laughed and shrugged. So people wanted to be like her, huh? Not a bad thing when you're selling spirituality.

"COULD YOU TELL US ABOUT HOW you met Sara?" The Today's Show host, Joan, tried to pass the question innocently to Janie. Janie knew better than to get frazzled by this dimwit in high definition makeup and hair extensions.

"Sure, we roomed together during college where we met in the theology department. She's a dear, dear friend." Janie heard herself talking, why did she sound like a seventy-year-old spinster? She hardly knew what came out of her own mouth these days, it felt like she had gotten so many personality makeovers just to keep up with the trends. She needed to do better.

"I mean, Sara's great. We've been working on joint projects for about five years now. In fact, we're going to be writing a book together soon. We're also co-hosting the next Cultural Yoga Symposium in San Francisco. It'll be a blast, and be sure to check out our social media pages for more info." Janie smiled, proud of herself for sounding better, less insecure.

"Great!" Joan beamed. "Everyone out there, make sure to visit Janie's website." The website address flashed between them on a screen. "So Janie, have you read Sara's latest book? It's turning out to be quite a hit, what are your thoughts?"

Janie's insides cringed at the mention of Sara's book. Sara was becoming a household name now, huh? "Yes, I'm so happy for her. She's a dear friend." The words had already come out of her mouth as Janie realized she lacked preparation for this interview. Veronica had been right.

The interview got more awkward and uncomfortable after that. Janie felt like the audience hated her and loved Sara, anyway, so what was the use of trying? Sara was a family woman and had it all. She was the perfect face of spirituality today. What had Janie become, and who cared? She had built a whole empire for herself, and seemingly overnight Sara had ruined it just like she had ruined their friendship in college. Without even caring or saying anything about it. It was all Sara's fault. No amount of spiritual connection to Sara's throbbing heart beat could make Janie feel better now. Joan's eyes seared knowingly into Janie as the interview wrapped up.

"Thank you, to America's leading spiritual guru!" she concluded. Janie hated the word guru. She was a yogini and shaman.

THE DAY OF THE SYMPOSIUM was hectic. Veronica ran around with Sara's agent, Beth, both of them making sure everyone knew what they were supposed to do as guests arrived. Sara checked in briefly for wardrobe, and she left afterward to nurse a mild headache before show time. Beth had never heard of Sara getting headaches before. They were entering the big leagues now, and she supposed things were going to get a bit more stressful for them all. She handed Sara two Advil and told her to feel better, she'd knock on her dressing room door half an hour before start.

Janie was in a great mood that day, better than usual. Veronica was relieved. Janie was pretty hit-or-miss these days. Loving, hating. Excited, apathetic. Intelligent like her old self, or just plain trite. She was kind of mean sometimes. Saying cutting remarks like they were natural responses. Other times she was very appreciative of everyone, generating holiday spirit absent any official holiday. Veronica was happy Janie had come cleanly through her jealousy toward Sara, though. After the

Today's Show interview, which was pretty embarrassing overall, Veronica suspected the worst. But Janie increased her trips to Helena Heart and seemed at peace afterward.

"What did Helena suggest? Veronica asked Janie one afternoon. Janie smiled like Veronica had told a joke.

"Helena never suggests anything. She's a psychic and spiritual healer—she sees things, before they even unfold."

"Oh, okay, so what did she *see* for you?" Veronica tried again.

"Helena Heart said that Sara and I will have a reconciliation. We'll be able to feel a humble connection to each other once again, to appreciate the throbbing of each other's heartbeats." Strange, Veronica thought, those words were straight out of Janie's latest book. Janie corrected herself quickly. "That was just paraphrased, of course. I can't tell you exactly what Helena told me, that's private."

"Oh yeah, right. I didn't realize you and Sara were fighting right now."

"We're not. We were just distant for a while, it's hard to understand if you're not in it. It'll be better soon, though. I care about her and feel we have a lot to offer the world together."

Veronica stared at a table of nametags and smiled. Since that conversation, Janie seemed more at peace. Helena must have been right, things would go better for Janie from here on out.

SARA HEARD A KNOCK AT THE DOOR and managed to softly answer, "Come in." Her headache wasn't getting better with the Advil, it was getting worse.

What was she going to do? The symposium would be starting soon.

Janie entered, a look of concern on her face. "Are you feeling any better?" She crouched into the small space next to Sara's feet on the couch. On her way in, she had flipped on the overhead light, causing Sara to shield her eyes.

"No not really. Actually, the headache's getting worse. Do you mind turning the light off? It's hurting my eyes."

"Oh, you poor dear! What are we going to do, since the symposium's about to start?" Janie started to rub Sara's blanketed legs. "Maybe we should have skipped out on brunch this morning, maybe it's something you ate?"

"Yeah, it could be something I ate. Though I don't have a stomachache. Weird, I never get headaches. Hey Janie, do you mind turning off the overhead light? The corner lamp is enough light for me."

"Once I ate some bad food and actually got a headache—so you never know." Sara's frustration grew. Her request seemed to keep flowing directly in and out of Janie's ears. She didn't feel she had enough energy left to even repeat it. "Can I get you anything?" Janie continued.

Sara shook her head slowly. "Uh uh, I just need to wait this one out. Listen, I don't know if I can go up there right now. Maybe I can cover more of tomorrow's session if you take over today."

Janie nodded her head enthusiastically. "Yes, for sure, anything I can do to help. You'll probably be taking the whole weekend off." Even in her weak and dazed state, Sara's mind was confused by that comment.

"No, Janie, I don't need the whole weekend off. I'll feel better by tomorrow. Hey, I'm sorry, but do you mind turning the light off on your way out?" Sara closed her eyes completely, waiting for Janie to head to the symposium. It was almost show time, about 45 minutes left.

"Sorry babe, you'll be taking the whole weekend off. I know you're not feeling too well, but I can't turn off the light yet."

"What do you mean by 'yet'?" Sara asked, now starting to get very annoyed but having less and less energy to express it.

"I need to be able to see what I'm doing."

"What?!" Sara started to get up off the couch and was dismayed to find that her head wouldn't lift an inch. "Janie, I can barely move. I'm starting to feel really ill. Could you get someone?"

"Oh, you poor dear. Who would I get, though? It's too late anyway."

"Huh?"

"I've been meaning to tell you something, Sara. I tried to talk to you at brunch, but you wouldn't listen so we need to talk now. I don't know what this whole innocent act is of yours. I know why you came to Hollywood, why you've always been so jealous of me."

Sara's mind began to panic as she heard Janie's words drift around the periphery of her failing consciousness. She felt sure of something all of a sudden, and she had no strength to run. "Janie, what did you do to me?"

"After my Today's Show interview, I thought it was I who might be envious of you," Janie resumed, "and it was really tormenting me for a while. Did you watch it?" Janie waited, as if expecting a real answer from Sara. Sara's feet were kicking weakly, but she didn't have the strength to get up.

"Help! Help me, please!" Sara started to yell. It came out as a whisper instead.

"I talked to Helena Heart afterward and she helped set my mind at ease. I don't think your jealousy should come between us anymore, Sara, as we were always such good friends. We're both such warm, giving, and spiritual beings, don't you think? I think we should make up now. You know, I once read that if you don't feel a humble connection to your fellow human being, this is the illness to which you must first attend. I'm trying, Sara. I'm making a real effort to feel where your heart's coming from."

Sara's world grew gradually dimmer as Janie's words swam in and out of her mind. She couldn't catch much of what her old friend was saying anymore. Something about Sara's coffee at breakfast, a plan, drowsiness, Hollywood, reconciliation, college, Joe, the Spiritual Club, the book, and so on. A fragmented and nonsensical trip down Janie's memory lane.

The last thing she heard before the light finally went off were the words "spiritual connection."

THE ATMOSPHERE CARRIED THE CURRENT of change as the news flooded the T.V., the internet, and the radio all at once. It described how the beloved international philanthropist and yogini, Sara McGrath, was found brutally murdered in a dressing room in San Francisco. She was supposed to be co-hosting the Cultural Yoga Symposium, usually organized by herself but this year also headed by the primary murder suspect in the case, Janie Day-Smith. Janie Day-Smith is also a well-known celebrity yogini and shaman. The murder happened at a Hollywood hotel. Celebrities attending the symposium were devastated.

Veronica didn't need the never-ending news reel to tell her what had happened. She had come to Sara's dressing room a half hour before the symposium to check in on Sara's headache. Veronica knocked on the door, and not hearing a response, she opened it. She noticed Janie in there first.

Veronica screamed and dropped nametags to the ground that she'd been holding. Janie sat on the floor, in her familiar pretzel yoga pose. Who knew exactly how she had done it, but she was sitting in a pool of red looking absolutely at peace. It was almost like one of her private yoga sessions except that in her hands she held Sara's heart, taken from her now limp body. Janie stretched her arms out toward Veronica and announced to her, "See— Sara and I are best friends again. We're ready to start the symposium."

BULLY

MS. MARINA USHERED the remaining kids into the auditorium, a concerned look on her face regarding the subject matter of today's school assembly. A young man bumped into her rudely while dribbling a basketball inside ahead of him, a backward cap taunting her as he passed. She smoothed out the pleats of her long gray skirt and remembered that these people could hardly be called kids anymore. In middle school, she saw an infestation of growth spurts, potty mouths, and just plain talking back. These "kids" were nearly adults now, and they should know better. Her nerves were tested every day trying to help these students become all they could be.

When Ms. Marina first started teaching at Adler Middle School, she looked forward to molding this delicate age range. The kids were no longer finger painting or learning how to read as in elementary school, ever expectant of the next recess. Nor were the students applying to college, dating, and solidifying their ultimate fates like happened during high school. Middle school offered a chance to find oneself. It let you test out the waters, your potential, and your place in this world. Middle school was beautifully awkward in a way, Ms. Marina remembered of her own schooling.

While teaching over the last five years, however, she

came to see just how little respect these students showed toward their elders and increasingly toward each other. Today's important school assembly was going to address bullying. These last few months had been harrowing. One sophomore, Ella, had recently started cutting herself and was admitted to a psych ward by her parents. The culprit: Soccer jock, Danny. Danny could get any girl he wanted, but he'd become equally fixated on tormenting the less endowed females. He called Ella names and sicced his band of fully breasted followers on her too. Ella's parents didn't know when she'd be returning to school.

Pete was a young gay man who seemed the butt of everyone's jokes. It wasn't official news that he was gay, but everyone treated him that way. He probably wouldn't have minded the assumption given his skinny jeans, floral print tops, in-season scarves, and active involvement in theater. He unabashedly fit the stereotype and would most likely become a fashion designer some day. What did bother Pete, however, was being labeled in an insulting and derogatory way. His parents had started it at home and the sneering had somehow caught on at school too. Pete had been absent from school a lot lately.

Another student, this time a gap-toothed Indian boy named Sunjay, had gone from A's to D's in no time at all. Satellite camps of bullies waited around his locker to call him names, ranging from Turban Boy (though he didn't wear a turban) to Chief Brown Nose for knowing the answers in class. Sunjay, who was East Indian, couldn't get away from being stereotyped as either a terrorist or a Native American. It seemed like no matter how peacefully the yogis meditated in India, in America Sunjay was to battle against the constant stereotype of being a war monger.

Ms. Marina searched the crowd, and Sunjay was

nowhere in sight. He must have skipped school again to avoid his tormenters. She sighed. She herself had been bullied and made fun of as a child, but she had become a better and stronger person because of it. She intuitively sensed that not all the students at Adler were blessed with as strong of character as she had. It was her duty to help them through this tough time so they wouldn't be scarred for life.

She would have hated to grow up in today's culture where you could be made fun of both in person and online over social media. Who protected the students from these dangers? The parents seldom knew what went on at school until it got real bad. Teachers, like herself, did the best they could but they were blasted by school meetings, crammed syllabi, and noncompliant students. Teachers hardly had time left over to police each student's behavior.

"Quiet down please," the principal, Mr. Phillips, requested from the front of the auditorium. A reluctant hush fell over the gym after a few minutes, the students' attention held as if by a thin thread. If someone were to accidentally fart even, the whole atmosphere would be shattered. Mr. Phillips took the narrow opportunity to introduce the assembly.

"Students, we're assembling today to discuss the importance of preventing bullying at school. Bullying has been a real issue this school year, affecting many students, and Ms. Marina took it upon herself to arrange this assembly to address the issue." Scattered pockets of students erupted in chuckles at the mention of Ms. Marina's name. Even as an adult, Ms. Marina was seen to be somewhat of a nerd in a large body. She wore pleated skirts as if she were still a school girl, her uniformly bobbed hairstyle never changed, and her planner was her best friend. She seemed to be asking for it. "Anyway, please give your undivided attention to Ms. Marina." Mr. Phillips wrapped up half heartedly, sensing that the students' attention span was thinning as fast as his hair.

Ms. Marina assumed the podium to start the assembly. Her fears of public speaking bubbled up under the surface and threatened to undermine her authority as she prepared to talk. Today, the nerves were even worse than usual. What was going on?

It was her concerns about bullying that sparked a school-wide meeting a month ago and ultimately this assembly today. All the teachers agreed with her, it was time to do something about it. They just didn't want to carry the burden on their own shoulders. Beyond the "Teacher of the Year" award that she won her third year of teaching, Ms. Marina hadn't stood out from among the other teachers over the past couple of years. Maybe this was her chance to make a real difference at Adler Middle School.

Her slightly trembling voice bellowed over the microphone, filling the entire auditorium with a sense of honor, purpose, and duty. She would make herself heard today, and the bullying would stop once and for all. Isolated snickers sprouted in the auditorium, seeming to intensify the more earnestly Ms. Marina addressed the students. She decided to push on past the laughter, as the students would have to learn to respect her authority. Her conviction ironed out her shaking voice as she proceeded.

"What you think is funny now, may tomorrow bring you shame and regret." She paused for a few moments and let her statement settle in the air for full effect. All sound was sucked out of the auditorium. Ms. Marina stepped off the podium and traveled slowly into the open space where a picture of the school's Bulldog mascot was painted onto the hard court.

"Some of you take part in the bullying that is becoming a big problem at this school. What gives you the authority to hurt people in this way?" She looked at Marcy McLean, one of the students in her homeroom class.

Marcy had flouncy blonde curls, the latest fashion, and a never boring love life. The girl was self-absorbed with capital letters. She couldn't ever seem to put her damn phone down in class even during the most pivotal lessons, texting tidbits of "OMG" and "Totes Mcgotes, he's so hot" as if they were the most important announcements of the year. Ms. Marina confiscated her phone during class one day, "forgot" to give it back, and read all the texts during lunch. That's how she knew what Marcy was up to. Marcy also loved texting shit about other students. *"Danielle's so fugly, who would ever date her?"* *"Oh my god, did you hear what that skank Vicky did last night?"* *"Look, no one's sitting next to Jenny LOL."*

Ms. Marina walked over toward Marcy. Her gray pleats stopped short of Marcy's curls, which were bobbing up and down above her phone. Marcy's silent laughter at a funny text was surely being shared by another inconsiderate student in the audience.

"Does it make you feel powerful, is that why you do it?" Ms. Marina waited. Marcy hadn't heard the teacher's words but she suddenly sensed a strange ripple of fear spreading through her. The blonde hair on her arms stood on end and she gulped a couple of times before looking up. Ms. Marina was staring straight at her and the whole auditorium was silent. "Does it make you feel powerful, Marcy? Enlighten us."

Marcy shrugged, but she was starting to feel very queasy as if she could hurl at any moment. "Does *what* make me feel powerful?"

Ms. Marina laughed. "That's funny, Marcy. You're showing everyone here, as you've been doing all year, another form of bullying. Thank you for demonstrating it for us. When you text bad stuff about other students, it's still bullying—don't you think? I just wanted to ask you why you do it."

Mr. Phillips shifted uncomfortably in his seat as he watched Marcy's cheeks change in color from a slight rose to a mottled crimson. He had never really seen this side of Ms. Marina before. He didn't know whether to feel sorry for Marcy or happy that the students were paying attention to today's lesson on bullying.

Marcy didn't say anything. She sat there transfixed while Ms. Marina waited for an audible answer from her. The students were cringing, scared that they might be next. Even the ones who were regularly bullied didn't know what to think of this display. Just as Marcy's eyes started to tear up with the embarrassment she was feeling, Ms. Marina turned on her heel and walked back to the podium and mic.

"In just a moment, we'll be watching a well-put-together video about bullying. Before I start it, I want to express that some of the behavior I have seen from you students this year has been outright shameful. I'm very disappointed in what I've seen.

"When you emotionally or physically bully another student at this school for being different, you don't just hurt that student—you hurt us all. While bullying makes you feel powerful or authoritative as a person, it's really just cowardly at heart. It actually says more about your own self-esteem than that of the person you're bullying.

"I and the other teachers and staff members here expect more from you all. You're not little children anymore. You're young adults. If you'd like to be treated like young adults here, and not like small children in the way I just addressed Marcy, you must earn that respect." Ms. Marina looked over at the spot on the bleachers previously occupied by Marcy, and found she had disappeared. She was most likely crying in the bathroom and expertly fixing her makeup afterward, thought Ms. Marina.

"Anyway, I don't want you students to think about this today and then forget about it tomorrow. You have to change as a group and start respecting one another more. Do unto others as you would have them do unto to you." Ms. Marina finished with the Golden Rule, wondering if she had remembered to phrase it correctly from her own elementary school days. What exactly was "unto" anyway?

Ms. Marina asked Mr. Phillips to turn off the overhead lights, pressed Play for the video, and sat down quietly in a chair to watch. The students waited numbly, mentally itching to escape the auditorium and move on with classes and life. No one would talk about it much afterward, but today was turning out to be a very strange day.

A recess setting panned onto the large white projector screen, fully equipped with a jungle gym and see-saw that Adler's student body hadn't seen since 3rd or 4th grade. A tall blonde kid about eight years old shoved a smaller brunette boy onto the concrete. "Ouch!" the brunette boy exclaimed as he began to cry. Mr. Phillips rolled his eyes, realizing that Ms. Marina had picked out a bullying video for elementary-aged children rather than middle schoolers. What universe was this woman living in? Mr. Phillips felt a twinge of guilt for "bullying" Marina in his mind.

The video lasted thirty minutes too long, and Mr. Phillips jolted from his seat to turn it off once the credits rolled. The lights came back on and he quickly thanked the students for coming and dismissed them to their next period. Just as the auditorium doors opened, he caught Ms. Marina frantically approaching him from the corner of his eye. "Mike, Mike—I had some closing remarks I wanted to make after the video…"

Mr. Phillips found a smile from somewhere inside of him and turned to address Ms. Marina. "Julie, I really appreciate you putting this together today. The students…heard your message and I'm sure the assembly will spark some change." He nervously ran his hand through what barely passed as a hairstyle on his head. He had started his position as principal with a thicker mop, but more strands were going extinct each year. It was definitely the stress. He suddenly felt the need to shield what was left up there from Julie Marina.

"Thank you Mike, that means a lot. I definitely have more to say, and I didn't get a chance to fit it all in today…I mean, this has been a huge problem for the school and with the increasing absenteeism…"

Mr. Phillips nodded. "Yes, I know. We just had to let them out at some point. We were moving past an hour, and they have to finish out the school day." He turned back to ejecting the video, hoping Julie would take his hint and leave to finish out her school day too. After a moment, his eyes darted back to where she was still standing, waiting. This was getting awkward. What did she want?

Putting the video back in its case, Mr. Phillips tried to break the ice with "Have a good rest of your day, Julie. See you tomorrow." He looked toward Ms. Marina with finality in his eyes.

Ms. Marina smiled very warmly, almost too warmly, and held his gaze. A subtle feeling of dread punched Mr. Phillips in the gut. "Mike, I know you care as deeply about this issue as I do. It's just a little strange to me though, that you seemed to merely want to touch the surface of the bullying problem with this assembly today. I thought your introduction could have been a little more—heartfelt."

Mr. Phillips was getting tired of all this. His subconscious was beating around the bush in determining whether he felt bullied by Julie at the moment, if you could call it that. She was acting quite fiendish and rabid about something.

"Julie, I care about this, okay? Believe me, I'd like to witness less bullying around here too." Mr. Phillips wondered why he should have to explain himself to this woman, if you could call her that. He helped her arrange the damn assembly, and she still wanted some nebulous "more." He had no idea what that more was, and that's what felt dangerous. She was still waiting, and something was simultaneously tickling his brain. Might as well just say it.

"I do wonder if that episode with Marcy was necessary, however." He heard those eleven words pinball through his mind as a small bell of alarm rang out. What was he getting himself into? Mr. Phillips had made it his mission as principal to avoid a few choice female teachers as much as possible, in order to prevent confrontations such as this one. While he cared about the bullying situation at Adler, he had let Julie be in charge mainly to appease her. He hadn't anticipated in advance that she would turn psycho on a student at the assembly.

A wave of reactions was spreading through Ms. Marina's face, but the end result was not yet readable. A flash of anger dissipated as if it had never existed and the warmth returned with an expectant smile. "And what would you suggest is a more appropriate gesture toward a student who is texting out insults during a bullying assembly?"

"Julie, you don't know she was texting bad things about anyone, let's not get carried away. I agree that it's probably not the best time to be texting, but that scene was somewhat humiliating for her. Could you see that?"

"And being ignored during my own assembly wasn't humiliating for me?" Ms. Marina amped up the tone of her voice a couple levels, making Mr. Phillips want to cover his ears. Julie decided to keep mum about how she'd read Marcy's insulting and pointless texts during school that one time. That knowledge would unravel her whole argument, and the victim here was her, not Marcy.

Mr. Phillips sighed, nearly ready to give up. "I don't want to argue about this, Julie, we're on the same page about stopping bullying at Adler. I'll do my best to support what you're doing, but as principal I'm just asking that we not single out individual students publicly. Let's use these assemblies to address all the students, and handle specific situations one-on-one privately. You can definitely talk to Marcy about not texting at school, and I'm sure she'll understand. Make sense?"

Ms. Marina nodded, and Mr. Phillips couldn't read whether she'd truly understood at all. She was still holding on to something.

"Well, would it be okay with you if we held one more assembly before the end of the school year? I don't think the students could get too many reminders on how important it is to keep Adler bully-free. It will put us on the right footing for next year."

Mr. Phillips agreed. He didn't really want to have

another assembly, but if Julie covered the topic without ostracizing a student next time, it could make up for what happened with Marcy. He just didn't trust Ms. Marina, but she was here to stay for now. Often the teachers were harder to teach than the students because they assumed they had nothing left to learn.

"Great, Mike! Looking forward to working with you again for the next assembly. Thank you so much for everything, and have a wonderful day!" Ms. Marina flashed him her most caring and empty smile and left the auditorium like a victor. Who knew what exactly she felt she'd just won.

Mr. Phillips looked down at the D.V.D. case in his hands. "Say No to Bullying!" it screamed at the top in red letters, right above a picture of a pint-sized class of students holding hands with each other and their smiling teacher. Was any of this helpful, he wondered to himself as he stood alone in the auditorium on top of the caricatured Bulldog.

A FEW MONTHS PASSED, made up of an inefficient flow of days in the mind of Adler's top teachers. There were never enough class periods to do everything you wanted and on top of that, teachers like Ms. Marina were afflicted with perfectionism. She was in the midst of putting together the school's second assembly on bullying, and the faculty and staff buzz hinted that she might get Teacher of the Year for a second time. There was a lot to do before June came around and heralded summer break.

Ms. Marina had strengthened her foothold on being the school's bullying expert by profusely writing blog posts and articles on the subject, which she circulated among her peers. She even scoured the library and waded through journals of adolescent medicine for reputable sources on the despicable behavior. The more she researched, the more she knew she'd found her crusade at Adler, and a worthy one at that.

Ms. Marina had felt different all her life, just like many of the bullied kids felt here at Adler. People were learning in today's world that different was okay, that in fact it was valuable. People are like snowflakes, Julie thought to herself. Each one unique and one in a million. She felt fulfilled again, like all was going well in life and she was helping to make a real difference for the youth— tomorrow's leaders.

Mr. Phillips mainly stayed out of her way and let her pursue her interests in whatever way she chose. He would help out with simple tasks if she asked him, such as in getting the word out about her bullying blog. He really was turning out to be a peach. Julie had at first been concerned about his conviction after the assembly a few months ago. She had wondered if he really cared about the bullying situation at Adler to begin with or if he was just going through the motions. She hoped he understood now that middle school wasn't for the faint-hearted. Teachers and staff had to be as strong as the middle schoolers to get through it. Sometimes that meant unapologetically laying down the law.

The teacher's lounge was filled with frenetic energy on the Friday a week before Easter. Teachers were giddy with coffee, filled with anticipation of time off, and sparked by the conviviality that accompanies holiday months. Teachers who might normally go out of their way to piss each other off, lose patience toward one another, or just plain ignore each other were inspired instead to break bread together around the dining table. Someone had even ordered pizza and pint-sized bottles of soda, pulling out paper plates and plastic cups. The hallways were quiet and slowly drowning out the earlier stampede of students leaving for spring break, but the teacher's lounge was a happening place. If the hallways had been less deserted or the lounge more subdued, the following events could have been avoided.

It wasn't long before the conversation landed on the bullying assembly that took place earlier that year. There were still some problems with bullying at school, but the assembly had been a real…eye opener for everyone, including the students. A few bullies, such as soccer jock Danny, were no longer seen prowling the halls for fresh meat. The teachers knew it would take time, but they were appreciative to Ms. Marina for spearheading the movement. The high fives she'd received from teachers after the assembly were the first ones she'd ever experienced.

In the teacher's lounge, Ms. Clemens was the first to bring up the subject. "Julie, I just have to hand it to you again, your assembly really changed things around here." The other teachers nodded eagerly in unison. "Yeah" and "absolutely," Ms. Marina heard echoing around the lounge, accompanied by the pitter-patter of enthusiastic applause.

Ms. Marina smiled modestly and brushed a strand of hair behind her ear. She waited for the clapping to quiet down before responding, "Thank you so much, everyone. I hope my efforts will make a real and long-lasting impact on bullying at this school." The feverish nodding continued for a few moments. Then a hushed awkwardness started to spread through the room. No one knew what to say and it seemed an inappropriate time to bite into a piece of pizza. Ms. Marina suddenly noticed that her hands were empty and she didn't know what to do with them. They nervously took to smoothing out the pleats of her skirt. Ms. Clemens broke the awkwardness as quickly as she had engendered it.

"Marcy McLean's been different in class lately, and I noticed she doesn't play with her stupid phone anymore." Other teachers nodded.

"Yeah, I noticed that too," Ms. Mancuso agreed. "She seems a lot less ditzy too, wow sometimes I wondered about that girl."

Ms. Daniels wanted to share too. "I heard that she wants to be a model someday. Her mom told me during parent teacher conferences that she'd made a deal with Marcy. If Marcy could get all A's this quarter, she'd be able to enroll in modeling classes." Teachers rolled their eyes and laughed.

"Did she do it?" Ms. Mancuso inquired.

"Naw, her phone probably got in the way of that goal," Ms. Daniels guffawed as if she'd made the funniest observation in the world.

Ms. Marina felt her heart thudding in her chest all of a sudden. She hadn't thought about Marcy in a while and the girl had slid into the background of her homeroom, no longer announcing her presence like she used to with a flip of her blonde curls. Ms. Marina's pleats were already smoothed and now her awkwardness was turning into an unexplained fear. She needed to say something, anything. The teachers were looking right at her and wondering why she was so quiet, she was sure of it.

"Model, huh? Well, I guess in reality she'll be flipping our burgers and making our fries some day." Ms. Marina felt the wave of laughter spreading through the room in approval of her joke.

"Seriously, I look at her sometimes and wonder how many brain cells are left there. They really should do a study looking at the correlation of phone use to I.Q." Ms. Clemens said with a pitying look on her face. Many teachers had opinions about Marcy and they took turns sharing them.

The gas eventually ran out on the topic of Marcy, and silence was about to return. "To be a model, you need personality not just looks. Hey, who do you think is the prettiest student in the school?" Ms. Mancuso threw out to everyone.

"Definitely Christy Loya, you know that volleyball player? She's gorgeous and applies herself in school. She's one of my best students." Ms. Clemens smiled knowingly at the fact she'd just shared.

"Gosh, Marcy doesn't hold a candle to her," Ms. Marina egged on. She knew there had been a reason she'd called out Marcy's behavior at the assembly. All the teachers shared her viewpoint about the situation. That girl would have to learn, and better now than later in life.

The conversation was rolling now and it was impossible to keep track of who exactly was saying what. It was a hungry reel of insights and observations, things the teachers had kept to themselves all year long. The tidbits seemed to validate each teacher's existence at Adler Middle School. Behind the scenes the teachers saw, heard, and remembered everything. Adler Middle School was truly possible because of them and their watchful care.

"Who's the smartest student at Adler?"

"Oh, definitely Jimmy Choo. He's going to make it to Harvard someday."

"The laziest?"

"Cal Rinna, you know him? He sits in the back and dozes off half the time. Talk about burgers and fries."

"You know who's the worst at math? No offense, but I think Jake Smith's parents might want to take him back a year. I've been hinting at it for a while, they think he's smarter than he really is. Some parents are so stubborn, believing their kids can do anything. You have to be realistic though, you know?"

One teacher chuckled. The lounge being full of female teachers today, she thought it appropriate to ask, "Who do you think is the hottest male student?"

A few teachers gasped, but Ms. Clemens piped up. "Some of those boys are so tall, you can almost see what they'll look like as grown men. Yeah, I've spotted some hotties." She blushed.

"Randy Long is incredibly good looking. I'd say he's the hottest." The teachers were now scrambling over each other's words to fit new comments in.

"Most nervous and anxious?"

"That would be Brook Summers. Her foot starts tapping so hard before tests, I get worried she'll crap herself." Several teachers' eyes opened wide like saucers at the choice of words, but conversation carried on and the new tone of speech along with it. It was reaching a nonsensical pitch without any real continuity.

"I hate to call anyone dumb, but really that kid Newton…"

"I think Joanne is the one most likely to get knocked up…"

"Most embarrassing, that would be Stewart in my class…what about yours?"

Imitations were starting to pop up too. Ms. Marina started with a spot on impression of Marcy checking her phone during class. Then the teachers were trying to out-do each other with who could do the best so-and-so.

Before anyone realized how late it was, the clock

reached 6:30 p.m. They had all been talking and entertaining each other for over two and a half hours.

"Wow, time flies when you're having fun!" Ms. Clemens smiled, resting her hand on Ms. Marina's shoulder. "I actually have to get going." The teachers swallowed down any residual laughter and pizza, tossed paper plates in the trash, and grabbed coats. The voices diminished to subdued chatter as everyone wished each other a good spring break. One by one the teachers of Adler Middle School filed out of the lounge into empty hallways and toward their cars. More than one had a queasy stomach and didn't know why.

ADLER'S STUDENTS AND TEACHERS either recharged their batteries over spring break or depleted them even further. Ms. Marina spent a lot of her time working on the next bullying assembly. Marcy's parents hardly saw her over break and noticed that their daughter was uncharacteristically down in the dumps these days. They thought they'd seen her crying once or twice but she wasn't in the mood to talk about it. Mr. Phillips went fishing and tried to get as far away from school as possible.

The first day back felt like culture shock, and Mr. Phillips sat at his office desk a bit dazed when his assistant walked in the door. "Mike, Julie wants to talk to you today about the upcoming bullying assembly. What do you want me to tell her?"

Mr. Phillips sighed in response, which he'd been in the habit of doing a lot lately. He had ample time to think over break, about everything. He knew what he had to do. "Thanks for taking the message, Melissa. I'll stop by

Julie's classroom this morning and talk to her. By the way, here's a special announcement for lunchtime. I'll explain later, but we need this sent out over the P.A. system." He handed Melissa a folded note, not his usual style for an announcement. Melissa snapped it in her clipboard for safekeeping and confirmed that she'd meet with Mr. Phillips later on. She could read the look on his face and tell that something was up.

"Hey Mr. P!" a student yelled out as Mr. Phillips walked toward Julie's classroom. "Good morning, Joe." Mr. P replied. The student kept walking in the opposite direction but glanced back over his shoulder first. Mr. P seemed different today.

He entered Ms. Marina's classroom, his eyes immediately drawn to a blue banner positioned above the chalkboard. It read "Positivity is Contagious!" What did that even mean? There couldn't be anything farther from the truth, from what Mr. Phillips knew.

"Julie, I need to speak with you for a moment," Mike alerted the bustling teacher. She looked up at him like he was an old piece of gum stuck to her shoe. Once she realized the message her face was emitting, she managed to make a few minor adjustments to find a suitable smile. After all, she needed something from Mike this morning.

"Yes, actually I was just about to come to your office to talk. I have some important requests for the next bullying assembly..." Julie carried on, but Mike cut her off abruptly.

"Julie, the bullying assembly will take place today."

"Today?" Julie blinked, incredulous. "But I'm not ready!"

"I know you've been planning it for a while, but something has come up and it's timely that we have the

239

assembly today instead."

"Why, Mike? Are you trying to sabotage what I've been working on? You acted like you cared this whole time."

"Julie, I'm informing you of this beforehand as a courtesy. I'm the principal of this school and if I'm changing the schedule, you better believe there's a damn good reason." Ms. Marina cringed. He had sworn at her. She waited with a slightly sad and far off smile, knowing that Mike's guilt would soon kick in and he'd take back what he'd said.

He didn't. "I'll see you later today at the assembly. No preparation on your part will be needed as I'm running it." Mike turned and walked out without further explanation.

Ms. Marina stood there fuming. She would let the teachers know later on what a traitor Mike was, and he'd better watch out since they were on her side now. What a bully he was.

THE AUDITORIUM FILLED with students who were mostly sick of hearing the word "bully" at this point. Maybe that's how the school planned to handle bullying, just wear all the students out with assemblies and slogans like "Say no to bullying!" Even after two weeks off, the students looked worn out and ready for the end of the school year.

Ms. Marina stormed up to Mr. Phillips, who was about to stand at the podium. She noticed he didn't even have the projector screen set up for a video or presentation. Had he even prepared for this? She should have known he didn't taken bullying seriously.

"Mike, I'm ready to do my presentation now if you'll let me. I have everything here at school and I would just need a couple extra minutes. You could do the intro while I get it all ready."

Mike looked at Julie in a way he never quite had before. She recognized what it was and wished she could erase what she saw in his eyes. He didn't have an ounce of respect left for her. He dismissed her to her seat and she wandered there, a new foreboding feeling replacing the anger.

The students hushed as Mr. Phillips grabbed the mic and walked out to the Bulldog. He was a tall, regular looking man with peppered hair that was thinning. Most of the time he blended in with the school's walls and outside of the occasional "Hey, Mr. P!" he didn't know whether he was appreciated at Adler. There was nothing outspoken about him, yet today he had an aura of extreme storminess and peace surrounding him all at once.

"Is it enough to stand against something?" Mr. Phillips asked. He started pacing back and forth as he spoke, as if he were in his own living room. He didn't say anything else for a few moments.

"Is it enough to stand against bullying? I see propaganda everywhere these days. Say no to drugs, right? Say no to tobacco. Say no to cancer and to bullying. Say no to child hunger and poverty around the world." He stopped speaking again as if trying to wade through his thoughts. The students were still, and they waited.

"I realized over break that you can stand against everything that's supposedly 'bad' and still not do anything to change a bad situation. Just because you're *against* bullying, does that really mean anything?" Mike's words hung in the air like a sudden change in atmospheric pressure.

His steps carried him toward a spot in the bleachers. The spot was occupied by Ms. Marina.

"Ms. Marina brought to our attention the dangers of bullying at the last assembly, did she not? Do unto others as you would do unto yourself. Respect people's differences and resist the temptation to hold power and authority over others through bullying."

Mike stopped and stared Julie straight in the eyes. Julie's palms were sweating now, and it felt like Mike was putting her on trial. The ungrateful bastard. He didn't seem to have any intention of pacing away from her yet. She'd speak to the school's board of trustees and superintendent later on about this backward presentation. Who knew what he was getting at here.

"Ms. Marina also emphasized that when you bully others, it's a reflection of your own low self-esteem, not a deficiency in the person you're bullying. Did you not speak those exact words, Ms. Marina?"

Ms. Marina looked around the auditorium, all eyes on her. She was getting very irritated now. "Of course I did!" she said. She felt the need to take back control, Mike was rather unpredictable at the moment and had a crazy look in his eyes. She motioned to Mr. Phillips to hand her the mic so she could take over from here. He welcomed Julie to stand next to him.

"Yes, Ms. Marina will take over from here." Instead of handing Julie the mic, he put a small cell phone up to it on which he had pushed Play.

Out of the device streamed a voice, which was then amplified through the auditorium's loud speakers. It was Ms. Marina's voice along with a few other teachers who joined her and were more difficult to identify. They were talking about Marcy.

Those moments were uncomfortable for everyone, but for different reasons. Marcy felt no worse than she had upon overhearing the school's teachers talking about her in the lounge. She had been about to leave for break when she caught the mention of her name. She had then eavesdropped around the corner, out of sight, and was able to grab most of what was said using her phone. Crying, she'd rushed straight to Mr. Phillips's office to tell him. She didn't know who else to turn to. First the assembly earlier in the year, now this.

Marcy was torn up over it, but Mr. Phillips was comforting and said he'd take care of it. He asked if he could replay what she'd recorded to others, and she'd agreed on the condition that he left out the parts about other students. She'd already been publicly burned and she didn't want other students to have to go through that.

Many of the teachers were squirming in their auditorium seats, unsure whether the student body could identify their individual voices or not. One thing was for sure, though, that Ms. Marina's voice rang loud and clear. She'd been so vocal about bullying lately that it would have been hard to mistake her voice for someone else's. As her tirade about Marcy ended, Mr. Phillips pressed Stop on the phone. Julie's face looked horrified and her cheeks turned a deep crimson from the humiliation.

"Ms. Marina, did that make you feel powerful—is that why you did it?" Mike walked away from her without waiting for a response.

He resumed speaking once he'd reached the Bulldog in the center. "The world calls teachers the unsung heroes, right? We uphold and celebrate the youth. We shield them from bullies in any way we can." His eyes locked with Julie's. She looked down at her pleats.

"Students—not every teacher is your hero or role

model. In fact, sometimes what we teach you may be wrong or backward. One student overheard this conversation before break and learned that the hard way. What I can tell you is that it doesn't matter what we think about you. No matter what happens in life, lock onto what you think about yourself. There will be bullies in life, and they're not always easy to spot. They're also not always your peers. They can be a teacher, a professor, a family member, your best friend, anyone. They may not even overtly say something bad about you, sometimes they simply declare that you don't exist at all. If you believe what they say about you, that's when they have you." Marcy, who was seated in the same spot as the first assembly, nodded to herself.

"I can't stop all occurrences of bullying at this school or in the world. If I was promising you this, I'd be lying. In the real world, you can't always control what happens and I know you students are smart enough to know that. Hell, you probably know it better than we adults do." Mr. Phillips glanced over at where Julie had been sitting and noticed that she had disappeared.

"What I can say is don't spend your whole life railing against what you're not. Know what you are and that will help you get where you want to go. A lot of people will have a lot of stuff to say, implying that they know who you are and what's right for you. They don't know anything about you, remember that. Don't just stand *against* bullying, stand *for* something first—for yourself."

Mr. Phillips didn't know if he'd articulated his thoughts well, but he didn't have anything left to say regardless. Sometimes it just comes out how it comes out, and maybe it's better that way. He dismissed the students and lingered in the auditorium as the space emptied.

Marcy walked over. "Thanks, Mr. P," she said to

him, "I actually made it through this assembly intact." Her smile was tired and relieved. Spring break hadn't been all that relaxing, and she would head home to finally rest now.

"You're welcome, Marcy. See you tomorrow." Mr. Phillips handed Marcy her phone and then turned to the center of the auditorium, alone. His eyes settled on the school's Bulldog until the painting blurred slightly out of focus. Who said it always had to be a dog-eat-dog world?

Ms. Marina was never spotted again at Adler Middle School.

NOT THE SAME

I RODE THE F-TRAIN to Fisherman's Wharf. People were coughing, sneezing, and sniffling in the damp air, and I felt their germs entering my lungs with every breath. I tried to breathe through my nose; maybe it could act like a filter.

The wharf was relatively quiet, even though it was a sunny day. Families, mostly tourists I guessed, strolled listlessly through the maze of shops in a fugue state, disconnected from their bodies, themselves. A middle-aged white man with a bald head and generous beard rode down the boardwalk in a Segway, bumping 90's rap by some one-hit wonder artist pretending to be a gangster. A group of teenagers smoked cigarettes and glared, desperate for attention, feigning worldliness. Two children ran screaming like maniacs along the docks, giant cookies clutched in their hands. I ignored them all.

I attached the 300mm to my Nikon, and zoomed in on a couple leaning over a balcony on the second floor, in front of a Japanese restaurant. They were watching the sea lions. He looked as if he had just gotten off work, his shirt unbuttoned, tie undone and hanging around his neck, shoulders slumped with an invisible weight. She turned towards him, open and questioning, but did not speak. Click. His expression had been tired, cynical, but he turned to her and softened, pulling her close with an arm around her shoulder. She leaned her head on his shoulder. Click.

Eventually they moved on, and I continued through the wharf, past the shops and restaurants, and toward the back alleys. Behind one of the many seafood restaurants, a back door opened and a middle-aged man with grease stains on his apron carried out two large trash bags. He brought them to the dumpster and set them down. He stood there for a moment, gazing out at the ocean, unconsciously tracking the movement of first a seagull, then a far off ocean liner. Click. He leaned gently against the dumpster, the setting sun casting a long shadow against the wall behind him and causing him to squint. Click.

I found three more before the light ran out. Five total, not bad for one day. I thought with pleasure of getting home and into the dark room I had created from my walk-in closet, and adding them to my collection. I liked to develop my photos the old fashioned way.

I wasn't delusional. I knew that they were just pictures, that taking them didn't really change anything, but still they meant something to me. It was an act of preservation; not for the sake of expression, but for protection. Not for an audience, but for myself. Call me naïve, but I never quite understood why people called photography creative, when the photographer wasn't creating a picture, only capturing it. I never considered what I did to be art.

I slung my camera over my shoulder, and walked toward the train stop.

I SENSED HIM BEFORE I SAW HIM, out of the corner of my eye. Instinct told me not to turn and look directly, but for what I lacked in vision, my mind was able to fill in the rest. He was tall and pale, wearing a long gray overcoat and white-blonde hair cut short, standing still near a bench at the entrance to the wharf, tightly coiled energy disguised by a relaxed and casual posture. My gait slowed slightly as a matter of caution, but I continued to walk as if I hadn't noticed anything. I felt his eyes tracking me.

"Hey you," was all he said. His voice was quiet and sounded as if marbles were rolling around in his throat.

I kept walking.

"You with the camera." More pronounced.

I stopped walking, turned and looked in his direction. We stood about ten feet apart facing each other. I felt a cautionary tingle spread from the middle of my body up my neck, down my arms and through the tips of my fingers. I said nothing.

In the fading dusk, his bright blue eyes glowed like orbs with their own light source, beneath a wide brow and heavy lids. His nose was thin and slightly crooked. His colorless mouth turned upwards on one side, in a knowing half smile.

"I've been watching you."

I still didn't reply. I could hear my heart beating in my ears.

"Yessirree. Watching you, watching others. The watcher being watched." He laughed then, marbles rolling around, clicking together, making a sickly sound.

"What do you want?" I asked, surprised at the steadiness of my voice.

"What do I want?" He threw up his hands in a theatrical shrug. "The same thing you do, of course!"

"I doubt it."

His smile faltered a little, but recovered quickly.

"No, no. I am sure of it. I've seen you, I know what you're about. We are both after the same thing."

I hesitated to ask, but went ahead. "Oh? What is that?"

His eyes glowed even brighter. "Isn't it obvious? Isn't it so simple? Life! I like to watch too, just like you. But watching isn't enough, I want to have it. I want to take it for myself, to own it, let it fill me. Yes, we are the same, you and I. It is good to finally meet someone like me, who understands how I feel. The world can be such a barren place, filled with falsehood and artificiality. Real, pure life is going the way of the dodo! You and I, we see the sadness of that, and we do what we can to keep life alive." His grin was repulsive.

My stomach had turned queasy. Suddenly, the ground felt unsteady, as if I had just gotten back from a long boat trip. My body felt weak and weightless.

"No," I said, mustering up what courage I could. "I don't think you and I are the same at all." With no small effort, I turned away from his piercing gaze, felt his eyes pulling at me like magnets, needy and expectant.

"Wait!" he called after me. "Don't you see? You are just like me! Two peas in a pod!"

I kept walking.

I DIDN'T TAKE EVEN ONE PICTURE for the next three months. My dark room stayed completely dark. I went to my job, out for the occasional drink with coworkers, watched a lot of television, read a couple of paperback mystery novels. My camera sat on an end table near the door, watching me, asking like a cat to be let out to explore the world. Eventually, I put it on the top shelf of my closet above the coats.

One evening, I was absentmindedly watching the 6 o'clock news when a story came on about the discovery and capture of a murderer who had a history of victims going back over four years. Missing persons are a relatively common occurrence, especially in a big city, and since the murderer had no real pattern for choosing his victims, until now no one had even known he existed.

He had been found randomly, on a tip from a neighbor who saw him carrying an unusually large and heavy looking object wrapped in a comforter from the trunk of his car at 2 in the morning. Upon searching his apartment, sixteen bodies were discovered in the basement, mostly women, but also a few men and children. They had been strangled, and their bodies had been drained and preserved in formaldehyde. The media had dubbed him "The Poser," as he had positioned his victims in his furnished basement performing activities of daily life like reading a book, conversing at a dinner table, sitting together on the couch. All of them had been reported missing at some point, their whereabouts a mystery until now.

I think I knew already, as there was no real shock when I saw him, though the hairs on my forearms stood on end. The television flashed a picture of the murderer. The hair was a little longer. The skin was more grayish than pale in the well-lit mug shot photo. But the luminous blue eyes, those were the same.

I turned off the television and went into my bedroom, opening up the drawer where I kept all the photos I had taken. I gathered them up and placed them in a paper grocery bag, then put on my shoes and a coat, and left.

There was a green dumpster outside of my apartment building, sitting in an alley. I lifted up the black lid.

My arm stayed that way for a while, fully extended, holding the dumpster open. A sedan rolled leisurely by. Sparrows sang playfully and flew loops among the trees lining the street. A young girl laughed from somewhere in a nearby yard.

I closed the lid, and walked to the street. A few minutes later I hailed a cab into the city, cradling the bag under my arm.

THEY CALLED IT "CITY LIFE." My suggestion of "Not the Same" didn't have the right feel to it, they said. I told them that was fine, to call it whatever they wanted. Most of my photographs were enlarged, but were otherwise unchanged.

The Golden Gate Art Gallery achieved a level of fame and exposure far beyond anything they had ever seen before. The show ran for four months straight, drawing full crowds on a daily basis. It was featured in two front page stories in the Life and Arts section of the Times, and was reviewed favorably by almost every art magazine across the country. I took the paychecks happily, but told them I didn't want my name associated with it, that they could credit the photos to Anonymous, or make up a name of some imaginary person. I didn't care.

I wasn't an artist.

ABOUT THE AUTHORS

Jason Petersen and Aarti Patel live together in the Bay Area with their son and practice naturopathic medicine. They enjoy writing fiction on the side and like to explore themes involving individuality, society, and health.

Made in the USA
San Bernardino, CA
15 May 2016